OUR 2ND FIRST DATE

PAMELA DEAN

OUR 2ND FIRST DATE

Tammy

Coming back here was never part of the plan—but neither was cancer. Now that Dad's gone, I'm starting to see just how much this town has changed. Back in 1985, Bower was a thriving farming community in Northern California. Ten years later, it's clear something shifted.

While the estate gets sorted out, I take a job as an aide in the special education class at my old school. I don't expect to love it, but I do. My student, Donny, is incredible—his antics provide a welcome distraction from the weight of my grief.

This town may have lost its farms, but it hasn't lost its ability to surprise me. Some surprises are good. Some are bad.

And some are named Sam Ford.

Sam

Coming back to my hometown was at the top of the list of things I swore I'd never do. But I need to be here. I need familiarity, something I've only found here. Farms that once thrived have folded. Processing plants are shuttered. Recognizable faces have disappeared.

I thought knowing every back road and street corner would make it easier. It doesn't. Especially not when I see her.

Tammy Little was my first crush. By the time I worked up the nerve to ask her out, it was a week before graduation. I doubt she ever understood what happened after that—why I left the way I did.

I never forgot that night.

And I sure as hell never forgot her.

ONE

Tammy

HOT AS HELL

THE HEAT RADIATING off the sidewalk could probably cook an egg. People say that, but has anyone actually tried it? Maybe that could be a class project. I tip my head back so the sweat drips away from my face. I should've worn my hair up, so at least some air could reach my neck. School should start in late October here in Northern California. Like after the rice harvest.

I can't believe I moved back here. I mean, I wouldn't have said no —he needed me, but now? Now I am questioning my sanity. I wipe the sweat from my brow and glance around at all the parents dropping off their kids, and the ones who are walking up to the school on their own.

There are more of those. Bower Elementary is in a pretty run-down part of town. Hell, if I'm honest, the whole town has become run-down. It hasn't been the same since I left for college, and I don't really understand why. It seems like Bower just sort of gave up. The houses all show wear, peeling paint, trim boards hanging loose. Some stores I remember from when I was a kid are closed now and that makes me so sad. I loved growing up here, and until I learned to drive, I thought all places were like this. I couldn't imagine a world where people didn't grow something, where dads didn't smell of tractor grease and sweat.

Dusty boots and faded jeans were like the uniform of my childhood until I got to high school. Driving opened up the world to me because it meant I could go to the bigger towns around here and raid their libraries. My wallet held not just my driver's license but something far more valuable to me. Four different library cards. I had one for Chico, Oroville, Bower, and Gridley.

Bower's library, which was tucked into an old cement building, consisted of a few children's books and every copy of farming literature known to man. Well, that's probably an exaggeration, but compared to the bigger city libraries, it was painfully limited. I remember the first time I climbed the steps with my dad, the promise of stories dancing around my head and heart. I left with a new copy of *Frog and Toad* that I didn't want, but my dad loved reading with me, and a copy of *Beezus and Ramona* by Beverly Cleary. It didn't take me long to burn through that series and start annoying the librarian with questions about when the new books would be in.

My desire to get some new books to read fueled my first solo drive to Chico, a college town north of here. I felt a sense of freedom that came from the unread stories, the imaginary worlds, and the characters I would meet. People who lived in places where shops stayed open late, with cafés where music spilled out the door. Where cities had sidewalks and hustle and bustle. I guess I finally got that in spades when I moved to Washington, D.C.

I didn't think I'd ever come back here for more than a visit; Thanksgiving or Christmas, sure, but this extended stay on the surface of the sun wasn't something I had envisioned. I take a deep breath and blow it out, not ready to think about the choices that lay before me now that he's gone.

I glance over at a beat-up Lincoln Town Car that pulled up a few minutes ago. The kids got out right away and ran towards the school, but now the car is off, and the man who was driving is nowhere to be seen. I scan the parking lot and spot him leaning into the window of a

Ford Pinto. He slapped hands with the driver, and if I hadn't been watching, I would've missed the baggie that passed between them.

Classy. Drop your kids off, then pick up a dime bag. I roll my eyes as sweat drips into them. I curse at the sting, then glance at my watch again.

"No bus yet, Miss Tammy?" the school nurse asks as she scurries past me. She's running late today. Must be having trouble with her daughter again.

"That's why I'm here in this blistering heat, Rhonda. Waiting on good ol' 43," I say to her quickly retreating back. It's not that she doesn't care, she is just trying to get inside. I'm envious as she grabs the door to the main building. They have a great air-conditioning unit in that part of the school.

Bus 43 is never this late. I wonder if something happened, or if maybe Donny isn't coming today. His family isn't always great about letting us know that he's going to be absent. Knowing my luck, as soon as I walk away, the bus will pull up and he will lose his shit if he doesn't see me. I love that kid more than I should; I know that. We aren't supposed to get attached, but it's kind of hard not to when he is just so fucking amazing. Since I started working here, I've learned a little about his home life, and I admit it's kept me up at night more than once.

"Hi, Miss Tammy!" a little girl calls out as she walks past. She has a firm grip on her brother's hand since his favorite thing to do is dash into the library and hide.

"Hey, Kathy. Good job with your brother." I nod my head towards the squirming boy in her grip, and she beams.

"Thanks, my mom said if I can get him into class I get an extra Oreo when I get home from school!" She tightens her grip further and I see the little boy give up. She turns to him and says, "I'll share it with you, Richard. Now come on. Mrs. Lenox is waiting for you."

She waves over her shoulder as she tugs him toward the kindergarten classroom. I scan the parking lot again and glance down at my watch. The bell is going to ring any minute, and still no sign of the bus. Fuck, why is it so hot? It's not even eight thirty in the morning. I need to bring a change of clothes, or at least a different top. I glance around and take a sniff of my pits, not sure if I remembered deodorant. Seems like I did, but I'm sure Donny will let me know if I stink. Kids are brutally honest. It's one of his best assets if you ask me.

I finally hear the bus before I can see it, so I walk out to the curb, adjusting my apron a little. It has three pockets and is the most valuable tool for this job. I have candy in one pocket, tissues, Band-Aids and Donny's favorite dinosaur toy in the other. The third pocket has a zipper to keep him from picking my pocket. That pocket is where I keep my highlighter, my pen, and a pencil with a nice, fat eraser. Donny is obsessed with erasers, and if given the opportunity, they are snapped off and squirreled away somewhere. I've lost enough of them and still don't know where he's putting them.

As soon as the bus comes into view, I sigh and prepare myself for whatever mood he might be in. It's a Monday, so if he had a good weekend with his mom, then he will be fine. If it was his dad's turn with him, all bets are off.

I see the top of the knit pom-pom hat and cuss. "Motherfucker! Oh, hell no. It's 98 degrees out!" I whisper-yell to myself as the bus pulls to the curb and the door opens. He's going to get overheated, then have an actual meltdown. I don't wait, I charge onto the bus and point right at Donny. "Take it off!" I say in a stern voice. I blame my thin patience on the fact that sweat has been pouring down my back for the last ten minutes.

He is unaffected by my bad mood; in fact, he squeals with delight and starts laughing, then holds his hands over his hat.

"Donny, I'm not kidding. It's too hot for the hat!"

"Hot for the hat! Hot for the hat!" he repeats back as he bounces in his seat.

I mumble more cuss words under my breath and make my way to the middle of the bus where he's sitting. I hold my hand out and he slaps it, then puts his hand up for a high five. Not what I intended, but I'll go with it. "Okay, now give Miss Tammy the hat."

He shakes his head and squeals again. "Hot hat!" His smile is huge and so fucking adorable, I melt a little more than I was earlier. Donny has jet-black hair that is currently smashed under a blue-and-white knitted snow hat. His big brown eyes are dancing with joy and possibly mischief.

I narrow my eyes at him and say, "Okay, listen, you can wear it till we get to Mrs. J's room, but then you have to give it to me. No hats in class."

"No hats in class," he repeats as he stands up.

"Donny, Mom or Dad this weekend?" I ask as I walk backwards, keeping my eye on him.

"Dad! Dad! Dad!" he chirps.

Great, that means no lunch, probably. I stand on my toes and look for his bag. "Where is your backpack?"

"Backpack!"

I turn and walk the last few rows to the front of the bus. Usually, Miss Francis is our driver, but I see a guy about my age in the driver's seat instead. That must be why the bus was late. "Hi, did Donny have a backpack when you picked him up?" I ask.

The guy is writing something on a clipboard and holds up his finger, indicating either he's number one, or he wants me to wait. Rude either way. I let out a sigh, wanting to get off this stupid metal heat trap.

The bus driver has long hair tucked behind his ears, and he's wearing a ratty Giants baseball cap. I notice he has his ear pierced too and chuckle to myself. When I was in high school, there was a thing where, like, if you had your right ear pierced it meant you were gay, or was it the left? I couldn't remember then either. Donny is bumping into the back of me, anxious to get off the bus.

Without turning around, I say, "Space, please." He stops, but I can practically feel him vibrating behind me. If he hears the bell— just as that thought crosses my mind, the late bell rings and Donny starts to rock and whine.

"Sorry, I'm sure that is super important or whatever, but Donny wants to get to class. Can you just tell me if he had his backpack or not?" I say, then quickly turn and hand Donny his plastic dinosaur. "We wait, Donny."

"Okay, done. What was your question?" the guy asks, finally looking up from his clipboard. He has intelligent light blue eyes that don't really match his brown hair or scruffy almost-beard. There is something familiar about him, but Donny's whine from behind me stops that train of thought.

"Did Donny have a backpack or lunch or anything when you picked him up?" I thumb over my shoulder at Donny hoping he hasn't put the whole dinosaur in his mouth already.

"No, he didn't. Shit." He glances over at Donny. "I mean shoot, was I supposed to check for that? Some lady was standing at the curb with him, and she wasn't holding a backpack."

I glance back at Donny wondering if he got it wrong. "Donny? Mom's or Dad's?"

"Dad, dad, dad dad," he chants around the dinosaur that is firmly lodged in his mouth.

"Okay, thanks. I'll figure it out."

The bus driver holds out his arm, blocking me from leaving as he says, "So for the future, should I ask that woman for his backpack? I can make a note." He points to his clipboard.

"No, that's okay. I'll ask Mrs. J to reach out to Donny's parents." I go to step off the bus, and Donny turns to the driver, saluting him before following me down the stairs. Huh. I've never seen him do that before.

I hold out my hand, and Donny slides his tiny middle finger onto my palm. Ugh. That's wet. I sigh and wrap my hand around the only part of him he will let us touch and lead him over to the buildings that make up our special education wing. Really, it's three portables that were set at the back of the schoolyard on what used to be part of the playground. There are basketball court lines that disappear under the building that intrigued Donny for a whole week last year. So far this year he hasn't paid them any attention, although we are only one week in.

We walk up the ramp and into class just as Mrs. J is singing the good morning song. Our class is not full, with only seven students, but there are rumors floating around that we might get another kid soon. It's a good little group, but there is always room for more. I am primarily Donny's aide because he is considered nonverbal and needs more assistance, but when we are in here, I help with all the kids.

"Miss Tammy!" Mrs. J sings at me. "What's the weather like today? Is it sunny? Is it cloudy? Is it hot as he"—she stops and winks at the kids—"heck today?" They all burst out laughing, and Laura bangs on her desk with her cup, glee evident all over her face.

"I am sweating, I am fanning." I make a fanning motion with my hands and stick my tongue out like I'm panting. "It's hot as heck today!" I sing back as Donny darts past me to his spot on the rug. I see he has taken his hat off and put it in his cubby by the door, so I cross to him and reach in my apron pocket for a piece of candy. I hold it in front of him and say, "Good job remembering the hat, Donny." Then I hand him the candy. He trades me one very wet dinosaur for the Now and Later. Watermelon, because it's his favorite.

I sit cross-legged next to him and listen to the rest of the morning routine. She starts the day the same way all the time: the hello song, which we missed thanks to the late bus, then the weather song. She says hello to each student and waits with the patience of a saint for them to respond in whatever silly way they have agreed upon. After that, we say the Pledge of Allegiance.

I got really lucky being assigned to this classroom. Mrs. J, or C. J. when we aren't at work, is amazing with the kids and a lot of fun to be around. She has more energy than anyone I've ever known and can switch gears on a dime, something I've learned is a valuable skill here.

After the morning circle is done, all the kids start independent work time, so once Donny is at his desk with his tasks, I help move Laura's wheelchair over to her area. Her work looks different from the other kids but it's still important for her to do this independently, so I step away. She arches and tries to turn to see where I'm going, but I just say, "Work time" as I walk away. She reaches for her first bucket and throws it on the ground, hoping I'll come back. I did the first few times, but realized she was just trying to get me to stay with her.

"Bummer. Try again," I say. She can't see where I went and I watch as she bangs her cup a few times in frustration, but before long she reaches for the next bucket. "Good job working, Laura," I say, then scan the room for Mrs. J.

I spot her by the toy bin, so I walk over. She holds up a dinosaur that is missing its head. "Do you think we should ask Donny's mom on the lookout for this in his poop?"

"Darn it, sorry, I handed that to him yesterday for like a second. That kid is fast."

"Brontosaurs have tiny, delicious heads. It was only a matter of time." She tosses the headless toy into the trash can and continues to rummage, looking for something.

"Donny doesn't have his backpack or a lunch. He said Dad when I asked who he stayed with, but the bus driver mentioned a woman at the curb this morning."

"Did Francis, say anything else? Did she know the woman?" She stops digging and looks up, a little concerned.

"No, well, it wasn't Francis. There was a sub. He might take over the route though because he was taking notes on things and asked about what he should do in the future if there is no backpack."

Mrs. J makes a noise like a hum and twists her lips to the side. "Damn. Francis was my boots on the ground. Okay, I'll call transportation and see if I need to break in a new spy. There are a few things Donny will eat in the fridge, and I think today is taco day. He will eat the shell but not the meat, and he might eat the lettuce."

"Okay, I'll grab an extra one when I get lunches today. Thanks, Mrs. J."

TWO

FIRST DAY

I WAIT until the aide has walked away with Donny before I drive off. He was a cute kid. The first thing he did when he climbed onto the bus was run his hand up my arm, pushing my T-shirt out of the way. He must have been curious about my tattoo, and it seemed like he wanted to check out the rest.

My notes from Francis show that he doesn't like to be touched and that he is mostly nonverbal. He and I have one thing in common, so I figured we'd do alright. I helped him lift my T-shirt and pointed at the tank. "That's a tank." His eyes darted to mine, then back to the tattoo. "I was a soldier," I said, saluting him. His eyes grew big, and he smiled. I watched as he repeated my motion almost perfectly. That surprised me.

I looked past him for the woman who was with him on the curb, but she was nowhere to be seen, so I shut the door and told him to take his seat. He sat in the first row, but then quickly got up and moved to the middle of the bus, just like Francis said he would. So far, so good, except the kid was wearing a fucking snow hat, and it's hotter than hell today. I kinda forgot that about this town, but my bad memory is why I agreed to come back. I had enough of the dry desert heat to last me a lifetime.

I make my way back to the yard where they keep the buses and wonder what kind of excitement I'll find there. I'm a trained mechanic, so when I got this job I was told it would be a mix of things, but I didn't really understand I'd be picking up kids from shit-hole apartments. I'm betting that was a hell of a lot easier than dropping them off there. The woman who was standing with Donny was clearly not someone he was comfortable with. Based on the way he was standing and how he jumped up and down when he saw me coming. She must have barely waited for him to step toward the bus before she turned and went back inside the crappy first-floor apartment.

I park Bus 43 and give myself a minute to stand and stretch my left leg. I get stiff quickly, but the bus routes are short. Most of my day will be spent here, repairing the dilapidated fleet of buses. I grab my clipboard and use the lever to open the door, stepping out into the furnace of a day. Fuck, it's like not even nine a.m. and the thermostat reads 92 degrees. It's expected to get up to 110 today. I grab the bandana from my back pocket and wipe my brow. I should do some squats or lunges or something to keep my hip loose, but I don't want to draw attention to myself on the first day.

"How did it go, Sam?" a voice over my shoulder says, startling me. I didn't see anyone else here when I pulled in. I take a few breaths, trying not to let that rattle me. What is this guy's name again? Starts with a T . . . or was it a R? Luckily he's wearing coveralls with his name on a little white oval above his heart. Mike. Fuck, not even close. I lift my clipboard and write Mike Yard, then draw an oval around it to help me remember. That's not his last name, but it's helpful for me to remember where I know him from.

"It went good, Mike. Just dropped off my last student, no problems. Although I do have a question."

"Yeah? What's up?" Mike walks toward the garage where they have a small bus up on a lift. All the tires are off, and there is an oil pan catching the sludge dripping out. I follow him, tucking my clipboard under my arm.

"The high school students that I picked up were fighting. Nothing too serious, but I had to pull over and make them move to opposite ends of the bus. Can I implement a seating chart going forward? I didn't like that I had to wait to find a safe space while they punched each other in the face."

Mike barks out a laugh. "Trevor and Garrett? Jesus, those two haven't changed a bit. Sure, yeah, see if that works. They've been trying to kill each other since about second grade. It was a little easier to manage before they got so big. They're cousins, you know?"

"No shit? What do they do at family gatherings?"

"Same thing." He shrugs, his gaze darting to the bus that's lifted. He squints and steps up to the bumper. "Oh, hell, is that a dent?" He turns to me for my opinion, so I step closer.

"Yeah, looks like a small one."

He stomps off toward the small office at the back of the garage, so I run my hand over the dent. It's not big or noticeable. I lean back and look towards the office when Mike's yelling grows louder.

"He told me he ran over nails. That front tire popped because he hit something! There's a dent in the fender and everything. I don't have that kind of budget for him to be demolition derby driving my buses. I want him gone!" He pauses and rubs his hand over his face, and his shoulder sag. "Well, find me another one like Sam and do it quick."

That's nice to hear, I guess, but I've worked here for like three hours. He has no idea of the baggage I have. I sure as hell can drive a fucking bus without hitting anything though, so maybe he has a point. He hangs up with whoever he was yelling at, but the phone rings right away.

"Transportation, this is Mike. This morning? Route 43 was our new guy, Sam. There a problem, Mrs. J?"

That perks me right the fuck up. Shit, what did I do wrong? I was a little late getting to Donny because those cousins were fighting, but he was there before the bell. Francis didn't mention anything in her notes about what to do if you're running behind, so I didn't radio in. Maybe I should have called in and told someone I was having a problem. I didn't want them to think I couldn't handle—My thoughts are cut off by Mike holding out the phone to me.

"Mrs. J, Donny's teacher, wants to ask you a question." He has his hand over the receiver so she can't hear him. "Nice lady, quit acting like you got sent to the principal's office."

I take the phone and say, "Sam Ford here," stopping myself from saying Sergeant Ford.

"Hi, Sam, my name is Clara, or Mrs. J. I wanted to check in with you about Donny and ask if you had any questions?"

My shoulders relax a little, and I blow out a breath. "Um, no. Francis gave me a bunch of notes about him, and they all seemed pretty accurate. He was my easiest student this morning, actually. Cute kid."

"That's great to hear. Donny loves the bus, but sometimes if he has been at Dad's, he's a little wound up," Clara says. I think back to that aide asking him where he had stayed. I made a note about that because I wondered why she was curious.

"That makes sense. I don't know if it was his mom who was with him at the curb this morning, but I picked him up at the Terraces Apartments."

She laughs and says, "You would think that would help me, right? Both his parents live there. His mom and dad are quite interesting. I believe his mom is in 201 and dad is downstairs in 105."

"Oh. Well, a tall, thin woman was with him this morning."

"Yeah, that's partly why I called. That's not Mom. Did you see a dark-haired man, late fifties, around anywhere?"

"No, just the tall, thin woman."

I hear her sigh before she says, "Okay. So Donny's father somehow manages to be quite the ladies' man. I'm not trying to be mean, but that dude is no prize. I'm betting Donny had a rough night. Are you taking over the route that Francis had?"

"Yes, ma'am, going forward, is there anything else you need me to know?"

She runs through a few things with me, but nothing that Francis hadn't already told me. I scan my notes and put a star next to each item that Mrs. J. reiterated.

"Thank you, that's all very helpful. I'll be out front to pick him up after school."

I hang up and get to work helping Mike replace the tires on the lifted bus, then while he finishes the oil change, I read the list of problems waiting for me. Brake job, transmission leak, nothing too crazy.

I keep busy until it's time to repeat my bus routes from this morning. Mike let me know that I'd be taking a student in a wheelchair this time. Normally she's on my morning route too, but she didn't need the bus to get to school since she had an appointment. I read over the notes from Francis to settle my nerves a little. Laura has cerebral palsy that affects her ability to walk and speak, but she's sharp as a tack and funny. I blink at that, wondering how you can tell.

When I pull up to Bower Elementary, I can see the aide from this morning and a few other adults waiting with the kids. Donny is sitting on a blue bench holding his snow hat onto his head while the aide is trying to tug it free. He's laughing, so I guess this is a game he likes, but the aide doesn't seem to enjoy it as much as him.

A woman with long hair streaked with grey stands and waves when she sees me. I watch as she holds a finger up to the rest of the group, then she comes over and climbs onto my bus.

"You must be Sam! We spoke this morning. I'm Clara." She thrusts out her hand, so I turn in my seat a little so I can be polite. I shake her hand gently, but she gives me a squeeze that lets me know she's got some strength.

"Nice to meet you, ma'am."

"Clara or Mrs. J, please, ma'am makes me feel old. Donny pointed out that I am getting grey, so I don't need any more confirmation on that front. Are you able to lower the lift for Laura, or do you need help?"

"No, ma'am, I mean Mrs. J. I can handle that. Thank you, though." I glance out the window as I walk back to open the back door and lower the platform that will hold Laura and her wheelchair. There is a woman with bright red hair cut into a blunt, smooth bob, and I chuckle to myself. It looks like a helmet. She is playing peek-a-boo with Laura, but Laura doesn't seem to like it. She's arching away and I swear she just rolled her eyes. That makes me smile.

Mrs. J walks back to the group and brings Laura's chair over to me, and I catch what she is saying. "I know Laura. I'll talk to her. You aren't a baby. I think that Miss Georgia likes to play that game, but we know it's stupid, don't we?"

Laura leans forward and smiles, making a little noise. Mrs. J runs her hand over her hair and smiles down at her. "Laura, this is your new driver. His name is Sam. You be nice and follow the rules. No dancing in the aisle when the bus is moving, okay?" The little girl laughs, and I see the twinkle in her eyes.

Mrs. J turns to me and says, "Her parents will be waiting at the house. It's a long driveway, so don't think you've made a wrong turn." She starts to walk away, then snaps her fingers and turns around, and adds, "Oh, and Donny's mom will be out front this afternoon. Short woman with dark hair and a cigarette hanging from her lip, with possibly another one lit in her hand. Her name is Bea." She walks off without another word, and I glance over at the aide from this morning. She stands and holds out her hand to Donny. He gives her one finger, his middle finger, actually. That's kinda funny.

I get to work securing Laura's wheelchair to the platform, then bend at the waist and tell her, "No peekaboo, I promise, as long as you follow the rules and don't dance. If I see any dancing, I'm going to stop the bus and come back here and peek-a-boo your socks off." I tug on her chair a little to make sure the straps are tight enough and look down to see her smiling up at me. Yeah, we are going to get along just fine.

When I get back to the front of the bus, the aide is waiting with Donny at the curb. He is holding a perfect military salute, so I return the favor, and he smiles, climbing the stairs to the bus. When he reaches me, he does what he did this morning and pushes my T-shirt out of the way to see my tattoo.

"Hey Donny, we ask before we touch. Ask, please. Can Donny touch?" she says.

To my surprise, Donny looks up at me and says, "Can Donny touch?" Of course his little wet hand is already all over my bicep, but I nod and say, "Yes. You can touch."

I'm so busy watching Donny I almost miss the way the aide is looking at me. She has her head cocked to the side, and her eyes are narrowed.

"Are you Sam Ford?" she asks.

"Yep, that's me." I lift my gaze and study her face more closely, then my gaze darts to her name tag. "Wait, Tammy Little? Is that you?"

Her eyes fly open wide, and she nods. "Holy crap, it is you! You look so different; I didn't recognize you."

I'm about to say the same thing to her when Donny says, "Holy crap!" as he sits in the first seat on the bus, then gets up and moves back to the middle.

Tammy hangs her head, shaking it a little. "I'm gonna lose my job for teaching that kid new cuss words, I swear. Good seeing you again, Sam."

She turns and walks away without another word. Well, damn, after all these years, here she is.

THREE

Tammy

SO MANY QUESTIONS

SAM FORD.

Never thought I'd see that guy again, let alone driving a bus. I figured he'd be a catcher for a major league team by now. I don't want to admit it, but I scanned the local paper when I came back to check if he was mentioned. He wasn't, of course, and no one ever talked about him or his family, so I gave up wondering.

I was a little busy though; maybe if I had more time, I would have discovered that he was still living here. Well, here in Bower, but not at his farm—that's been vacant since I got back into town. I know that because I may have taken the long way so I could drive past Ford Nut Farm with Dad when I came back. There was a big plywood for-sale sign that looked like it had seen a few years of weather sitting at the bottom of the long driveway.

I walk back into our classroom to grab my purse and see Mrs. J. bent over the toy bucket again. "Did you lose something in there, or have you become obsessed with the toys?"

"Yeah," she sits back on her haunches and blows a strand of hair out of her sweaty face. "Well, I didn't. Laura threw that water weenie and I swore it flew into the toy bin. I don't want Donny or Will to get a hold of it. No telling what that liquid is."

"I'll help look." I set my purse down, dropping to my knees to crawl around looking under the desks and bookcases.

"That new bus driver seems nice. I hope he sticks around," Mrs. J says, as she blindly swipes her arm under the media cart. That's brave. No telling what's under there.

"He went to school here, so there's a chance he might." I flop onto my stomach and stretch my arm out, feeling under the bookcase with my hand. I pray the squishy thing I'm touching is the toy. I have to adjust myself to get closer, but finally wrap my hand around it only for it to squirt away. Damn thing.

"It's under here, Mrs. J. It ran when I tried to grab it, but if I use a ruler, I should be able to get it out."

"Nah, just leave it. It's safer under there. Not sure why it made Laura so mad, but she chucked it pretty quickly." She sighs and straightens up, her back audibly cracking. "Ugh, I'm getting too old for this."

"Are we sure she wasn't aiming at a certain someone?" I ask, scooting back away from the bookcase so I can stand up too.

She snaps her fingers at me. "Thank you for that reminder. I need to speak with Georgia again about infantilizing Laura. She's small for her age, and I get it that the sippy cup and diaper don't help, but Jesus, our girl is smart. She probably threw the weenie at Georgia."

"Well, if Sam can get Donny here on time tomorrow, I'll run the morning circle if you want to take a moment to educate the staff on Laura's awesomeness." I wink at her, and she smiles back.

"That's helpful, thanks. So did you go to school with Sam?" she asks as I'm pulling the strap of my purse up to my shoulder. Usually, I'm in no hurry to get home to my big empty house, so I'll hang around after school prepping for the next day or helping clean up. Today, I actually need to go. I have a meeting with the attorney. My least favorite thing.

"Yeah, well, just high school. We went to rival elementary schools because he lived on the other side of Highway 99. His family is the one that owned Ford Nuts," I explain. Clara Jorgenson and her husband Adam moved here around the time I left for college, so she should recognize the name.

I watch as her face morphs into sadness. "Oh, damn, really? That's too bad."

"What? You didn't like them?" I glance at my watch, because I am going to be late if I keep asking questions, but her response surprised me.

"Oh no, nothing like that. I mean, the town isn't too fond of Wilton Ford, as you know, with what he did, but I doubt they blame his son. You better get moving, or you'll be late." She nods at the door behind me, and I give her a tight-lipped smile.

"Right. Okay. See you tomorrow."

The drive to Chico isn't terribly long, but without a working radio and that bombshell statement bouncing around in my head, it lasts forever. What the hell happened with Sam's family? I rack my brain trying to remember if he had brothers or sisters but come up short. I mean, even if we went to the same school for four years and had exactly one date our senior year, I didn't really know very much about him. He was someone I considered a friend, but thinking back to our conversations, they always seemed to be about trivial things. I don't think we even talked about what we wanted to do after high school. We laughed a lot; I remember that. He was really kind and funny as hell. I wonder if I was just enamored by him, surprised he was even talking to me. I was the nerd, and he was the jock, and if we hadn't been paired together for our senior project, I'm sure he wouldn't have even known my name. Tale as old as time, and about as cliché as you can get. My mind drifts as the rice fields fly past my window.

"Tammy Little, your partner will be—" I remember the sharp intake of breath next to me, and glancing over to see Destiny crossing herself like that would ward off having me as her partner. "Sam Ford."

The teacher continued pairing up students, but for me the entire room went silent. I couldn't look at him. I bet he was rolling his eyes or whispering to his buddy next to him. Who was that? Fuck, he was an asshole. I remember that much.

Curtis Donovan. The name slams into my memory like a locker banging open. That's who he was sitting by. That little fucking creep. Curtis, unfortunately, did go to my elementary school, and his favorite pastime throughout fourth grade was throwing grasshoppers at me. He hit me in the face with one that was so big I felt its wings vibrating on my cheek as it tried to get away.

By fifth grade, he had moved on to calling me fun names like Tammy Whammy and Tammy Big Butt. I was a chunky kid and carried that extra padding until sophomore year of college when, for some reason, I grew an inch and lost the weight. I was a late bloomer, so who knows what kind of hormonal weirdness was going on, but most of my friends in college had the opposite issue. The freshman 15 became the sophomore 20 for them.

I wonder what Sam did after graduation. Did he leave and come back like I did, or did he stay and help with the nut farm? Maybe I'll go to the library after the meeting and see if they have the old newspapers on microfiche. I imagine something as big as a tragic event happening to one of the area's largest almond and walnut growers would be in the paper.

I put my blinker on and exit the freeway, then wind my way through to the downtown area where my attorney has his office. He's nice enough, but to be honest, I really hope this is the last time I ever have to see him again. His office is in an old house that has been renovated into office spaces. I'm not sure what his budget was, but he must've spent a pretty penny on the air-conditioning unit. My nipples harden the second I walk in the door. Jesus Christ, you could hang meat in here.

I step to the desk and notice his receptionist is wearing a sweater. A fucking turtleneck sweater. "I'm here for my appointment with Mr. Rolland, Tammy Little."

"Yes, hello, Miss Little. He's just finishing up with another client, and he will be with you shortly."

I nod, then take a seat across from her and watch in amazement as she blows on her fingers and rubs them together before she starts typing again. Poor lady.

The door behind her opens, and two men walk out, slapping each other on the back and laughing. "Thanks for coming by. That property has been sitting for so long I didn't think we would ever find a buyer. I'll let the executor know that this time, the offer is legit."

Mr. Rolland waits for his other client to leave before addressing me. "Hello, Miss Little, sorry to keep you waiting. Right this way." He motions to his open door, and I stand then follow him in. He leaves the door open, something I noticed the first time I came to see him. Well, I was a blubbering mess that day, so he probably wanted to make sure his secretary could come help if I melted into the floor or something.

"I have the final papers here for you to sign." He grabs a folder off his desk and opens it, then turns it so I can read it. "This portion of the rice field here"—he taps the map that is with the papers, then continues—"that will be absorbed by the neighboring farm like your dad wanted. A bigger company that can handle the harvest has purchased as well the other fields, but." He stops and looks up at me before softening his voice. "I understand that your dad didn't want that, but since you weren't keen on becoming a rice farmer—"

I hold up my hand to stop him, yet again. I told my dad no a hundred times growing up, then broke his heart a million times again as cancer ravaged his body and his spirit. "No. I can't. Thank you for trying to parcel it out. I'm glad that the one close to the house will be a family-owned one."

He nods and gives me a sad smile. "It's hard to lose a parent and even harder to navigate all of this." He waves his hands over the pile of papers on his desk. "But the good news is that the house is paid off, as well as your student loans and, of course, the part of your dad's hospital bills that the VA didn't cover. There was enough left over to honor your request for a scholarship. Per your request, it will be called The Littlest Rice Grant, and students who attend Ag colleges, like Chico State, will be eligible to apply. It will cover their first year. We have it in an investment fund, and hopefully, if it does well, this scholarship will continue on for years."

"That would make my dad really happy. Thank you."

He smiles, and we go through the details as he gets my signature on various forms. As we are just about finished, I realize he might know what happened to Sam's family since he deals with the estates of a lot of ranchers in the area.

"Hey, do you remember Ford Nuts?" I ask as he shuffles the papers back into their folder.

"Yes," he says hesitantly. "Why do you ask?"

"Oh, I just ran into Sam Ford. We went to school together. When I came back last year, I saw his family farm had a for-sale sign at the end of the drive. I can just ask him though, if it's confidential."

"It is, and it's complicated. How is Sam doing, if you don't mind me asking?" He folds his hands together on top of his desk, and I see he's wearing the same expression he wore the first day I was here.

"Um, he seems good. He's driving the bus for the school where I work."

"Oh, well, that makes sense. I hear he's a damn fine mechanic. At least the military gave him something good."

I nod and smile because I have a feeling that if Mr. Rolland knew that I know nothing about Sam, he wouldn't be sharing any information.

"Well, unless there is anything else, Miss Little, I'm going to have to let you go. I have a meeting soon."

"Of course, sure. Thank you so much for all your help." I reach my hand across his desk, and we shake hands. Then I return to my car, knowing these little nuggets about Sam Ford are going to drive me up the wall. He was in the military? I get a flash of Donny saluting him and groan, of course. Now that makes sense. Why didn't that occur to me?

Something happened after I left town, and it wasn't anything my dad mentioned when I called or when he wrote. His letters were always the same upbeat stories about the rice fields and the workers. I guess I should not be surprised that he may have kept a big event from me since he hid his cancer for years. Dad must've known what happened to Ford Nuts that made the whole town angry, and he didn't think I should know about it.

THAT'S the thing about dying: You get out of a lot of explaining.

FOUR

KNOCK-KNOCK

AUGUST FINALLY GIVES way to September, but the heat isn't ready to loosen its hold on the north state. I've gotten better at managing the bus route and haven't been late since that first day. Separating the cousins helped a lot because now we sail straight from their houses to the high school.

Donny and Laura are easygoing, and I find myself really looking forward to my time with them. I discovered that they both like knock-knock jokes. I say, "Knock-knock," and Donny repeats that. I say, "Who's there?" and Donny, most of the time, will repeat, but sometimes he gets stuck on the "knock-knock." Laura seems to think that is pretty funny, so maybe he's doing it on purpose.

I pull up in front of the school and a little smile tugs at my lips because Tammy is there waiting like always, fanning herself and holding her long brown hair off her neck. She looks different from the last time I saw her; still beautiful, but there's something in her eyes that wasn't there when we were teenagers. Fuck, I'm sure my eyes tell a different story than they did when I was eighteen.

I lift a hand to wave at her, and her lips curve up a little. She dips her head a little like she's embarrassed or shy about seeing me, which is funny to me since our interactions last about five minutes twice a day. I wonder if she remembers our date or if she thought about it over the years like I did. The laughter, the music, the feeling that our entire world was about to open up for us. That warm June evening, it was like I was indestructible. Was it only me who felt it?

When I pull the lever and the door opens to the morning heat, she looks up at me and hits me with the same big smile I'd get in class after we started to get to know each other.

"He's wearing the hat again," I say as she steps toward the bus.

"Yeah, I saw. I was laughing to myself, wondering what it will take to get that damn thing away from him," she loudly whispers to me, leaning in like we can share this little secret.

I glance back at Donny, but all I can see is the blue pom-pom of his snow hat. Makes me sweat looking at him. "Is Mrs. J coming for Laura?" I glance over Tammy's shoulder but don't see the teacher.

"No, she's busy. I can take them both. Let's have Donny wait till Laura is ready," she says as she hands me a small plastic dinosaur. I've seen her give this to Donny when she wants him to wait, so I nod and walk to him in the middle of the bus.

"Hey, Donny. Miss Tammy says she wants you to wait. She is going to get you after I have Laura out." I hand him the dinosaur and when he takes it, he immediately put it into his mouth. He doesn't look at me or really acknowledge my words, but I know he understands. He has a new dinosaur backpack today. Since I started this job, I have seen him with four different backpacks. I wonder if this one will last.

Laura smiles up at me as I get to her platform. "Hey there. Thanks for not dancing in the aisle, Miss Laura. I really appreciate that. You ready for school?"

She makes one of her cheerful noises, and I grab the washcloth that's clipped to her chair to wipe her face. She's such a cute kid. "Okay, hang on. Going down, First Floor: Women's underwear, toilets, and barrels of monkeys. Please watch your step, the monkeys have been known to poop on the floor." I use my snobby voice and she squeals and bangs her cup. This girl loves her poop jokes. Once I learned that, my mornings got a lot more fun.

We ride the platform down, and I bend to unhook her chair. The air hits my back as my shirt pulls up, so I quickly straighten, and turn so I'm facing the other way. I tug my T-shirt down and look around. Tammy is busy talking to a student and no one else is around, so I breathe out a sigh of relief. It's dumb and probably a little vain, but I haven't gotten use to the way my back looks. Maybe I never will. It doesn't hurt as much as it used to, though, so for that I'm grateful. I know a lot of guys come home with worse, or didn't come home at all.

"Miss Laura, can you wait for me to go get Donny?" Tammy asks, stepping closer to us. Then she says to me, "I'll be right back."

She turns and goes to the front of the bus, only stepping up to the first step. "Donny, dude, let's go." She motions to him, and he jumps up and runs to her. It's clear to me she is his favorite person. I've seen him interact with Mrs. J and both of his parents, and none of them hold a candle to Tammy Little. That's another thing he and I have in common. I had such a crush on her that started the first day I laid eyes on her in ninth grade. I was always too chicken to ask her out, but right before we graduated, I finally got the nerve. Best date I ever had, well, best night I ever had.

She walks back to me with Donny, holding onto his middle finger. She tries to pull away so she can push Laura's chair, but Donny whines. "Dude, we have to get Laura to class! I can't hold your finger and push her. That takes two hands."

"Two hands!" Donny cries as he steps closer to Tammy with his hand extended.

She bends down so she can look at him and says, "Donny, you can keep Dino until we get to class if you let me push Laura, or you can help push. Which is it?" She holds up one finger and repeats, "Keep Dino" then holds up another finger and says, "Help push."

Donny touches her second finger, showing he wants to help push.

"Okay, give me Dino." She holds out her hand and quickly stows the very wet plastic toy in her apron pocket. Donny steps to her side, and together they maneuver Laura toward the portables.

"See you after school!" I call after them, and Tammy stops and turns to me.

"Thanks Sam. Have a good day." She gives me a quick smile that I try to memorize. The way her eyes crinkle a little now is different than the smiles I got in high school. I like these better; there is more behind them.

After getting the platform back up, I drive Bus 43 back to the yard, realizing only once I pull in that Donny doesn't have his backpack. No wonder he goes through these so fast. I walk back to where he was sitting, and sure enough, it's there on the seat. Looks empty, so I think about leaving it there until I pick him up but I grab it and pat it down to make sure he doesn't have lunch in there or anything. As soon as I pick it up, I get a whiff of marijuana.

No fucking way. I shake my head and unzip the backpack and see a small ziplock baggie filled with dried green flakes.

Damn it.

I put it back in the backpack and carry it to the shop to ask Mike what the hell I am supposed to do with this.

When I walk in, he's on the phone and I hear him say, "Oh, he just got here. Is it a dinosaur backpack? Because he's holding one. Okay, yeah, we have it. Does Donny need it now, or can we give it to him this afternoon?"

He pauses and waves me over. He reaches for the pack when I reach his desk, and repeats, "A salad? Okay, well, sure, if that's his lunch, we might be able to run it back over."

I shake my head and unzip the backpack, pulling out the baggie. Mike's eyebrows lift to his hairline, and he says, "C. J., I'm going to have to call you back." He puts his finger on the switch ending the call, but the receiver is still in his hand.

"What the hell is that?" he asks, pointing with the phone receiver to the baggie I'm holding.

"It sure as hell isn't a salad." I toss the baggie onto his desk and put my hands on my hips.

"Damn. I wonder where he found it." His eyes go wide. "I wonder if he ate any of it? Did he seem okay? Shit, I need to call Clara back." He grabs the phone and dials before I can even answer.

I wait while he tells Mrs. J about the drugs I found. It's frustrating only hearing one side of the conversation, but I get the general idea about what will happen next. He pulls the phone away and asks, "Who was out front with him today?"

"Dad. He was alone this time."

Mike repeats what I said and nods and says, "Uh-huh, yeah. Okay, no, I will call the district. Let's see what they want to do. Okay, yep, I'll call you when I know something." He hangs up the phone and tips his head back, blowing out a breath.

"Anything I can do?" I ask.

"Nah, I need to call over to the district office and let them know what you found. I imagine they will call Child Protective Services as well as Mr. Hawthorn's parole agent." He levels his gaze at me and squints like he's thinking. "They might want to talk to you, but I really need to send you to Sacramento for a couple of parts. Think you can go now and be quick?"

"Sure. I can do that."

"Take the truck; you're picking up a set of rims and a few other boxes. I think there is a new seat too, but that's probably wishful thinking on my part. It's been on back order for a while."

"Okay, no problem. Same place I went to last week?"

"Yep." He sighs and sits down, scrubbing his hands over his face. "Fuck, I do not want to make this call."

"That's why they pay you the big bucks," I say, waving over my shoulder. I snag the keys to the truck off the rack by the door and head out to the beat-up district-owned pickup.

I spend the drive trying not to worry about what will happen with Donny. Instead, my mind wanders to what Tammy has been up to all these years. Well, to be honest, that is how I spend a lot of time since realizing we live in the same town again. She is taller than I remember, and I'm not sure why she is so thin now; I really liked her curves. That's not something you can ask a person though, so it will remain a mystery. Not like I have plans to talk to her outside of work. I'm happy with the arrangement we have, even if it makes the weekend seem like ten days instead of two. I guess I shouldn't be surprised that she still does it for me—she was the most beautiful and interesting girl at Bower High.

I admit I drove past her dad's rice farm a few times in the last week. I'm not sure if they still live there, since I don't know what Tammy drives now. Her beat-up red Chevy truck isn't there anymore, or her dad's truck either, but that doesn't mean anything. Fuck, I feel like a stalker. Good thing she doesn't know what I drive these days, or she might have seen me being a creep.

I get back to the yard with the parts in time to have lunch and start an oil change on one of the buses. Mike and Curtis are working on one of the vans, so I don't get a chance to ask him about Donny before it's time for me to do the afternoon route.

Curtis was in a few classes with me senior year and played on the baseball team with me. Guy is a real selfish prick, always has been. I was glad to hear he has nothing to do with driving the bus routes; he's just a mechanic here. While I was off busting my ass in the Army, good ol' Curtis Donovan was spending his time in jail for a felony DUI. Like I said, total prick.

I pull up to the curb and see Tammy standing by Laura's wheel-chair. Donny is not with her, and for a minute I feel a little panic wash over me. Fuck, I wish I could have asked Mike what happened. I open the door and wave, then walk to the back of the bus to lower the platform for Laura's chair. Tammy wheels her over and waits for me to step off the platform. I'm about to ask about Donny when I see him out of the corner of my eye. His mom is talking to Mrs. J by the office, and I watch as Donny spots the bus, then me and Tammy. He bolts and runs at full speed towards us. Mrs. J sees him and lunges, but she's too slow to get ahold of him. Donny's mom is oblivious and is waving her arms around while yelling something.

Tammy turns just in time to catch Donny before he crashes into her. He ducks behind her and holds onto her back pockets. She freezes and takes a deep breath before saying. "Donny takes deep breaths."

I watch as she calmly breathes in deeply and then out slowly. She does this a few times, her arms at her sides, until Donny does one on his own. She still isn't looking at him; she's just letting him hide behind her. "Deep breath in, slow breath out." She does that, then says, "Donny's turn."

I watch as he mimics her, and on his last breath out, his shoulders relax a little. "Tammy's turn," she says, then does the breathing. I admit I am following along as well until Laura bangs her cup on her tray, snapping me out of it. I bend and quickly fasten her chair to the platform with the straps, keeping one eye on what's going on next to me.

Tammy doesn't turn or acknowledge the banging; she just says, "Donny's turn." This time I see her hold out her hand and he slips his middle finger into her palm as he takes his breaths.

Mrs. J waves and Tammy nods, like they have some unspoken secret language. Tammy slowly dips down to her knees and takes a few slow breaths with Donny. She smiles at him and quietly says, "Good job, Donny. Do you want to ride the bus?" She holds up one finger, then adds, "Or ride with Mom?" She holds up a second finger.

Donny bats at her first finger, then turns and looks up at me with the most hopeful expression I have ever seen. My heart cracks wide open.

"It's cool with me, little dude. Let's get you on the bus." I step around Laura's chair and hold out my hand on reflex, then realize he probably won't give me his finger like he does Tammy. I look to her for guidance, but she's watching with curiosity. Slowly Donny slides his finger out of her hand and gives it to me. I feel ten fucking feet tall as I lead him to the front of the bus. Once he's seated, I close the front door, then walk back through the bus to get Laura.

"Thanks, Sam. We told his mom he wanted to ride the bus, but she came anyway. She can meet you at the apartment complex. I'll let Mrs. J know. Do you drop him off first, or Laura?"

"I drop Laura off first. It takes me about ten minutes to get to her house, then another five or so to unload her chair. Donny lives only like two blocks from her. I'd say I'll be at the apartment in twenty minutes?"

"Got it. Thanks, Sam." Tammy turns and jogs over to Mrs. J and Donny's mom. I see her wave toward the bus, and his mom nods, then wipes her hand over her face.

"Knock-knock," I say as soon as we pull away from the curb. No answer, so I wait, then try again, "Knock-knock. "

"Knock-knock," Donny says so quietly I almost don't hear him.

"Who's there?"

"Who's there?" he says, and I smile.

"Dwayne!"

He repeats, "Dwayne!" A little louder.

"Dwayne the bathtub, I'm dwowning." I don't wait for a laugh because that is my least favorite knock-knock joke, and really doesn't deserve a laugh. Laura bangs her cup, but Donny is silent.

"Knock-knock," I say, and this time Donny copies me right away with his normal voice volume.

"Who's there?" I say and he copies me.

"Lettuce."

"Lettuce Lettuce Lettuce," Donny says, making me laugh.

"Lettuce in, it's cold out here!" I say.

"Cold out here! Cold out here!" he chirps back. That also earns a cup bang from Laura. I feel myself relax into their simple joy.

FIVE

Tammy

TROUBLE AND PIZZA

FUCK, what a day.

I guess it was only a matter of time before Donny's father got arrested again, but man, that was rough. Poor kid had more than one meltdown, so we spent a lot of time outside just walking around and doing our deep breathing. I couldn't get him to eat when it was lunchtime because he wanted his "salad." By afternoon snack time he settled enough to eat a little. Mrs. J was able to explain to me what Sam found when Donny was with the speech therapist.

I ran groups while Mrs. J went to the office to talk to law enforcement, and because Donny is super smart, he picked up on the tension in the air. Even Laura was thrown off by it all. At first, it seemed the other students didn't notice, but it's like dropping a rock in a still pond. The waves eventually reach the shore.

Justin pushed all his work onto the floor, then crawled under his desk and refused to come out. Mandy ripped a page out of the coloring book, which is not a problem to anyone but her; then she spent the next hour looking for tape. Ed enjoyed that Mandy was upset, so he followed her around trying to find the tape before she did so he could throw it in the trash. Something he let her know every few minutes.

It was one of those days I missed my old job. Around two o'clock, I would have given my left breast to walk down the quiet, sterile hall that led to the archive room where I spent my time. Instead, I was dodging pencils being thrown at my face, trying to find a roll of clear tape and digging a clipboard out of the cupboard so at least one kid would be happy. Justin appreciated being able to continue to work on the floor, so that was a win. I made a mental note to buy ten rolls of clear tape and maybe some earplugs, and a helmet.

I rub my temples, waiting for Mrs. J to finish speaking with Donny's mom, then I follow her back into the classroom. Georgia is there resetting the kids' work for Monday, and she doesn't look up or smile when we come in. I can only assume she didn't like being told that Laura doesn't like peek-a-boo. Too bad, lady, this is not about you.

"So, great job with Donny today. Let's incorporate more outside time into his schedule for next week. He may be right back to his usual self by Monday, but I want to be ready if he's not. Can you think of some academic or IEP goals that can be done outside?"

"He has a goal to match, and he's reluctant to do the tasks we have for that. I could find stuff outside, like categories, you know? Like matching three sticks that are the same length, or finding five brown leaves. Would that work?"

"Yes, if you can throw in a challenge or two. Check if he knows that the longer stick doesn't belong. That's close to the size stuff we have in here." She snaps her fingers like she just had a great idea, which she often does. "Take some of the letter cards and have him place a letter on an object, like the "s" on the swings." She stops and sighs loudly. "You've got all weekend to think up more things, so you can put it all on the back burner and come have a beer with me?"

I glance over at Georgia, and Mrs. J catches it, saying, "Georgia, it's been a rough week. Would you like to grab a beer with us?"

"No, thank you. I don't drink," she says as she fills Laura's buckets with tasks. I cringe at her selection. They are all essentially the same, and Laura hates that. When I set her up, I try to mix up the activities. Like, if she has a color sorting task, I won't add any other sorting tasks. I'm not sure why that doesn't occur to Georgia.

"Okay, suit yourself. I need to finish up a few things. Want to meet at the Pizza Palace at four?"

"Sure, then I can go home and change. I have all kinds of Donny on my shirt. He used the corner of my apron to wipe his nose more than once today, so I'm taking it home to wash."

"Good idea. Okay, see you later." Mrs. J nods at me and disappears into the small room where her desk is kept. I'm pretty sure it was supposed to be a supply closet, but she managed to get a desk and a chair in there.

"Bye." I grab my purse from the cupboard and contemplate telling Georgia how I prepare work for Laura, but as she slams the last bucket into place, I think better of that.

"Have a great weekend, Georgia. See you Monday."

I get a noncommittal *hmmm* noise from her, but take that as her goodbye. Stepping outside I groan at how hot it still is. There was a magazine at the grocery checkout yesterday, and everyone on the cover was wearing sweaters. "Excited for Fall" stretched across the bottom of the picture. I wanted to yank it off the shelf and jump up and down on it. I bet it's cool in Washington, D.C. right now. Well, maybe not cool, but cooler than this oven. I think it was usually around seventy to eighty degrees in the fall.

Here in Bower? It's currently ninety-two, and that is an improvement. This past week we have seen cooler weather. The morning news weather guy seems pretty excited about it, but it's still so fucking hot. Sorry, Anthony Watts, get back to me when it's in the seventies. I'll be super excited about that.

I drive to my house and park in the driveway because I know I'm going right back out. Normally I pull my little Toyota into the garage, parking it next to my baby. I'm glad my dad didn't sell it when I left for college. I told him he could, that I'd probably never drive it again, but when I came back to take care of him, he proudly led me out here to show me Big Red was right where I left her.

Big Red is a 1968 Chevy C10 step side. My dad bought it the year I was born and drove it every day until I got my license. I helped him change the oil, fix flats, change spark plugs, you name it because he always said it was my truck; he was just borrowing it until I could drive. He tried to keep up with her maintenance while I was gone, but when he got sick, all the extra stuff fell away. He hired people to help with the rice, but eventually he needed me. Neither of us had the energy to tackle fixing my truck when I returned, so I bought a small commuter car that was easier for him to get in and out of, pretending that it was what I wanted.

I climb out of my car and jog up the steps to the old farmhouse that raised me. I run my hand along the wooden banister and get a flashback of the night Sam Ford took me on a date. I close my eyes and can picture him standing right here, hands stuffed in his pockets, looking all kinds of nervous as he asked if he could kiss me goodnight.

And what a good night it was. In the years since, I can honestly say no guy has ever taken me on such a great first date. Too bad it was all for a dare. Even knowing that, I still look back on that night with such fondness. Sam was my first kiss, and in that moment it didn't matter to me why he had asked me out or why he was kissing me. My heart allowed me to be delusional in those moments, and I am grateful for that. I like to imagine that by the end of the night he was having fun, but who knows.

The answering machine is flashing when I walk past the den, but I'm not going to check it. It's probably Kyle again. He tends to call me when he's between girls, checking if I'm coming back. I made the mistake of telling him I was only staying to finish up things with the attorney, so it's really my fault for giving him hope. Even if I go back to D.C., I wouldn't want to date him again.

I take a quick shower and feel a hundred times better by the time I go back downstairs. My Keds are by the couch in the den, so I sit to pull them on, deciding it won't be the end of the world to listen to the machine.

"Hey, Tamara, just checking on you. There's a big fundraiser coming up, and I have a plus one if you are going to be in town. Either way, call me back. I miss your voice."

Called it. Kyle.

I pat myself on the back and grab my purse without calling him back. I need a whole pizza and a pitcher of beer, but I'm sure I'll have one beer and two slices. Damn my responsible self.

The Pizza Place is packed. I chuckle to myself and say that a few more times. I think the kids are rubbing off on me. It's four o'clock on a Friday in a small town with exactly two restaurants, so it's really not a surprise. I see C. J.'s van and shake my head at her bumper stickers. She has one that is so faded it's almost unrecognizable, that says Carter/Mondale '76. There are a few Grateful Dead stickers and one that says *This is Not an Abandoned Car!*

I don't see her in the parking lot, so I head inside and spot her right away. Her long black hair is split into two braids that drape down her back, and it looks like she made it home to change too. She's wearing a tie-dye shirt under cutoff denim overalls with very worn-in Birkenstocks.

I freeze when I see who she is sitting by at the bar, wondering if I should just turn around and leave. Damn it. I really want a beer and pizza; I don't know if I have the energy for Sam Ford right now.

Before I decide either way, he turns his head slightly and sees me. He has that ratty baseball hat on, but now it's turned backwards, his long brown hair spilling out from under the bill. It's wavy and thick and surprising. I would never in a million years have pictured Sam with long hair. It didn't surprise me that he joined the military, didn't really surprise me that he came back. But the long hair? Complete shock because guys around here do not have long hair. The earring is surprising, too. I should ask him about that, because that seems very out of character.

He lifts his chin and gives me that slow smile that used to melt me instantly when I was a teenager. I lift my hand in a little wave and weave through the crowd to get to them. Just as I reach the bar, Sam stands up to offer me his stool.

"Oh, that's okay, I can stand. How are you, Sam?" I ask because I want to seem unaffected by his presence, and it seems that is what a normal person would say when seeing a coworker.

"I'm good, but I was just leaving. Taking my pizza home to eat. This is a little too crowded for my taste." I watch as he slides a small pizza box off the bar. With his free hand, he pats C. J. on the shoulder. "Thanks for telling me all of that. I really like that kid; I hope his family can get their act together soon."

"They might. But don't hold your breath, Sam." She gives him a sad smile.

"Good seeing you, Tammy. Enjoy your night." He dips his head a little, and I watch as he turns to go, his left leg catching a little as he walks. It's slight, other people probably don't notice, but I watched that boy walk down the hall for four years. He's limping.

"Bye, Sam," I call after him, but he probably doesn't hear me over the crowd. I indulge my inner teen and watch him as he walks to the parking lot. I keep watching, not letting him leave my sight until I see him climb into a black jeep.

When I turn back around, CJ's smirking at me. My stomach tightens, and I'm sure my face turns all the shades of red. I couldn't have been more obvious if I had tried.

"Sam and I went on a date in high school!" I blurt out, like a complete idiot.

"Really? Is that why you followed his ass all the way to his car? Must've been some date." She chuckles a little, then pats the stool next to her.

God, I'm so lame. I slink over to the bar and sit next to her, ready to explain, but she launches into what happened today instead.

"Bea seemed a little drunk when she came to pick up Donny. I'm glad that she allowed him to ride the bus home. Sam said he was fine on the bus and that when he pulled up to the apartment, Donny's mom was calm and smiling."

"That's good to hear. I really worry about that kid."

"It's the hardest part of our job. When Paul and I lived in Berkeley, I took the train to Oakland every day to teach at one of the elementary schools in a rather rough area. Seeing drug deals happen in front of the school and by parents that were picking up kids . . ." she stops and shakes her head. "Well, it can break you if you let it. I decided I needed to be the best teacher I could be for these kids. At least for six hours of their day they would have consistent expectations, food and love."

"Is this where I admit I lay awake at night worrying about Donny?" I ask.

"Me too, kiddo, me too." She waves the bartender over and orders another beer for herself, then looks to me.

"Do you have Sierra Nevada on tap?" I ask, and he rattles off what they have. I go with the Pale Ale and shift on my stool a little, my legs sticking to the wood as I do.

"It's a special kind of heat up here, isn't it? I've lived here nine years and haven't gotten used to it yet."

"I was born here, lived in this oven for seventeen years and I can tell you that you don't ever get used to it."

"Do you miss D.C.?" C. J. asks.

"Sometimes, but mostly just the weather and some of the restaurants," I say with a laugh. The bartender comes back with our beers and the pizza C.J must've ordered.

"I hope you don't mind; I knew it was just going to get busier." She nods toward the pizza.

"I don't mind a bit. Let me know what I owe you." I reach for my purse, and she shakes her head.

"This is on me. You saved my ass today covering the groups and walking around with Donny." She pauses and looks over her shoulder before continuing. "Georgia was pretty mad when I talked to her about Laura. I might see if we can move her in to help with the reading groups for a little, give her some time to cool off. I don't want her to quit. As much as I wish she was better at her job, at least she shows up every day. Before you two I had subs constantly. I was told I might get a third aide, but watermelons might also start growing on the moon . . ."

"I won't hold my breath." I laugh, then add, "Yeah, she seemed pretty mad after school. She's fantastic with Ed and Justin. Mandy seems to gravitate towards her at reading time, so perhaps having her do things like that will help. I can handle Laura and Donny in class."

"If you're in there, I have no doubt. It's days like today that make me want three more aides." Mrs. J takes a bite of pizza and nods for me to do the same.

We eat in comfortable silence and I think, I hope, I have dodged the whole checking-out-Sam conversation, but I'm not that lucky.

"So tell me about this date with Sam." She wiggles her eyebrows at me and smiles.

I wipe my mouth and grab another piece of cheese pizza. The mozzarella is melted to perfection, and one piece is not enough. Plus, if my mouth is full, I can't answer her. I take a big bite and shrug, hoping that she gives up. I don't really want to talk about it, but not why she may think.

"He seems like a nice young man. I didn't realize the Fords had a kid. When the rumors of the affair and all that other stuff started circulating, I remember being grateful they didn't have young kids. I guess Sam was already gone when it happened?"

I finish chewing and swallow hard, reaching for my beer to wash it down. "I actually didn't know that. We had that one date at the end of our senior year, but we both left right after graduation."

That's not a lie; it's just not all the details. We graduated on the first Friday in June, and I was gone by Monday. I'm not actually sure when Sam left.

"So you aren't going to give me more details?" she asks, cocking her eyebrow.

"No, because that's really all there is to it. I was eighteen when we last saw each other."

She makes a noise like she doesn't believe me but thankfully drops the subject. We spend the rest of the time talking about the kids and things she wants to incorporate into her curriculum.

AFTER MY ONE beer and two pieces of pizza, I stop at the store to get more milk. I'll do my big shopping later this weekend, but there is nothing worse than not having milk for my cereal and coffee in the morning. I park my Toyota and grab a basket, because who am I kidding? Now that I'm here, I'll be getting more than just milk.

"Hi, Miss Tammy!" There are arms wrapped around my thigh the second I walk in the store. I glance down and see two red bows holding back the thickest black hair on earth. Each ponytail must weigh five pounds.

"Well, hi there, Monique! How are you doing?" I give her a little hug and look around for her parents.

"I'm good. Mom said I can get ice cream. Do you get ice cream?" She's tugging me towards the back of the store, and I still don't see her mom or dad.

"There you are! Monique, you can't run off like that!" An out-of-breath woman comes up to us, putting her hands on her hips. She looks young, like late teens or early twenties.

"Aunty, this is Miss Tammy! She works at my school. She pushes me on the swing sometimes, and she likes ice cream too."

I wave at the woman and smile. "Hi."

"Hey, thanks for grabbing her." She holds out her hand and Monique takes it easily, waving at me over her shoulder.

"Bye! See you Monday!" I say, then turn to push my cart towards the milk section, pausing to quickly grab a carton of Tin Roof Sundae ice cream. The best ice cream known to man. Well, next to that one at 31 Flavors that has the ribbons of peanut butter running through chocolate ice cream. Wait, pralines and cream is also good. Should I get that too? When I was little, I liked the bubble gum one, but now that sounds gross.

"You know, if you stand there much longer, the ice cream is going to melt." A deep voice over my shoulder shakes me from my thoughts.

"Sorry, I was just—" I grab the Tin Roof Sundae carton and turn to find Sam smiling at me.

God, did I really forget how handsome he was? I mean, I know it's been ten years, but how did I forget that face? Even though I have seen him twice a day for weeks, we have never been this close. His eyes are still that beautiful sky-blue. Right now they look very much like the sky that spans out over the rice fields on a clear summer day. His smile is broad and almost too perfect, except he has this little scar on his upper lip. I never got a chance to ask him how he got that. He's been clean shaven since that first day, making me wonder if he was so nervous for his first day that he forgot to shave.

"Still your favorite?" He nods towards the ice cream I'm holding.

"Huh?"

"That was your favorite, if I remember correctly, unless you can go to Baskin-Robbins, then it's the chocolate peanut butter one."

I blink at him, then shake my head a little and look around. Like I stepped into an episode of *Candid Camera*.

"There are some things I can easily remember, Tammy." Another smile crosses his face, and I see his gaze dip to my mouth, but then he quickly looks away.

"Yeah, that's right. Wow, Sam, I can't believe you remembered that."

"Well, we drove all the way to Chico talking about it, so it kind of stuck in here." He taps the side of his head.

"Right, and you like rainbow sherbet! Do you know I have never met anyone else who likes that?" I say with a laugh.

"It's the superior ice cream, no matter what anyone thinks."

"Sure, Sam. Whatever you say." I finally step aside and let him get to the ice cream. I wait for him to grab a carton, then ask, "So are you liking the bus driver thing?"

"Yeah. I do. I work at the yard for the rest of the day, and sometimes that's a nice break, but other times that drags out because I can't wait to be with the kids, you know?"

I smile at him and nod. "I do. I feel pretty lucky I get to hang out with them all day."

"I bet. Your dad must be happy to have you back," he says, and I try to hold my expression, but my smile falls.

"Dad passed away," I say. I mentally count the months before I add, "Almost a year ago now." The pain still sits in a little corner of my heart.

"Damn, I'm sorry. I didn't know." I can see he's uncomfortable, so I force the smile back into place.

"It's okay, Sam. Why would you have known? Not like you and I have talked or anything." I shrug.

"True," he says as he drops the ice cream in his cart. "Would have been nice if we had. You are someone I thought about a lot over the years."

SIX

BRAVERY IN THE FROZEN FOODS

WHY ON EARTH did I just say that? I couldn't look at her to see what her reaction was. Would she have wanted to keep in touch? I glance down at her hand, like I have done before, no ring. That doesn't mean she doesn't have someone though.

"Yeah, that would have been nice, Sam. I, um, thought about you too," she says softly. God, how she says my name still makes my heart soar. "I bet you've had some interesting stories to tell over the years. I heard you joined the Army?"

"Yep, right after graduation." I grab onto the shopping cart with both hands as that uncomfortable dread starts seeping in. I don't mind talking about my time served, or even the war. It's the fake gratitude, the "thank you for your service" from people who really don't mean it. Not that Tammy would be one of those people, but hell.

Her gaze flicks down at my white-knuckle grip then back up to my face, and I see a little shift in her posture. She takes a deep breath and blows it out slowly. "My dad was in Vietnam. First wave of troops actually. He got injured almost immediately and was home and back at the farm almost before people realized he had left." She stops and gives me a genuine, soft smile. "I hope you didn't see any combat, and if you did, I'm so sorry."

I let my grip loosen a little on the cart and I nod. "Thank you. Gulf War actually. Wish I could say my experience was different from your father's. I was—" I stop and glance around, trying to balance how I feel versus how many times I've had to tell this story. It's different because it's her. Why the fuck that is true is beyond me at the moment.

"Sam." She's shaking her head like I don't have to tell her, and all of me wants that to be true, so I nod my head. I look down the aisle, then back at her.

"So are you going to eat that whole carton of Rainbow Sherbet tonight, or does it take you a few days? Because after today's events, I think I'm gonna big-spoon this whole carton." She tips her head down to her cart with the Tin Roof Sundae ice cream.

I relax my shoulders and smile at her. "I'd like to say it will take me a few days, but today was kind of a whole-carton kind of day, wasn't it?"

"It was. I keep expecting things to get easier, you know? Like I'm building this wall around my heart so that Donny doesn't take over, but that little pom-pom hat-wearing kid gets me right here." She thumps her chest. She then turns and opens the glass door to the ice cream freezer and grabs a carton of Pralines and Cream. "It really might be necessary, and I like to be prepared."

That has me laughing. "It is good to be ready for all situations, Tammy."

"That's true." She looks down the aisle as if she wants to go, but I'm not ready for this to be over. This ease and strange feeling of familiarity between us, even after ten years, is not something I want to lose to my empty apartment.

"Jeeps are good for eating ice cream," I blurt out like a fucking dweeb. Inside I cringe as my soul shrivels up, but hopefully what she sees in front of her is a casual dude looking to share some dessert.

"Are they? You know, I heard that once, but without the scientific data to back it up, I really will just have to take your word for it."

"I have a Jeep. It's black. Topless at the moment, because it's still warm out." I will myself to stop talking, and for the moment I'm winning. That moment will blow away like dust in the wind if she doesn't say something soon.

"Topless? How nice." Her eyes twinkle with mischief, and my stomach flips a little.

"Yep. I don't put her top on until November. I mean, that's how I did it at Fort Irwin."

"Is it hot there?"

"Worse than here, yes."

"So coming home is like a break in the heat? That's wild to me. I had forgotten how bad it is here."

"Yeah, so do you want to?" I swallow hard, then clear my throat. "Eat ice cream in my Jeep? To prove a point. Science and all that."

That earns me a laugh. "I'd love to. I wasn't looking forward to the big, empty farmhouse."

She pushes her cart away before I can respond to that. I follow her as she grabs a gallon of milk and a few other things. After we both pay, she lets me take the lead to the parking lot. I don't have the doors on so even though there is absolutely no reason to walk to the passenger side with her; I do. She sets her bag of groceries down and grabs the roll bar, swinging easily up into the seat.

"Were you going to give me a boost?" She laughs when she notices me standing there.

"I really don't know." I shake my head and walk around to the driver's seat, tossing my bag into the back.

"Well, I appreciate your support either way. You always were a gentleman."

I pull out of the parking lot, turning to head to the levee, but Tammy reaches over and puts her hand on my arm.

"Sam, stop!" She laughs and covers her face with her hands.

"What is it?"

"Um, can we actually go back to the store? My car is there." She bursts out laughing and I do too. I kind of like that she was so excited to be with me that she forgot everything else.

"Oh, right, yeah." I turn the wheel and get us back to the parking lot. She points at a small, grey Toyota.

"That's me. Let's stop by my place first; I want to put my groceries away, and I'm betting you don't have big spoons in here."

I look down at her hand that is still on my arm and register the warmth, the softness, just everything about it. I clear my throat and try to act like a normal fucking person and not someone who hates to be touched by everyone but her, apparently.

"Sure, yeah. I have, um, I have some plastic spoons in the glove box, but yeah, they aren't big."

"Sam, we can't eat ice cream with a tiny, breakable spoon. There is no way those could handle the amount of Tin Roof Sundae I want."

I chuckle and watch as she climbs out of my jeep and into her car with her groceries. I flip the blinker on and follow her to her house. I wonder about what just happened. Like, like that has to be a good sign that I got her so flustered she forgot her car, right? I'm going to take it as a win, even if it's small.

"I'll be right back." She hops out of her car, grabbing her bag from the back seat.

"I'll be here," I announce. Once she's out of sight, I lower my head to the steering wheel and bang my head gently a few times. The light pouring out of the front of the house catches my eye, and I turn to watch her. The big bay window that is visible from the front of the house is, if I remember correctly, the kitchen. When she was in high school, that window was filled with plants; now it's empty. It was one of the things that made me think she had moved.

"Okay, sorry that took me so long. I got two big spoons and some water because I don't know about you, but ice cream always makes me so thirsty. I also brought a blanket. Maybe that was dumb. It's like eighty degrees."

I smile at her, waiting for her to stop rambling, and when she finally does, I ask, "Ready, then?"

A big sigh comes from her, and she says, "Yes. Ready. Let's test this Jeep theory."

I pull out onto the road in front of her house and drive towards her father's rice fields. I remember there are a couple of good-sized turnouts where I can park. Not like there is a lot of traffic, but still, better to find a safe spot.

She's quiet as we drive, and it feels comfortable, like ten years apart hasn't changed anything. Out here among the flat expanse of rice fields, I can almost pretend nothing has changed.

"So tell me, when did you come back?" I ask because I have wondered that since I saw her on that first day.

"Last year. My dad got sick, and I came out to help. I don't know what was worse: that the cancer took him so fast or that I didn't come sooner. Still beating myself up over that one." She pauses and gives me a little smile before continuing. "How about you, Sam?"

"About six months ago. I, um, had to be here. The doctors thought it would help." I pull off the road and back in so we have one field behind us and one in front. The crickets and frogs are loud as they sing their nightly songs, not bothered at all by the crunch of my tires on the gravel.

I reach back and grab our bags from the back seat, and she takes her ice cream. She wastes no time pulling off the lid and digging her big metal spoon into the top. She takes a huge bite, and I have to look away as she slides her lips over the spoon.

"Oh, my God. This is better in a Jeep." She hands me the other big spoon and blushes a little. "Sorry, I should have waited."

"It's okay." I pry off the lid on mine and dig in. The warm night air, and the music of the nightlife around us does make everything better. I feel myself relaxing and tip my head back to rest on the seat.

"Do you feel like it's helping to be here?" she asks after a few more spoonfuls.

"Somewhat. Yeah. It's nice to be around familiar things." I'll leave it at that because no one wants to hear about the troubles I've had since the Gulf War. Maybe she would listen, but I don't want to talk about it, so I change the subject. "Can I ask what kind of cancer your dad had, or is that—"

"No, it's fine. He had bladder cancer that had spread. 'Metastasized,' they call it, just a fancy word for it took over his whole body. I'm convinced it's because of all the chemicals he was subjected to in Vietnam, but of course the military is fighting that."

"What do you mean?"

"Well, I filed a claim because I think Agent Orange caused it. The military started accepting some responsibility in 1991, but Dad never filled out any of the paperwork when he first got sick. He kept saying that it wasn't their fault. Now that he's gone, it's a little more challenging to get them to do anything."

"That's a bummer. Did he go to the VA for his care?"

"Nope. That's the other problem. Dad liked to doctor shop. Right until the diagnosis, when he was forced to see an oncologist, he went to so many doctors. I think he knew he was really sick and was just hoping to get someone to tell him he was fine."

"I can understand that." Pausing when she looks over at me, the big spoon turned upside down in her mouth. "I don't agree with it, but I can understand it."

She nods and takes another big bite. I don't like the direction this conversation is going, so I change the subject again. "So, do you think Donny's mom will take good care of him? She seems like kind of mess."

Tammy leans back in the seat and kicks off her sandals so she can put her feet up. She has her toes painted the brightest shade of pink I have ever seen. God, she has pretty feet, small and perfectly shaped.

"I bet you want me to say yes, but honestly, Sam? I'm not sure. That woman is a disaster. The only good thing I've seen them do is stay in the same apartment complex so Donny could have some consistency."

I take a big bite and think about that for a little bit. Donny always wears clean clothes, and if he wasn't wearing that damn ski hat, I bet his hair would be combed. It seems like his mom and dad are trying their best to raise him, but what if their best isn't enough?

"So you knew him last year too?" I ask.

"Yeah, I started in January. He won't wear a jacket, so be prepared for that. It was raining, and I hated seeing him get soaked every day, so I gave him that hat. I thought at least his head would be dry." She shrugs a little and takes another bite of her ice cream.

"So that's why he wears it. It came from you!" I laugh and shake my head.

"Yeah, C. J. is giving me endless shit about it. She says I should have seen it coming. I didn't realize then how important his patterns were. I get it now." She rolls her eyes at that.

"Who is C. J.?" My mind is instantly frantic. That name isn't familiar.

"Sorry Mrs. J. Her first name is Clara, so we call her C. J. some-times." She cocks her head at me as I blow out a breath.

I wish I had my notebook to write that down. Now I'll be worried about calling her the wrong name. I dig into my ice cream and take a big bite, hoping that we can move on from this.

"She won't mind if you call her that, or Mrs. J. You can pretty much call her anything, I promise. She's really cool."

I nod with my mouth full of ice cream, taking my time to swallow. "I haven't gotten used to calling people by anything but Mr. or Mrs. The Army really drills that whole respect thing into you, you know?"

"Boy, do I! My dad was the same way. He called all the workers by their proper titles for years. I didn't call a grown-up by their first name until I was in college!"

That makes me laugh, and I relax my shoulders and rest my left foot up on the door frame. My hip is bothering me, but I don't want this night to be over. I roll my head and watch her as she takes another bite. It's so weird that she is here, in my Jeep, back in this town. She looks the same, but so different, and I don't know how both of those can be true.

"You're staring at me," she says, her head mirroring my own.

"I am. I can't believe it's been ten years. I see you like you were in high school, then I blink and you're old."

She laughs and chokes on the ice cream she had just put in her mouth. After a few sputtering coughs, she wipes her mouth with the back of her hand and glares at me. It would be more convincing if she wasn't smiling. "That's rude. You look old too, by the way, and what's with the long hair and earring? Are you a hippie now?"

I smirk at that, but I don't really answer, and because she is perfect in every way, she doesn't push it. We fall into a comfortable silence, listening to the music of the rice fields.

"When are you going to harvest?" I ask as I scrape the last of my ice cream from the carton.

"Not mine to harvest. I sold it all." She twists in her seat, pulling her knees up to her chest. "It's weird to see all of this and know my dad won't be involved anymore."

"Shit, I'm sorry. I should have known."

"No, it's okay. A lot of people thought I would cave and take over his fields. I have told him since he started asking, I think I was around ten years old, that I had no interest in farming."

"I never did either, although my parents weren't asking me to take over the nuts."

"You're lucky." She looks like she wants to say something else, but she stops herself. I'm sure she's curious. Hell, I'm wondering exactly what happened too. By the time I got back, the almond and walnut orchards were for sale, and my parents' home was condemned. I hadn't spoken to either of them since the day I left for boot camp, so I probably have the same questions as everyone else. I guess my sister swooped into town, hired an attorney to handle some of the shit and left two days later. Mario was pretty vague when he said the farmers around here don't blame me for what my father did. I shake off the feeling that always comes when I think about my parents.

"Thanks for this, Tammy. I think this was way better than eating ice cream alone."

"It was, you were not wrong about it tasting better in a Jeep." She pauses and looks over at me with a lazy smile. "Do you remember the HoHos?"

A laugh escapes me before I have time to think. "Fuck, I had forgotten about that. I still say Twinkies are better."

"Both are disgusting, but if I had to eat one now, HoHos all the way." She pushes at my arm, and I want to capture her hand, entwine our fingers and listen to the music of the fields. I don't. I keep my arm on the center console, though, just in case she wants to touch me again.

"I don't understand you," I say, shaking my head like I'm disappointed.

"Did you keep in touch with anyone from school?" she asks as she repositions herself in the seat, feet up on the dash, toes wiggling.

"Nah, how about you?" I wince as my hip protests being in this position for so long. I discreetly use my left hand to lift my leg a little, moving it off the doorjamb.

"Don't laugh when I say this." She dips her head, and I wish I could see the blush I know is spreading across her face. "But I kept in touch with Mrs. Kendal."

"No shit?"

"She was so cool. She is actually why I got my degree in Library Science."

"Wait, you became a librarian? That makes a lot of sense, actually."

She pushes on my arm again playfully but doesn't pull it away like she did the first time. She rests her hand on my forearm, and I'm instantly back in my truck ten years ago. James Taylor was singing "Everyday" and Tammy had slid her hand down my arm, causing my universe to flip on end. The feel of her soft, gentle fingers dancing over my skin was like a shot to my heart. It was everything and not enough, but the eighteen-year-old me froze, scared to make a move.

I reach over and rest my hand on hers and turn my head to face her. She's looking out over the rice fields, and when she doesn't glance my way, I continue. "I mean, you were always reading or researching something. Right?"

She squeezes my arm and slips her hand free as she sits up a little in her seat. "Yeah, but I didn't become a librarian. I went more into the research side of things."

"Okay, still cool. Is that what you were doing before you had to come back?"

"Yes. I worked at the National Archives in Washington, D.C."

"That's impressive! Was that a fun job?"

She shrugs and gives me a weak smile. "I guess. It was my dream job. At least I thought it was. I was good at it; I had friends, dated a little, but . . ." She stops and blows out a breath before continuing. "There was a part of me that was relieved when Dad called me asking for help. It was like this quick flash of 'oh, good, I can go home now.' Does that make sense?"

"Kind of. I am more at ease here. It's familiar. I know where everything is. Even if I didn't go to my childhood home, there is this entire valley that is filled with my memories, my childhood, me."

SEVEN

Tammy

REASONS TO SAY NO

I LET my gaze linger on Sam for a minute before I look forward again, staring out across the fields where Dad worked so hard. I think something happened to Sam during the Gulf War. He's made a few comments about needing to be back here and then there are the notes I've seen him take when someone tells him something. Plus, he kind of panicked when I called Mrs. J by her nickname.

I won't ask. My dad taught me soldiers don't always like to talk about why the toaster popping makes them sweat. Or why the sound of the crop duster coming in low makes you duck for cover. Not every time, mind you, only those days when the dark shadows of the past creep into the light.

Those days, you take deep, slow breaths and hold still, offer a hand to hold, a smile, and if willing, a hug. Hot chocolate works too, even in the summer months. Nothing, and I mean nothing, beats a puzzle laid out on the kitchen table. The slow, steady placement of piece after piece brought Dad back quicker sometimes than the deep breaths or hugs.

"Mrs. Kendal is actually the one that suggested I become an archivist. She said I had the necessary attention to detail and the patience. She even wrote me a letter of recommendation for my master's program."

"I can see that about you. You notice things that other people miss. I was so grateful to have you as my partner for that senior project."

"So, can we talk about the fact that you have an earring now?" I ask, hoping that is a safe subject. I can't help but notice the blue stone in his ear that matches his eyes. He always has his hat on, and his hair tucked behind his ears.

"See? Observant. I forget it's there most of the time. I got it after I left Saudi. I wanted something that was intentional. Same with the tattoo."

"Intentional?"

He shakes his head and a small smile creeps across his lips. "I knew you'd pick up on that. I got injured. About a week after I got to Saudi Arabia, actually." He looks at me for a bit before continuing, his gaze searching, curious. "I don't know what happened. I mean, I know what they told me, but have no memory of the accident. Actually, I have no memory of anything past my first few days there. The things I remember about those days are like clips from a movie."

Sam continues to watch me, and it reminds me of how my dad would share a story about Vietnam and wait for my reaction before he'd continue, like he needed to be sure I was listening and understanding what he was telling me. I'm tempted to ask questions, or tell him I understand, but I don't do either. I lean back in my seat and roll my head towards him. I rest my hand on his arm again, hoping he is okay with my silent way of telling him I'm here.

He looks down at my hand and takes in a ragged breath before covering my hand with his. "My tank hit a landmine. I was thrown out because I was standing up. I was looking around half out of the hatch. We were moving from one site to another. No engagement, no enemy in sight, then everything went wrong."

I squeeze gently on his arm, and he relaxes his hand over mine. I know I have touched him a lot this evening, and I am hoping this means he's okay with it. My dad was always patting my hand or giving me a hug. He needed that physical reminder that I was there. When he was near the end, I sat for hours holding his hand. We didn't talk or cry. I just held him, studied his wrinkled, calloused hand, committing it to memory.

I actually didn't know I was a touchy person until I started working with Donny. He freaked out the first time I patted his shoulder. I felt so bad. We were walking back to class after recess, and he stopped to check out the lines on the pavement. I reached over and tried to move him along. His whole body went rigid, and he ducked away from me, shoving three whole fingers in his mouth. He wouldn't let me get even an arm's length to him for the rest of the week. C. J. felt terrible that she hadn't mentioned his touch aversion to me, but I should have known. I should have seen the signs.

"I was the only one to survive the blast."

His voice is so quiet as he says that it causes me to sit up a little and turn towards him. My eyebrows draw together, trying to find those magic words that will make him understand I hear him, I care. There aren't words to erase the pain, though I know that, so I simply say, "I'm so sorry."

He nods and removes his hand from mine. I let my hand slip away from his arm, and I wish we weren't sitting in this Jeep. I wish I could climb into his lap and wrap him in my arms. My sweet Sam. The boy in my science class, who was charming and smart and shy, is a man now, hurt and scared of the past.

"It is what it is. I hope you don't mind, but I'm getting pretty sore sitting here, so I need to take you home."

"Of course. Sure, thanks for this, Sam. It was really nice."

I get a grunt for an answer, and I wonder if he is regretting telling me what happened to him. I don't want things to be different between us. I like how comfortable it is, how easily we slid back into what we had senior year, before our date.

We are quiet as he drives back to my house, so when he parks in front of my garage and says, "Where's your truck?" I jump a little at the sound of his voice. I had been so lost in my memories.

"Oh, it's in there. I told Dad to sell it when I left, but he didn't."

"I'm glad he didn't. That truck was so fucking cool."

"Oh yeah? You liked Big Red?" I ask, and he barks out a laugh.

"Big Red? That's a great name for her, hell yeah, I liked her." He turns to look at me, and a little quieter he says, "I liked her a lot. I'm glad she's still around."

I blink at him, unsure if we are still talking about my truck. "Yeah, me too," is all I can manage to say.

My heartbeat stutters a little, and I'm pretty sure I'm blushing for no good reason. It's been years since I've felt that flutter, that attraction that comes from a place deep inside blooming without thought. I shake my head to clear that, because even though we are older, I'm sure Sam sees me like he did in school. We were good friends then, and we have to be only that now. He doesn't need me crushing on him when he has come here to heal.

I reach across and grab his arm, giving it a little squeeze. This time I watch his face as I do it for a flinch or anything that would let me know this isn't okay. I see none of that. Instead, I see his gaze drift from my hand up to my face. He lingers on my lips for what feels like an eternity, and out of nerves, I let my tongue dart out across my lower lip. His eyes close and he turns away, so I remove my hand.

"Sorry, I, um, I'm a touchy person and it occurs to me you might not like that."

"I don't."

I swallow and start to apologize again, but he cuts me off.

"Not usually, but it's okay if you touch me. My arm or my hand, I mean, so far it hasn't bothered me. But yeah, usually that's a problem. I guess I feel comfortable with you."

That sends warmth straight to my gut. "I'm glad. But tell me to stop anytime. Okay?"

"I won't," he says, before I can even finish that sentence.

I nod and smile. "Okay, Sam. Thanks again for tonight. I'll see you on Monday."

"See you on Monday, Tammy."

I climb out of his Jeep and hurry into the house, not wanting to linger or look back to see if he's watching me go. It's not until I hear the crunch of gravel as he drives away that I remember my blanket is still in his Jeep. I laugh to myself when my dad's voice rings through my head, "People leave things behind where they want to be again."

He said that to me often as a kid, probably because I constantly forgot things like my jacket at school. I used to think he was trying to make me feel better, but damn, do I want to be back in that Jeep with Sam.

THE NEXT MORNING I am in the kitchen making breakfast. While I remembered to get milk at the store last night, I didn't know I was out of cereal. French toast it is. I'm mixing the eggs and milk when the phone rings.

I reach for the cordless and tuck it between my ear and shoulder as I sprinkle cinnamon into the bowl. "Hello?"

"Glad you didn't change your number."

"Sam?" I almost drop the phone into my egg mixture.

"Yeah, it's me. You forgot your blanket in my Jeep. I can swing by with it if you'd like." His voice is deep and warm, and that little flutter happens again.

I glance at the big bowl in front of me and say, "Sure. If you hurry, you can have French toast with me."

"On my way," he says, and I hear the click of the receiver. A laugh bubbles out and I set the phone back on its charger before jogging back upstairs to brush my teeth and put a bra on. I don't bother changing out of my PJs because they are cotton shorts and a T-shirt. I pull a brush through my hair and rush back downstairs just as I hear him pull up.

I put my hand over my heart and take a deep breath and wait for him to knock. I wasn't nervous last night, but now I'm all jittery. The soft tap on the front door made me jump even though I was waiting for it.

I pull it open and see Sam standing there, faded jeans hugging his thick thighs and a black T-shirt that hangs loose on him. My blanket is folded and tucked under his left arm.

"You must really like French toast," I say as I step aside to let him in.

"Something like that," he says with a wink.

The butterflies take flight as I step closer to him to close the door. I expect him to move, but he doesn't. He smells clean, like a mix of Irish Spring soap and something else. I want to bury my nose in his neck and try to figure it out, but I don't because that would be weird and I am desperately trying not to look weird in front of Sam.

"Come on in. I was mixing the eggs when you called. How many pieces would you like?"

"Three? If that's not too many."

I glance back at him as he follows me through the house. He looks nervous, but maybe that's how this new version of him looks when he's in someone's home. Sam from high school walked through here to meet my dad, and he had the swagger and confidence of a prince.

"Three is fine. Should I make bacon too?"

"I can do that," he offers, and I watch as he looks around, taking in the farmhouse. Not much has changed since he last saw it. There is still a small Formica-topped table with two chairs shoved against the wall by the pantry. The wallpaper is still peeling up at the edges around the doors and windows, although it's probably worse now than it was.

He opens the fridge and grabs the package of bacon while I get out another pan. When we meet at the stove, I notice he still has my blanket tucked under his arm. I chuckle at that.

"Want me to take that, or should I start calling you Linus?"

He looks at me with a confused expression, then down at his left arm where my blanket is nestled. "Oh, right. Here."

He hands it to me and our hands brush, giving me that swooping sensation in my stomach. I really need to get it together. This is embarrassing.

"Thanks for inviting me over. I hope it wasn't too much for me to call this morning."

"Not at all." I give him a small smile and tuck some of my hair behind my ear.

"It's been such a long time since I've felt comfortable like this with someone, and I want you to know how grateful I am for your friendship. In high school and, well, now, if that's okay."

It's like the air just got let out of my tires, but I don't show that to him. Instead, I turn and say, "I feel the same way, Sam. I'd love to be your friend. Since I came back, I don't really have anyone I'd call a friend, and a friend is a good thing to have." I wonder if maybe I could fit the word friend in there one more time. I mentally punch myself.

"I find that hard to believe, Tammy. You were always so well liked, and popular."

"Ha!" I bark out, unable to restrain myself. "I was not popular, Sam, then or now." Glancing over at him, I see he's shaking his head in disbelief, maybe, or maybe he just thinks I'm funny. I'm not. I am an idiot.

I should have said, "No, Sam, I don't want to be your friend. I was actually hoping since I am no longer the nerd I was in high school we could try that date thing again." Instead, I dipped the bread into the egg mixture and heaved a big sigh.

"Deep thoughts over there?" Sam asks.

"Not really, just wishing I had this bread that I'd get at a bakery back in D.C. It was thick and buttery, and let me tell you, it made the best French toast." I smile at him and a little at my ability to side-step all the things I want to say.

"That sounds good, but I'm sure whatever you have will be a

thousand times better than the microwaved breakfast burrito I was going to have." He heats the cast-iron skillet, testing it now and then by holding his hand over it. When it's hot enough, he peels the slices of bacon apart and gently sets six pieces in the pan. The sizzle is so satisfying I almost miss the tear that has slipped down my cheek.

Sam turns to say something to me but stops and cocks his head before asking, "Something wrong?"

I swipe at the stupid tear that slipped out and drop my egg-soaked bread onto the electric skillet. "Oh, this?" I point to my face. "Don't mind me, just emotional about how you make bacon."

Sam laughs and says, "Sure, I can see that. Why?"

"My dad used to do that. It's dumb because it's probably how you are supposed to check if the skillet is hot, but I always touched it quickly. It always made him yelp, so of course I did it again." I wipe away another stupid tear.

"Your dad was a smart man. I'm sorry you lost him."

"Me, too."

We finish getting breakfast ready in a comfortable silence. I grab plates and silverware, then quickly set the small table for us. I haven't sat here in ages. Dad and I started eating in front of the TV when I came back, because these chairs were hard for him. The padding has long since worn down in the seat and back, and the vinyl is cracking. It's nice to know that Sam won't judge me for the condition of things like Kyle would have. He was such a perfectionist. An old, cracked chair would never have been acceptable. He wouldn't understand that each little tear, each bit of stuffing that found its way out was a memory. A piece of my past, a reminder of what a wonderful childhood I had.

Sam settled in across from me at the small table, our feet knocking a few times before we found an arrangement that worked. "I guess I never realized how tall you are."

He chuckled and shook his head. "Well, you barely noticed me until we became partners on that project, so that makes sense."

I scoffed at that, making him smile. "I noticed you; I just didn't really talk to the jocks." Dragging the bacon through the last bit of syrup on my plate, I pop it in my mouth.

"I wasn't a jock; I just played baseball my junior and senior year. That doesn't make me a jock." He points his fork at me.

"Well, I spent all my time in the library, and that most definitely made me a nerd." I say with a laugh. "Finished?" I ask as I stand up from the table. He nods, and I take both our plates to the sink.

"So wait, if I hadn't played ball, you would have talked to me more?" he asks, crossing his arms over his chest. His thick muscles bulge with the movement.

"No." The answer comes out before I can stop it.

"What?" He stands and crosses to me in two easy strides, concern etched across his face. God, he is so handsome. "Why not? Did you think I was an asshole or something?"

"No, that was not it. I just was really," I pause and grab the towel off the counter so I have something to hold on to. Maybe if I am just honest, this will be easier. "I was really shy, and you were the hottest guy in school. A lot of girls were afraid to talk to you; it wasn't just me."

EIGHT

REVELATIONS AND REGRETS

I BLINK A FEW TIMES, trying to process what she just said. "Really? That's not true."

"Oh, come on, Sam, now you're just being ridiculous." She tosses the towel on the counter and walks out of the kitchen. I follow her and watch as she climbs onto the old sofa. She crosses her legs as she sits, so I move to the far end of the couch.

Last night, after burying my face in her blanket trying to inhale her scent, then feeling like a fucking creep, I decided to ask Tammy to be my friend. I don't know if I'm ready for more than that, to be honest, but a lot of that decision was because I thought she had never been interested in more. Not back in school, and certainly not now.

"You have a mirror, right? That, and you're Sam Ford." She rolls her eyes at that statement.

"What's that supposed to mean?" I lean back on the couch, stretching my arm across the back. Fuck, this couch is comfortable. My place is so small, there's a recliner, a small table, and my bed. I miss having a couch.

"You are the son of the richest nut farmers in the valley, played the sexiest position in baseball—catcher"—she laughs and continues —"who looks like that." She waves her hand in my direction.

"Okay, now you are pulling my leg. The pitcher is the sexiest position."

She raises an eyebrow at me and cocks her head.

"You know what I mean. All the girls go nuts for the pitcher. Gordon Walker was like the most sought-after guy in our school."

"That's because he had a huge—" She stops and covers her face to try and hide her laugh.

"And you have this information how?" I say, not even trying to hide my own smile.

"You'd be surprised at what you learn when you spend all your free time in the stacks. Most people didn't know I was even there. Oh! Like, for example, did you hear that Mr. Henderson's wife was having an affair with the janitor?"

I bark out a laugh. "Yeah, actually, I knew that, but only because Teddy and I were tight, and he couldn't keep his mouth shut. She was about ten years older than him and married. Unfortunately, he thought that was something to brag about."

"Gross," she says. I notice her old, stretched-out T-shirt has slipped down a little, revealing the top of her bra, so I look away quickly. Friends do not check out their friends' perfect tits even if they think about them all the time.

"So, do you keep in touch with anyone from our class, not counting the librarian?" I ask.

"No. Do you?" She looks down and sees her shirt has slipped, so I examine my knee as she adjusts the damn thing.

"Nah, well, wait, that's not true. I see Curtis Donovan every day. Does that count?"

She sits up straight, her legs untucking. "What? Why? Where?"

"He works at the yard." I pause, then ask, "Not part of his fan club?"

"That guy is a total dick," she says as she stands up. She walks over to the television, and I think for a minute she is going to turn it on, but instead she reaches for something above it. When she returns, she has our senior yearbook in her hand. Damn, I haven't seen that thing since I packed up my bedroom ten years ago.

"Open it to the back and read at what he wrote!" She drags her hand through her hair and paces back and forth while I fumble with the book.

Holy shit.

"He wrote that? Did you show this to anyone?" I scoot forward to the edge of the couch and I'm about to stand and join her, but she blows out a breath and sits next to me.

"No, what would they have done, anyway? I'm sure he would have said it was a joke."

"He's threatening you! Did your dad see this?"

"God, I hope not," she says, then shakes her head. "No, if he had, I'm sure Curtis would've suffered a permanent injury to the very body part he was offering to show me."

"He might still," I mumble.

"He's not worth it. Wait, he doesn't drive a bus route, does he? He won't sub for you or anything, right?" I'm upset at how panicked she sounds about that.

"No, he doesn't have his driver's license. He spent the last few years in prison for felony DUI."

"No shit? Really? Actually, that doesn't surprise me at all. Did you know he used to bring vodka in his Big Gulp almost every day?"

I shake my head, not at all shocked by that. "No, but that makes sense. He's a decent mechanic and, to be fair, it seems like he's trying to turn his life around. Mike at the yard is close with Curtis's family, so he pulled some strings to get him that job."

"Well, even if he's sober now, he's still a piece of shit. I'm glad I don't have to worry about him showing up at Bower Elementary." She wipes her hands down her face and groans. "He doesn't know I work there, does he? Please don't mention my name to him."

"I wouldn't. We don't really talk much. He asked me why I

looked like a hippie now, and I told him to mind his own business. Since then he only asks where things are."

That earns me a smile, and I feel my shoulders relax a little. I lean back on the couch and start to flip through the yearbook. The mascot was a wolverine for some reason. A farmer, or a duck, or a goose would actually make more sense. I flip pages until I get to the seniors and find Tammy right away. I don't realize she's watching me as I gently run my finger over her picture until it's too late. Deciding to own it, I say, "This is a really good picture of you."

"Thanks. It turned out better than I expected, to be honest." She scoots a little closer, so I let the book lie open on my lap so we can both see.

"Wow, I had forgotten about most of these people. Do you think they all still live here and I just don't recognize them?" she asks.

"Maybe you didn't recognize me, so that's a real possibility."

She punches me lightly on the arm, then flips the page to find my picture. Damn. My bow tie was almost as big as my face, but seeing this, I guess I do look different.

"See? That guy right there looks nothing like you now, his cocky smile and twinkling—" Her words fade out, but I hear "eyes," as she almost whispers it.

I see it too. Eighteen-year-old Sam Ford was good at hiding how fucked up his life was. It's not like I had it all together then, but I could pretend with the best of them.

"I was so excited to be a senior," Tammy says as she leans in a little more to turn the page again. I fight the urge to breathe deeply, wondering if she still wears the same perfume.

"Yeah? Me, too, but probably for different reasons than you. I wanted to get the hell out of my parents' house. You had it pretty good here; your old man was nice." That slipped out, but Tammy doesn't react to it. Instead, she turns to the middle where the sports team pictures were. There I am, down in a squat, catcher's mask tipped up and the goofiest smile on my face.

"See? Sexiest position in baseball." She taps my picture, then points to the other guys on the team. They made us all stand in ridiculous poses so our pitcher is mid-throw and unfortunately, I am suddenly very aware of what Tammy had said about my teammate.

I clear my throat and say, "Okay, whatever you say . . ." I trail off when I notice the note I left her under my picture. God, I was a cheese ball.

"You should've punched me for this. This right here is a punchable offense." I point to it and she laughs.

"I thought it was cute. Plus, every time I read it I could hear your voice, 'Catch ya later,'" she says in a deeper voice, trying, I assume, to sound like me.

"If I could've figured out how to draw finger guns, I probably would have added that. God, teenagers are so weird."

"For sure."

We sit and look through the rest of the yearbook, and I finally convince myself to leave. I'd stay here all day if she'd let me, but she probably has things to do. I need to go to the store and get a few things and then answer the letter my sister sent me last week. I don't know what she wants from me. I'm not setting foot in that house no matter what she thinks is there.

"Thanks again for last night, and today, Tammy. It's nice to have you back in my life."

"I feel the same way, Sam. Can I give you a hug, or is that too much?"

My whole body reacts to the thought of her pressed up against me, and I try to play it cool with a one-shoulder shrug. "Sure, we can try."

She steps closer and holds her arms out, waiting for me to make the first move, so I duck down and wrap my arms around her waist. She gently puts her arms under mine and places her hands on my back. I tense immediately, and she freezes.

"Too much?"

"Yeah, sorry." I step back, pissed at myself and embarrassed by my stupid reaction.

"It's okay. We can stick to handshakes or me touching those nice forearms," she wiggles her eyebrows at me and blinds me with the most beautiful smile.

"Okay, weirdo." When I laugh, her whole face lights up.

"See you Monday."

I nod at her and get the heck out of there before I do something stupid like ramble about why I don't like being touched.

It's surprisingly cooler today. I guess we will get our four minutes of fall before winter comes. I wonder what it would be like to live in a place that has all four seasons. When I joined the army, I went to Georgia for basic training. I thought I was going to die. It was over a hundred degrees and humid as fuck. Guys that came from that area laughed at all of us from California because there was no hiding our misery. I got used to it, thank God, because I wanted to go to Armory training and it was at the same base. I was in Georgia for the first five years of my Army career, then . . . I was deployed.

Those days in Georgia were some of the best days of my life. I'm glad I can remember them.

NINE

Tammy

TULE FOG HIDES THE TEARS

NOVEMBER IS my favorite time of year. The heat of the valley has finally given up, and the rice harvest is done. Fields get flooded, and then the birds come. The variety we get some years is downright amazing. Snow geese and Ross's geese in flocks so huge you almost can't see the field. My favorites are the great blue heron and the egrets. They are both majestic, but the heron has always reminded me of a tall wood fairy. The way they move so quietly along the shore, always watchful of danger, like they are the protectors of the birds who come to live in the flooded fields for the winter.

As I stare out across the street at what once was our rice paddy, it hits me that this is the first full season without my dad. He was here in body last year at this time, but it was only a matter of days before he slipped away. I glance at the jar of ashes on the counter and sigh. I promised him I would do this. I pictured myself walking across the street to the rice a hundred times, but now the thought of scattering him across that field, among the water and birds and soil that gave us so much, is almost unfathomable. It will be like losing him all over again.

I heave a sigh and swallow down the last of my coffee. It's barely light out and there is a thick blanket of fog, making the road almost impossible to see. No one would notice me, which is why he wanted me to do it now. I look at the blue porcelain vase that contains a man I once thought was invincible. "You really want to be duck food, Dad? This is your last chance to change your mind."

He doesn't answer, of course, but my heart swells as I remember his words: "Return me to the land, to the rice fields that saved me, from the rice fields that tried to kill me."

Vietnam took so much from him, not just the war, not the injury that sent him home. It planted that cancerous seed that grew until it consumed him. Although I guess I can't blame Vietnam for that. Agent Orange was an American poison.

I stop before my mind gets twisted into that unyielding knot, and I walk to the back door where I have my rain boots and pull them on over my thick socks. I slip Dad's Carhartt jacket off its hook and let it wrap around me, enveloping me in his scent. Then the tears start to fall, but that is not something I am going to care about. I have a job to do, and maybe this is a job that requires a few tears.

I turn back and grab the urn off the counter and tuck it inside the jacket, protecting it from what I do not know. The wooden steps off the kitchen creak as I make my way down them and to the side of the house. Here at street level, the fog seems thicker, and I wish I had grabbed my knit cap.

Out of habit, I look both ways, although it's doubtful I'd miss the lights of an approaching vehicle. It's quiet though, so I dash across the road and walk a few paces to my left, feeling for the fence post. There, the rice fields split with a narrow dirt check that is above the level of the water. I walk out into the mist, letting it swallow me whole.

"I miss you, Dad. I'm mad at myself for staying gone so long; I'm mad at you for not telling me sooner that you were sick. I know you wanted to let me live my life, but you took time away from me. Sometimes that hurts more than anything, that you knew but didn't tell me." I'll stop because this is turning into a bitch fest instead of a eulogy. "You were right about this, though. The fog is a perfect cover for scattering your ashes among the reeds. I imagine the pintails and mallards are still sleeping, but if they wake up and fly away, I hope they carry you with them. I hope you are looking down on this, on me, and that you know how very much I love you." The last bit comes out a little choked, but Dad wouldn't mind. I twist off the lid of the urn and step out into the field, my boots sinking into the muddy water. Then, holding my arm out to the side, I tip the vessel and make a giant sweeping arc. Tiny plunking sounds like rain falling on the roof of a car fill my ears for a moment, then the world is silent again.

"Goodbye, Dad. I love you."

I turn and make my way back to the path, slipping a little as I step up out of the water. I tip my head up and let all my tears fall, scattering drops of my pain all along the rice check. When there is nothing left to give, I walk back to my house to get ready for the week ahead.

Back inside the house, I shed Dad's jacket and my muddy boots by the back door, then head upstairs to take a shower. I did all my errands yesterday so Sunday would be free to release my father's ashes into the wild. With that finally done, I do feel a little lighter. I handled everything the way he asked me to, from the sale of his land to the scholarship and the deed to the house, finally paid in full. Even with student loans, I couldn't have afforded to make it, so Dad took a second mortgage on this place. I run my hand along the wall as I walk down the hallway. Framed pictures of my childhood stare back at me. Toothless, pigtailed girl riding on a John Deere with Dad, slightly older me with my nose buried in a book as I lean against the barn, oblivious to the world. Me with one of our countless barn cats laying in the grass on a hot summer's day, and my favorite one, that is, of me and Dad. It was just after harvest, my senior year in high school. We were leaning against Big Red and Dad had his arm draped over my shoulder. He has the biggest smile on his face, and I am looking over at him with all the love I held apparent in my eyes. I can't remember who took this, but I am so glad I have it.

I pause outside his bedroom door, breathe deeply before pushing it open. His bed is still rumpled from the last time he slept up here, and his wallet lies on the nightstand, stuffed so full I don't know how he put it in his pocket. I pick it up and laugh as the receipts fall out. Almost all of them are for gas, but there is one or two from the Pizza Palace. I toss them in the trash can next to the nightstand and pull out his driver's license, running my finger across his picture.

What do you do with these things? It seems wrong to throw them away, yet to hold on to everything he touched, all the things he needed in this life, seems like a selfish way to anchor him here. I go to put his license back in the worn spot where it lived for so many years, and I see the top of a black-and-white picture sticking out.

My breath catches a little. I haven't seen this for years. I pull it out carefully and stare down at the small picture of my mom holding me. She's standing next to a black Buick and her smile is bright. It's the only picture I have of us together. She passed away shortly after this was taken, and while I asked many times over the years for more details about why she died, my dad wouldn't elaborate more than to say, "God calls some of his angels home early and we don't always know why."

I set the picture aside and pulled the rest of his cards from the wallet. Tiny plastic reminders of things he won't need, his health insurance card, a business card for the guy who fixed the equipment on the farm and a laminated piece of paper with a quote from Bertrand Russell that says, "War does not determine who is right— only who is left."

That surprises me. I remember reading that quote to Dad when I stumbled across it in a book I was reading. I didn't realize it had resonated with him so much.

After a long, hot shower, I get into my warmest sweatpants, fluffy socks, and one of my dad's long sleeve T-shirts. I guess it's the finality of releasing his ashes, because I feel more settled today than I have in a long time. I also think I'm ready to tackle cleaning out his room.

This old farmhouse is too big for just me, but I decided I wasn't going to make any decisions about whether I would stay until summer. I need to ramble about this space alone to see if this life here suits me. I love my job—that's an easy one—and having Sam as a friend has proved to be a delight. He's come over a few times since that day we had breakfast, and we always have fun talking about high school or things we did when we first left the valley.

He seems a little more relaxed too, so maybe having me as a friend has been good for him as well. I pull the bottom drawer of my dad's long dresser open and sigh. Dad was very organized. This particular drawer contains his white undershirts, the next one up his socks, then the top one has his underwear. The other side holds his jeans. Three drawers of faded, ripped, and worn wranglers starting at the top with the newer ones, the bottom drawer holding the ones that really should be in the trash. I pull out a pair and laugh at the rip in the seat. I put those and all the other torn ones into the large black trash bag, then boxed up the rest for donation.

It doesn't take me long after that, and soon I have the entirety of my father's wardrobe cleared out of the dresser and closet, except for the few things I want to keep for myself. Next, I strip the bed and carry all the blankets and sheets down to the laundry room. This is good. It's like the fog of the last year has lifted a little, and I can see what is on the road ahead.

Too bad the valley hasn't gotten the same memo. Monday morning rolls around and the fog is so thick, I leave half an hour early for work even though it takes me five minutes to drive there. I get to work with plenty of time to spare, of course, so I spend a few minutes getting things ready for Donny. He has a new goal with his letters, something he seems curious about, so I pull all the tasks related to that. I have an uppercase/lowercase matching game and a few worksheets so he can practice writing each letter. Something that has always intrigued me about Donny is that when you give him any type of work on paper, he takes it very seriously. He is calm and practiced in his writing and more patient than he is with the other things we've tried. Mrs. J has a theory that he would prefer to be doing work like he sees the older students doing, so hopefully today we will start that.

I finish and head out to wait for the bus, feeling a little disoriented by all the fog. I'm glad Sam is driving Bus 43 now. He knows how to deal with this weather better than anyone else.

Cars dropping off students come and go, and still no bus. I glance at my watch just as the bell rings. Damn. I hope everything is okay.

"Tammy? Are you out here?"

I turn toward the voice just as Mrs. J steps out from the fog. "There you are." She sighs and hands me my purse. "I need your help. Donny won't get on the bus. Sam radioed the yard and Mike called me. Can you go see what is going on?"

I take my purse from her and nod. "Sure, of course, you'll be okay without me here?" I glance over her shoulder towards the direction of the classroom, although it's completely hidden from view.

"Yes, we will be fine. Justin isn't coming in at all today, and Mandy won't be here until after first recess. Sam has Laura on the bus, and Donny is just standing there refusing to board." She gives me a weak smile.

"I'm on it." I pat my apron and make sure I have his new favorite thing. "Be back soon."

I jog to my car and shake my head at the strange job I have found myself in.

TEN

HEARTBREAK AND TOY SPATULAS

I STAND and walk to the back of the bus to check on Laura again. "Sorry about this. Miss Tammy is on her way." I use her washcloth to wipe at her mouth, and she twists away. She is staring out the window, trying to see Donny. The bright blue pom-pom on the top of his hat is about the only thing I can make out from here. He's stepped further back towards the apartment.

I look down and notice Laura's blanket has slipped, so I pull it up, tucking it around her. She arches and makes a frustrated noise at me. "I understand. I feel the same way. I want Donny to get on the bus too."

I make my way back to the front of the bus and down the steps, peering through the fog.

"Come on, Donny. It's cold out here. don't you want to go see Miss Tammy? I bet she has your spatula." I am met with only silence. If not for his hat, I would think he had wandered off. Where the hell is his mom, anyway?

I hear a car pull up behind me, and my shoulders relax a little. Tammy appears out of the fog and gives me a little smile.

"Rough morning?"

"It appears that way. Thanks for coming, Tammy. He walked toward the bus like normal, but as soon as he was close enough to step in, he turned and walked back to where he is. He's done that like three times, and I kept thinking he was going to get on. I can't leave Laura and I know I can't grab his hand and drag him onto the bus. Sorry. Maybe I should have radioed it in sooner."

"No, it's okay. That's weird though, he's never done anything like this before." I watch her look over her shoulder at him, then she reaches into her pocket for his favorite thing, currently a miniature toy spatula.

"Miss Tammy is here, Donny," I shout and expect the silence to continue, but instead we both hear a little shuddering sob.

Then a quiet voice says, "Miss Tammy here."

"Shit." Tammy runs towards Donny and I follow her bright red cap through the fog. I can see she has bent down to talk to him, after a minute she turns and runs back to me.

"The door to his mom's place is open, and he keeps looking back at it. Did she come out with him?"

"No, he's been alone this whole time." My stomach sinks. "Stay here, Laura's in the back and she's getting pretty mad."

I don't wait for an answer; I jog past Donny and up the stairs to his mother's apartment. The door is open, so I call out, "Hello? It's me, Sam, your son's bus driver. Donny won't get on the bus, so I—" My words freeze in my throat. I take a few steps back until I am outside on the landing again, then I pull the door shut.

"JESUS CHRIST," I mutter and bow my head, trying to collect myself before I go back down there. My heart is racing and I feel a prickle at the back of my throat, like I might lose my breakfast.

I turn and pass Donny, who is still rooted in the same spot. Tammy's concern etched across her face tells me I am not hiding my emotions very well as I reach the bus. I climb the steps and grab the radio. "Yard, this is Bus 43. I need law enforcement at 165 Main Street. I have two students and their aide. We are safe."

I wait for Mike to come on and am grateful that he doesn't ask questions I don't want to answer on open airwaves. He simply repeats my request and tells me he's handling it. Tammy is standing right beside me on the top step of the bus when I turn around.

She gently touches my arm and whispers, "What happened, Sam?"

I lower my voice so Laura won't overhear, then say, "His mother is dead. I asked Mike to call the police. They will be here soon. We need to get Donny out of here."

"Shit. Agreed. Okay. Give me a minute." She drops her purse at my feet and runs to Donny. I can't see or hear what she is saying, but I don't have to wait long before she reemerges from the fog with Donny. He has his small toy spatula gripped in one hand and his middle finger of the other hand tucked into Tammy's grip. They climb the steps of the bus with Tammy in the lead. She stops and steps aside so Donny can sit in the front, then we wait. He looks at us, eyes rimmed red, nose runny and cheeks flushed. He stands up and goes to his usual spot in the middle. Laura bangs her cup on her tray, and I quickly climb into the driver's seat.

"I'll stay here and tell the police what's going on. Can you drive around, a little? Take the long way so I can try to be at school to get him off the bus?"

"Absolutely." The sirens in the distance are getting louder, so we share a glance, and she nods, grabs her purse and walks off into the fog.

I drive for a few blocks before I say, "Knock-knock."

No answer from the middle of the bus, so I try again.

"Knock-knock."

Still nothing, so I answer myself, "Who's there?"

I wait, my stomach clenching at the silence. Fuck, I want to pull the bus over and grab him. I want to hug him to my chest and cover his tiny body with mine, protecting him from what he saw, what he must have gone through. I can't, I know that. He doesn't want me to, just like I didn't want arms wrapping around me when I was at my worst.

"A broken pencil!" I say to the silence, and this time I see his hat move a little.

"Broken pencil, who?" I respond, then wait. Nothing, so I finish the joke, "Never mind, it's pointless."

That earns me a few cup bangs from Laura, but silence from Donny.

I try another one that I know he likes.

"Knock-knock?" This time I don't wait since I'm betting he won't answer. "Who's there?"

Laura makes a noise, so I continue. "Tank."

This time I wait. I am crawling along at a snail's pace along the frontage road. I drove in the opposite direction from our normal route because I didn't want Donny to see the police cars.

A very tiny voice says, "Tank," and my heart cracks wide open. I close my eyes for just a second and swallow hard.

"Tank who?" I say, my voice not as solid as I'd like. I wait another moment, more to settle myself than to wait for an answer.

"You're welcome!" I say with a little more bravado.

"Tank," the tiny voice says as Laura bangs her cup.

"Okay, let's see if we can make our way to school. This fog is pretty thick, but we should be there soon!"

I take a few more wrong turns on purpose, then pull up to Bower Elementary as Tammy darts across the parking lot. Mrs. J is out front and she has a whole bucket of candy under her arm. She came prepared for war, but the little dude has no more fight left in him. He goes easily to Tammy when she climbs on the bus, and I wait for them to exit before going back to Laura. I bend down and give her little scarf a tug. "You did great today, Laura. Thanks for being a good friend to Donny."

I lower the ramp and Mrs. J takes over as if it were any other day.

. . .

MIKE IS WAITING for me as I pull into the yard, and he taps on the door as soon as I stop. I pull the lever and the doors swing in; before I can even stand up, Mike is inside.

"So, what the fuck happened?" He crosses his arms over his chest and leans on the rail, clearly not moving until he gets an answer.

I sigh and turn to face him, and tell him everything, starting with how Donny tried to get me to follow him. It made perfect sense once I saw his mom. He didn't want to leave her; he knew he needed to tell a grown-up. He did amazing. My voice catches a few times as I describe that to him, but I regain my composure when I get to the part about Donny's mom.

"I think she had been gone for at least a day, Mike. What the fuck did that poor kid go through the last twenty-four hours?"

Mike wipes his hand down his face and shakes his head. "I don't even want to think about it. Listen, I need you to fill out an incident report. When you are finished with that I want you to take the rest of the day off."

"Hell, no. I'm not letting someone else pick up"—I stop because that makes no sense. I'm not picking up Donny after school with the bus. He won't be going home. Fuck.

"Come on, Sam." His voice is filled with pain and sympathy.

I follow Mike into the office and sit at his desk, where he already has a blank report and a pen. I'm almost finished with it when I hear Mike say, "Yeah, Sam Ford. He was the driver; he's filling out an incident report in there."

I look up as an officer is walking toward me. He's with the Sheriff's Department and he looks around my age. I stand and nod before saying, "Hello, are you looking for me?"

"Sam Ford?"

"Yes, that's me."

"I have some questions for you about what happened at 165 Main Street this morning. Do you have a minute?"

"Of course." I grab an extra chair and offer it to him, then sit back down and wait.

He flips open a little notebook and pulls a pen from his shirt pocket.

"What time did you arrive at the scene?"

"I get to the apartment every morning about seven forty-five. I think it was around that time, but I might have been earlier since I didn't have to drop off the high school students."

He lifts an eyebrow at me, so I explain. "I have four kids on my route. Two are high school students. I pick them up first, then I get Laura. I drop the boys off at the high school, then I get Donny. The boys are sick, so it was only Laura. I might have been there as early as seven thirty."

Fuck, now that I am telling him I realize I should have known something was really wrong, because as soon as I stopped in front of the apartment I could see Donny's little hat. I wonder now how long he was out there by himself in the fog.

I recounted everything: the way the apartment looked, where I saw her body, and how I backed out not touching anything. He asks a few questions, making me repeat things I already told him, but I understand. The last question surprises me, but I guess it shouldn't.

"Can you explain why you left the scene?"

I scrub my face with both hands and say, "Sure, I left because I had a traumatized seven-year-old who had been standing out in the cold for God knows how long. He spent the last, what, maybe twenty-four hours with his mother's body. I wanted to get him to school where his world could return to normal a little."

"That's understandable. Did you witness anyone or anything that seemed out of place when you arrived?" he asks, and I hold back my anger, but just barely.

"I couldn't see three feet from the bus. Has the fog lifted? Because this morning it was like pea soup."

"Right, I just thought I'd ask."

I deflate a little and shake my head. "The only thing that was unusual was that Donny was out there by himself. His mom wasn't going to win any awards for her life choices, but she was always with him for pickup and drop-off."

"Okay, and when you dropped him off on Friday, was she there?"

"Yes. I waved at her like usual and watched her and Donny walk up the stairs to the apartment."

"Is that normal for you to watch until your students get inside?"

"Yes, well, with him."

"Can you explain?"

I blow out a breath and shake my head again. "Not really. I really care about that little dude. It kind of—" I stop and try to think of a better way to say this, but there isn't one. "It kind of sucks to drop him off at that shithole apartment every day."

The officer nods and writes something down, then flips the notebook closed. "Thanks, Sam. It's good to see you again, I heard a rumor you were back, but you know I wasn't sure. You look great."

I glance down at his name tag and read his name: Henderson. Shit, I know him. "It's good to see you too, Kent. I almost didn't recognize you."

He stands and pats his stomach. "Yeah, I lost a bit of weight." He chuckles, sticking his hand out. I extend mine and shake quickly, not wanting him to pull me into some weird bro hug.

I follow him out of the shop and into the parking lot so I can find Mike and ask if I can stay and do some work. I really don't want to go back to my tiny studio apartment right now.

"Oh, hey, I saw your dad the other day," Kent says as he reaches for the door of his patrol car.

"Yeah?" That familiar chill runs up my spine.

"Over at the courthouse in Colusa. He said he's living out there now?" He asks this like I might actually care where that prick is living.

"You know more than me. Didn't know he was even in the valley anymore." I stuff my hands in my pockets, wishing he would just go. I can't deal with this right now.

"Oh, right. Yeah, so I guess you aren't aware that your mom is in India then?"

"Dude, I haven't spoken to my parents since high school graduation. She could be on the moon, for all I care."

"Right. Sorry. I kinda forgot how crazy that was. Seeing your dad brought it all back. Well, like I said, it's good seeing you again. Now that I know you're back, I'll have to recruit you for our baseball team in the spring. We need a catcher."

"Yeah, sure. You know where to find me," I say, forcing a smile. Just fucking leave already, would you? He smiles and finally gets into his car. Something happened here that involved my parents, but I can't find the energy to care. Mario has made a few comments here and there, and if I wasn't avoiding thinking about my shitty family I'd ask what he's talking about. That seems like too much work, though.

Mike lets me stay until lunch, so I get busy with an oil change and help Curtis with a brake job, but then, even I agree I need to get out of here. I'm worried about Donny, and Tammy and I can't seem to focus on anything else. Maybe I should stop by the school? Would that be weird?

I climb into my Jeep and pull out of the yard. I don't know the schedule at the school, and I don't want to disrupt an already stressful day, so I do the only thing I can think of: I drive to Tammy's house.

I pull in and angle my Jeep so I can watch the road, then I kill the engine and wait. It's twelve thirty. School isn't out for another hour and a half, but I'd rather sit here than in my apartment, so I lean back and attempt to get comfortable. This damp fog is making my hip hurt more than normal, so I get out of the Jeep and start to walk around stretching my legs when Tammy's Toyota turns into the property. She stops by the garage and gets out quickly, running to the house without giving me even a glance.

"Fuck," she yells, then I hear one thud followed by another. "Goddamn stupid fucking parents," she yells at the door. I jog over to the porch and make it up the stairs before she turns around and screams.

"Jesus Christ, Sam. What the hell are you doing here?" she says, clutching her chest.

I bend and pick up her keys, which are at her feet, and unlock the door for her. "I didn't know where else to go," I tell her honestly.

"Well, I'm glad you're here. Come in, we're getting drunk." She pushes the door open and stomps into the house, throwing her purse on the table. A vase wobbles as her bag skids to a stop next to it, but I grab it before it can topple. Tammy is opening and closing cupboards with enough force to break them, so I hurry after her.

"Where the hell is the tequila?" She spins on her heel and stomps off to the formal dining room. I hear more doors being opened and slammed shut. "There you are, Jose! You sneaky little bastard, you are coming with me."

She reappears, slamming a half-full bottle of Jose Cuervo on the counter. She opens the cupboard by the sink and pulls out two small glasses. They are the kind my mom used to serve us orange juice on Sunday mornings, as if it were the most valuable drink in the world.

Tammy twists off the lid on the tequila bottle and fills up each glass, sliding one over to me. "I don't have lime or salt." She says it like she wants a fight.

I reach for mine, not wanting to piss her off any further. "Don't care." I wait for her to lift her glass, then we both slam the shot back. I shudder as the alcohol slides down my throat, but Tammy doesn't even flinch. She pours another for herself, and grabs my glass, filling it back up.

"Uno más!" she says, tipping her head back and swallowing the whole thing in one gulp. I do the same with mine, this time without the shudder. The second one is always easier, which is why I don't usually do this.

She reaches for the bottle again, but I put my hand over hers, stopping her. "Slow down there, Miss Tammy. Let's take this into the living room." I grab the bottle and glasses from her and walk away.

I set the bottle on the coffee table and turn to wait for Tammy. A few seconds later she appears with an enormous bag of tortilla chips and a jar of salsa. A bowl is tucked under her arm.

Tammy sets them down, unties her apron and kicks off her shoes. She's wearing that red knit hat still, and her cheeks are almost the same color. Her grey sweater looks really soft, and I wish I could reach out and hug her. That's the second time today I have felt the need to pull someone into my arms. The doctor at the VA would probably say that's progress, but it's not about me. It's about protecting these people who have found their way into my life and my heart.

Tammy sits on the couch, and rips open the bag of chips. I help by dumping the salsa into the bowl, and we eat in silence for a few minutes.

"So where was she?" Tammy finally asks.

"On the floor in the living room."

"Fuck. Now I wish I had stuck around to find out more. I told the officers there was a body and explained about Donny and needing to get to him. I left before they really gave me permission to do so, but what else was I going to do? Did you see his face? That boy never cries. Never." She stops talking and pours us each another shot. I haven't had even a drop of alcohol since before I was injured, but if a day has ever called for it, I guess this is it.

I toss mine back and watch as she does the same. When she sets her glass down, I reach for her hand, surprising us both. She looks at me with so much pain, I can't stand it any longer, and I pull her to me, wrapping her in my arms.

"It's going to be okay," I say into her hair. She has her arms at her sides, and I realize I am pinning them down, so I let her go. She doesn't move back; she looks up at me with tear-filled eyes.

"They came and took him," she says quietly.

"Shit. That must've been awful." I reach up and stroke her cheek, wiping away a tear that had fallen.

"He was surprisingly calm. It was a lady he knew. His parents lost custody of him once before, and Donny went to a temporary emergency foster home for about two weeks."

I'm not sure what to say to that, so I continue to hold her face in my palm. I wait as she takes a shuddering breath and closes her eyes. We sit like that for a moment, then she slides back away from me, wiping at her face.

"I hate them so much. How the fuck can you do that to a kid? How can you be that fucking selfish? She must've overdosed, right? Or drank herself to death in front of him. Jesus, I want to punch her right in the face and I can't."

"I feel the same way." I lean back into the couch and rub my face. Three shots of tequila suddenly don't seem like enough, so I grab the bottle and pour us another round.

ELEVEN

Tammy

I CAN'T LET HIM GO

AFTER WE FINISH the first bottle of tequila, I make us an actual lunch instead of chips and salsa. I've been on a Mexican food kick lately, so the only thing I have on ready supply is ingredients for tacos, burritos, or nachos. My dad said they were all the same food, but on a different tortilla delivery system. As I carry the huge tray of nachos out to the living room, I see what he means. This could have been a burrito.

The platter slips a little as I set it on the coffee table, and it probably has more to do with the tequila than the overloaded plate. Sam has gone missing, but he emerges a few minutes later with another bottle of Cuervo.

"This guy was trying to make a break for it, but I captured him with my bare hands." Sam's eyes travel up my body in a way that I find very appealing. Especially since he mentioned bare hands. He licks his lips and sets the bottle down next to the food, crossing to me in two long strides. Stopping when his toes are touching mine, he smiles down at me. His boots long since removed, leaving him in wool socks that have the red toes, I feel them wiggle against mine. He has his baseball hat turned backward, giving me a better look at his beautiful eyes.

He reaches up and cups my face, then he leans forward like he might actually kiss me. I force myself to keep my eyes open; I want to see this. His gorgeous face this close, his full lips and beautiful blue eyes.

He stops, frozen inches from my mouth, he whispers, "He can't escape us, Tammy. We want him too badly."

I gulp and nod, my gaze flicking down to his lips then back up to his eyes. He steps back suddenly and proclaims loudly, "I also found this!"

I jump at the abrupt change and put my hand on my chest to settle my heart. Sam pulls a salt shaker from his front pocket and sets it on the table, then holds up a finger as he digs around in the other side of his jeans. A slow smile spread across his beautiful face as he pulled out a small, grayish ball.

I lean forward and squint a little at the object. "What's that?"

"I think it used to be a lime," he says, and as he tries to hold it up for me to see, he drops it on the coffee table. It makes a loud thunk as it hits the wood, and Sam and I lock eyes, laughter bursting out of us.

"That's a loud lime," I manage to squeak out, causing Sam to fold in half as he wheezes.

I collapse on the couch and sigh loudly and fight off a few more rounds of giggles. Sam drops down to his knees on the floor and makes a few attempts at sitting, but winces with each try.

I pat the couch next to me. "Sam, I don't bite. Come sit up here."

He sighs and heaves himself up, mumbling something that sounds like, he likes to be bitten. I need to lay off the tequila, or I might do something to endanger this friendship. Although the mind-numbing has been a nice way to forget about Donny, he's still there, and my heart just can't take it. The vacant look in his eyes will haunt me until the day I die.

"Why'd you get all serious over there? We have nachos and our friend Jose." Sam nudges me with his elbow.

"Just wondering what Donny is doing now. C. J. said he won't be at school anymore."

Sam bolts upright and turns to me. "What? Why not?"

"The foster home that took him is in Gridley. He will be enrolled there."

"Well, shit. That never occurred to me, that I'd never see the dude again. Fuck."

"I know."

"I don't think he understood that he wasn't coming back. C. J. packed up all his stuff in one of his backpacks and told the foster lady that she'd send his stuff to the new teacher. Donny just stood there with his little spatula, listening to all of it." I stop and take a breath before I continue. "I wish there were a way to be sure he understood, you know?"

"Yeah." Sam leans forward and dishes up the nachos onto two plates, then pours another two shots of tequila.

He hands me a plate and a makeshift shot glass. We drink and eat in silence. I need to eat, and after we're done I realize how hungry I must have been, since I inhaled everything on my plate pretty quickly. My mind is reeling though. Donny was the only reason I had planned on staying here. He needed me, and to be honest, I needed him too.

"So what now?" Sam asks. He sets his plate on the coffee table and takes mine, stacking them neatly.

"Now we drink until we pass out?" I shrug, like he should have known this.

"That's a today plan. What about tomorrow?" He rests his hand gently on my knee.

"I don't know if I can let him go, Sam." Saying that out loud feels good. I've been bouncing that particular thought around since Donny walked out of room 27.

"Does he have other family in the area? Like someone who lives here in Bower? Maybe he will come back." Sam leans back onto the couch, dragging his hand with him as he goes. I'm surprised he doesn't move it away, but grateful too. I wish I could climb onto his lap and wrap my arms around him.

"Doubtful. C. J. said there is no family. Dad is in jail for the next ten years, since it was his third strike. Donny's mom was not from around here. I mean, there might be a family member back east somewhere, but who knows."

"I wish I could have said goodbye," Sam says, giving my thigh a little squeeze.

"What if I take him?" I say quietly.

"Like kidnap him? I don't think that's the answer." He chuckles, but now that the words are out, I have a clarity that has fought its way through the tequila-induced fog.

"No, I mean, what if I adopt him? What if I become his mom?" A rush zips through me, and I feel more sober than I have in hours. I stand up and start pacing; I'm sure I sound like a crazy person.

"Really? Are you serious, Tammy?" Sam leans forward, placing his elbows on his knees. I can't read his expression, and maybe it's because I'm afraid he's going to talk me out of this.

"Yes. Why not? He needs a home, and it's not like I have any reason not to take him in." I spread my arms and waved them around a little. "Look at this place; there are four bedrooms upstairs and one down here that Dad used as his office. It's just me, Sam. I don't need a place this big." I stop and steal a glance at him. He doesn't seem like he disagrees, but I start talking again to make my case.

"It is either that, or go back to D.C. and my old job. I was only staying at Bower because of Donny. He needed me, Sam. Me. Can you even imagine? He loves me—I know he does. He trusts me, and that is more important than anything else in my life. I can't just let him go, Sam, I can't." The last word comes out in a sob, and the tears I had tried to stuff down all day release like the burst of a levee.

Sam stands and pulls me into him. He's solid and strong, and his arms are like heaven as they wrap around me. I bury my face in his chest and let the tears fall. Well, "let" is subjective and perhaps incorrect. There is no stopping them.

I don't know how long this goes on, but I finally take a shuddering breath in as we sink onto the couch. Sam still has me in his arms, and I snuggle into his neck. God, he smells so good. His skin is warm and I want to touch him, run my fingers through that hair. I slide my hand up slowly, stopping at his chest. His breathing hitches and he shifts a little, rubbing his fingers up and down my back.

I let my hand move up slowly, and I am about to put it behind his neck and dive into that beautiful long hair, when a hand shoots up and stops me.

"Shit, I'm sorry, Sam." I pull back and glance up at him. His eyes are wide and there is a panicked look on his face, but it fades, replaced with an expression I don't understand.

He loosens his grip on my wrist and sags a little into the couch. "It's okay. I um, I want you to." He closes his eyes before he continues. "I was burned; the skin back there is—" he stopped.

"I don't have to." I try to pull away, but his other arm pulls me in tighter.

"Please?" he says, his eyes still closed. "Just go slow. I'll let you know if I want you to stop."

I adjust myself on the couch, moving so I'm facing him a little bit more. He slides his hand off my wrist, trailing it down my arm. I take my time tracing my fingers across his firm chest. His eyes are still closed and he is leaning back against the couch, his head tilted up a little, exposing his throat. God, I could lick every inch of this man, and I would start at the little divot at the base of his neck where I can see his heartbeat.

I slide my hand up the side of his neck and feel nothing different, just warm, soft skin. When I move my hand a little closer to the center of the back of his neck, I notice the change. He sits forward, giving me full access. I let my fingers gently brush the rough, leathery feel of healed burns. I watch his face for signs that he's uncomfortable, or that he wants me to stop as I slip my hand up into his hair. This earns me a deep groan that shoots through my whole body.

"Fuck, that's so good, Tammy."

"Yeah?" I swallow hard as I scoot a little closer. "I'm glad." I rub a little more, then let my hand drift down to the neckline of his shirt. The burn scar is the same, not much on the right side, more to the middle and the left. That explains why I never noticed; when he's in the driver's seat, the burn is easily hidden from view, especially with his long hair.

"Can I take this off?" I ask, tapping the baseball hat with my finger.

"Yeah." Sam's voice is almost a whisper, and that seems to do the same thing as his moan earlier. My heart races as I imagine undressing him all the way. I want that, but I know that would change things for us. I can't afford to lose him too.

I take his hat off and set it next to me on the couch, trying to reach around him to massage his neck and shoulders, but he's too broad. "I'm going to straddle you, if that's okay? I can't do this the way I'm sitting."

He lifts his head and opens his eyes. Oh. I recognize that look. I remember that expression; it was how he looked when he leaned down to kiss me on my porch all those years ago. I swallow and lick my lips nervously. His gaze tracks my every move.

"It's okay," he says, and he tugs me a little so that I can climb on him. The sudden movement and being this close to him makes me a little dizzy. It might also be all the tequila.

Sam closes his eyes again and leans back. As he does, his hips shift a little, and I fall forward into him. "Sorry, I was trying to stay back a little and give you a little massage."

He shakes his head but doesn't say anything; instead, his arms wrap around my lower back. He pulls me closer so that I'm resting flush against him, chest to chest. My legs spread on either side of his hips; I try not to move.

"I haven't had a girl in my arms in so long. Please, just let me hold you." His voice is deep and pained, so I nod and tuck my face into his shoulder, breathing in his delicious scent.

TWELVE

STRICTLY RESEARCH

THERE IS A SOFT, delicious smelling woman wrapped in my arms, so I know I am dreaming. Women don't fall asleep against my chest. They don't puff little sweet breaths on my neck. I shift a little because my hip is on fire, and I open my eyes. It's dark but I know instantly I am not at my apartment. My gaze darts around the room as I fight a moment of panic at being in an unfamiliar place. The girl shifts on my lap and sighs, snuggling in again.

Tammy. I'm at Tammy's house, on her couch. She is on my lap, her face smashed into my neck. I have one arm wrapped around her lower back and the other resting on her upper thigh. My thumb is making gentle sweeps close to the juncture of her hip, as if in my sleep I knew where I wanted to touch her. I move that hand to the couch and stretch my other arm out, hoping it wakes her. It does not. Instead, she wraps herself into me more, wiggling her hips and sighing a little happy sound. Fuck. That's waking things up down south real quick.

I clear my throat and gently pat her on the back. "Tammy?"

"Hmmm?" she says, her lips tickling the soft spot on my neck. I can tell the moment she wakes up, her whole body going tense. She sits up and pushes back, one hand on my chest, the other on the couch.

"Sam?" Her voice is scratchy from sleep. "What are you—" She stops and climbs off me, which my hip is immediately grateful for, but the rest of me regrets.

"Oh, my God. I am so sorry. I must have passed out on you." She sounds a little frantic.

"It's okay. I crashed out too." I squint at the VCR, trying to see the time, but of course it's flashing 12:00. I don't know a single person who knows how to set the time on one of those damn things.

She squints at the VCR like I just did, then walks a little closer and looks up at the clock on the wall. "Shit, it's after nine. I am so sorry. I didn't mean to trap you here all day and night. Jesus, what kind of friend does that? I passed out on you like a koala." She pauses to look over at me. I am struggling to stand and stretch out my leg, but not having much luck. This couch is a very comfortable, soft pit.

"And look, now you can't even stand up! Oh, my God. Sam, I am so sorry." She rushes towards me and holds out a hand to help me up.

I wince as I finally stand and all the blood rushes back to where it's supposed to be. I steal a glance down at her. God she's beautiful with her rumpled hair and flushed face. I should probably let go of her hands, but I don't.

"Is your hip hurting?" she asks, her voice low and calmer now.

"Yeah, sleeping sitting up like that has made it kind of angry. Just give me a second."

"Okay." She squeezes both of my hands, and my mind flashes back to the rehab hospital. The therapist who worked so hard on getting my gait back to normal would stand this close to catch me if I stumbled. I hated it. I wanted to try on my own, not be treated like a baby learning to walk.

"I'm ready, let me take a few steps and it will loosen up," I say and Tammy immediately drops my hands and steps out of the way, giving me the freedom to try on my own without me having to explain.

I lean on my right leg and shake the left a little, then take a step. There's pain, but not more than normal, so I continue to walk around a little, each step getting easier.

"That's better. Just needed to stretch it out." I give her a smile and am rewarded with one in return.

"I'm so glad. Damn, I honestly don't know what happened there," she says, motioning to the couch.

"I think we drank way too much tequila after having a pretty shitty day," I say, wondering if she remembers that she basically said she wants to adopt Donny.

"It was a shitty day, wasn't it? It's probably for the best that we passed out. I was about to call C. J. and ask her how to start the process of adopting Donny. That's not a conversation you want to have while slurring your words."

"So you were serious about that?"

"Yes. Never been more serious about something." She spins and stops, grabbing her head. "Oh man, I need some Advil. Do you want some?"

"Sure, and maybe a sandwich or something. We missed dinner." I should go home, but for some reason my heart has other plans.

"Come on." She waves over her shoulder for me to follow her into her kitchen.

I watch her gather the things we need for only a second before I jump in and find the plates and some glasses. Tammy puts together two turkey sandwiches in no time flat. I pour us each some water and carry it to the small table she has in the kitchen. It's the same table that was here ten years ago when I came to pick her up for our first date. I noticed that the day I came for breakfast.

Not much about the place has changed, except of course her dad isn't sitting here. I lean back in the chair and let my gaze travel around the room. It's a nice-sized kitchen, smaller than the one at my parents' house, but this one is filled with love instead of flying glasses and shattered plates.

Right next to the coffeepot, I see a blue porcelain vase that I'm pretty sure is an urn. The lid is off and it's resting against the jar. There is a dish rag sitting next to them, like she had just cleaned it.

"I scattered his ashes on Sunday." Tammy's voice cuts through my thoughts.

"That must have been difficult," I say, then add, "Sorry, we don't have to talk about it."

She shrugs. "It's okay. It was sad, but also nice too, you know? I said my goodbyes." She pauses and adds, "Finally felt like I could move forward a little. I cleaned out his room, made donation piles, and actually took three bags to the dumpster. That man saved every receipt for every tiny little purchase."

I chuckle at that. "I think that is a farmer's habit. My dad was always after me to save the receipt when I got gas in the truck. I don't know how he figured the cost of me getting to and from school as a tax write-off, but he probably tried."

She sits down across from me, and I am hit with a sense of comfortable familiarity, like we have done this a thousand times. I watch her face and track the small smile creeping across her beautiful face.

"Thanks for being here today, Sam. Sorry again about getting you drunk and passing out on you." She dips her head and takes a bite of her sandwich.

"Not a problem. I think we both needed it."

This makes her laugh. "You needed me to pass out on you?"

I shrug. "Yeah, actually. Haven't been able to tolerate people touching me, and waking up with you wrapped all over me was"—I pause and make sure to catch her eyes with mine—"nice."

"Oh,"

"It's good to know I can do that," I say quickly because I can't read her expression right now and I don't want to ruin whatever this day has been.

"I'm happy to help." She takes another bite of the sandwich but doesn't look away this time. "Will you stay the night, Sam? I don't want to be alone. I know that probably sounds dumb, but—"

I cut her off. "Of course. That couch is comfortable. I can stay."

"I'm not asking you to sleep on the couch, Sam."

I raise my eyebrows, and she laughs. "I'm not asking that either; you can sleep in Dad's room. I just put fresh sheets and pillows out. Unless that's weird?"

"It's not weird," I say quickly, then add, "I'm happy to stay."

"Thanks, Sam."

I nod, and we finish our sandwiches in silence.

After cleaning up the meal. I follow Tammy upstairs, trying to keep a respectful distance.

"Dad's room is here." She pushes the door open and steps aside for me.

"Thanks." I reach up and run my hand through my hair, suddenly nervous. When I step inside, the clean, fresh smell hits me. There's a bed centered under the window that looks out over the front of the property, with two nightstands flanking either side. The quilt covering the bed is bright, happy colors, and even though it's adorned with flowers, it isn't overly feminine. The dresser top is clean except for a clock. It's a million times better than where I've been laying my head since arriving back in town.

"Is it okay?" Tammy asks, and I realize I'm frozen in the doorway.

"It's really nice, Tammy. Are you sure this is okay?"

"Yes, I want you to stay. I want to have someone enjoy how clean the room is."

"That I can do."

"The bathroom is across the hall here. It's, um, the only bathroom up here, so we have to share. I'm just going to duck in there and then it will be all yours." She turns to go, so I step farther into the bedroom. There is one wood-paneled wall that seems to have had a large, framed picture. I can see the outline of where it must have hung for years, the sun beating down on it, burning its memory in place.

THE REST of the walls are a crisp white with no holes made by angry fists. I don't know what it is about being here that keeps awakening my childhood demons. This farmhouse has never held the anger that mine seemed to have in spades.

I kick off my shoes and tug my T-shirt off without thinking about it. Might as well test this out. Part of me wants to see her reaction, but there is a little bit that wants to see my own. What will it feel like to have her eyes on me, or her hands gently tracing the scars and the thick, leathery patches?

"I set a toothbrush out on the sink for you, Sam. Is there anything else you need?" Her voice comes from over my shoulder, and I take a breath before turning to face her.

"No, thanks. I think that will be all I need. Should I, um, set an alarm, or can you wake me up?" I nod towards the dresser, and she smiles.

"If you can figure out that clock, be my guest." She laughs softly. "I'll be getting up at five. What time do you want me to wake you?"

"Five sounds good." I clear my throat and take a step towards her, then point to the bathroom like a tool. "Bathroom?"

"Yes. Good night, Sam." She turns and walks the few feet to the door to her room.

I let her go, even if I wish I didn't have to, but when I come out of the bathroom, her door is open. Not going to lie, I've always wanted to see Tammy Little's bedroom. I walk over and rap my knuckles on the doorframe. She's bent at the waist, gathering her hair to twist into a cloth scrunchie thing, and bolts upright when she hears me.

Jesus. She's changed into a tight tank top and very short shorts. No bra. I know that because I can see her very pert, hard nipples. I swallow and step into her room without invitation.

"Hi," she whispers. I stare at her beautiful face, her full lips and big brown eyes, my gaze travels over her body, lingering on her chest.

"Hi," I say as I step closer to her.

"Is there something you needed?" she asks in a hoarse voice.

I reach out and trail my finger down her bare shoulder to her hand, tugging her a little. She stumbles into me and I hear the air leave her lungs as a moan or whimper, maybe. I haven't wanted this for so long, I realize I'm a little unhinged.

"Is this okay?" I whisper in her ear.

She tilts her neck to give me better access, and I run my lips down the column of her throat. "Yes." Her response rushes out like a breath.

I notice her arms are still at her sides, like she's afraid to touch me. Hell, earlier I was afraid of that too, but having her on my lap, her fingers tracing over my scars, changed my fear into a long-lost emotion. For human contact, for touch, for her.

"Touch me again, Tammy," I say against her throat. I move up, kissing softly as I go until I reach her mouth. I slide my hands up to cup her face and pause a moment before our lips connect. Once they do, her hands move, pulling me closer, and we stumble together to her bed. Having her beneath me, kissing me like I am all she has ever wanted, is addicting and intense. Tammy was my first kiss, but there have been others over the years. I compared them all to her. To the way it felt like I was on a roller coaster when she'd touch me. The way my heart would swell when I made her laugh, or how fucking soft her mouth was when I finally got the courage to kiss her.

"God, Sam. You feel so good," she says, quickly diving back into our kiss. She starts moving beneath me, her hips seeking me out. I shift a little so we are more aligned, and she arches and moans into my mouth.

"Fuck," I pant, pulling back from the kiss so I can look down at her. The lamp on her dresser is on, casting a warm glow around the room and making her more beautiful than I thought possible. The delicate angles of her face, highlighted in the dim light.

"You are so fucking beautiful, Tammy. Always have been. You drove me crazy back then, too." I thrust my hips a little and she gasps.

HER HANDS SNEAK over my chest, and if I wasn't so turned on, I might have worried about her fingers mapping every inch of my back. I shove her tank top up just enough so that when I lay back down, we are skin to skin. I might go up in flames at how good, how right, it feels to be this close to her.

"Wait," she pants, but her hips haven't stopped moving; in fact, they have sped up and, to both our surprise, she stops, arches into me and lets out a moan that I feel all the way to my balls. She wraps her legs around me and pushes me in closer with her heels on my ass as she rides out her orgasm.

"Holy shit," she pants out, "sorry, I didn't mean to—"

I cut her off, pulling her tank top off then sliding down her body, taking her shorts with me as I go. She's not wearing any underwear, and it's my turn to groan. I slide my hand down her stomach and dip between her legs, tracing my fingers through her wet heat.

"Don't you ever apologize for something like that. Fuck, that was the hottest thing I have ever seen." I lower my head and kiss her stomach softly and slowly. I make my way farther down, and she spreads her legs to accommodate me. I plant light kisses at her center before letting my tongue slide over her. My fingers gently spread her so I can lick and suck. Her hands fly to my head, and she moans and bucks against my mouth. My cock is painfully hard, so I reach down with my free hand and give it a squeeze through my jeans just as she cries out in pleasure again. Jesus, I almost just came in my pants.

"Take those off now," she says, tugging on me and pushing me up.

"I don't have a condom," I tell her. "We don't have to do that. I just wanted to let you know before things got even more heated. I want to be careful with you."

"That's sweet. I'm on the pill. Are you clean?" She's propped up on her elbows, legs still spread. Her chest is rising and falling rapidly, and it's clear she expects an answer quickly.

"Yes." I quickly unbutton my jeans and shove them off along with my underwear. Before I can crawl over her, she sits up and wraps her hand around my hardened length.

"God, Sam. If I had seen this at eighteen, you would have ruined me for other men."

Before I can comment on that, she wraps her lips around me, sliding down and taking me in as far as she can. Her mouth is like heaven and my hips start to move. I tell myself to go slow and make this last, but I don't know how much more of this I can take.

"Tammy, if you keep doing that, this will be over very soon. I haven't done this is a long time." Tapping her shoulder gently to get her attention, she ignores me and keeps moving along my length. Her tongue is swirling each time she gets to my crown, and my eyes roll back into my head.

She stops long enough to say, "I want this, want to make you feel good like this." Then she dips her head again and sucks me so deep I see stars. My balls tighten and I let out a string of curse words, but she doesn't stop or pull off. "Tammy, oh fuck, I'm going to come, you better move or—" I can't finish the sentence because she is swallowing as the head of my cock hits the back of her throat. I'm done. I can't hold back and I grab her head as my orgasm hit like a freight train. It seems to be never-ending, but she continues to suck and swirl her mouth around me, taking every last drop.

When I give one final shudder, she gently releases me, then plants a soft kiss on my stomach and over to my hip where the scars from my surgeries start. She sits back on her heels and looks up at me, lips swollen, and she smiles.

I collapse on her, pulling her up the bed to the pillows as I bury my face into her shoulder and hair.

. . .

THE NEXT MORNING as I stretch out in a bed that actually fits my body, I smile. Smelling bacon and coffee that I didn't make on a small stove in a cramped studio, I stand and adjust myself before walking out into the hallway. I open the door and walk right into Tammy, who has her hand held up like she's about to knock.

She stumbles back, so I grab her around her waist and brace us both from toppling over. God, she is so right in my arms.

"Oh, you're up." She steadies herself by stepping back and placing her hands on my chest, but she doesn't push me away; instead, she lets her hands rest there. The warmth of her touch and her sweet scent are overwhelming me, so I pull her closer.

"Good morning." I hug her, unashamed of the fact that I am basically naked.

She makes a little noise that sounds like a contented hum and wraps her arms around me, her fingers moving around my scars with confidence.

"I could get used to this, Sam. You might have to move in."

I pull back and look down at her in my arms. She's smiling up at me like we hug all the time. Like I'm not currently pressing my very hard cock against her.

"Sorry I ran you over. I was trying to make it to the bathroom while you were still downstairs."

She steps back, and this time I let her, my arms falling to my sides.

"Well, I'll let you get to that. I, um, made breakfast. I hope you're hungry."

She seems nervous. I hope she isn't regretting what we did last night.

"Starved," I say, holding her gaze long enough to see the blush creep up her neck and onto her beautiful face.

"Okay, well, I'm ready. It's ready." She huffs out a breath. "Breakfast is ready." She gives me a little smile before turning to go back downstairs. I watch her go, then step into the bathroom and rub my hands over my face. I brush my teeth and wash my face, willing my dick to calm down. It seems that after more than a year of me avoiding physical contact, he has ideas of how he wants things to go now. I hope that is something Tammy wants. I did not get enough of her last night.

I glance at myself in the mirror. My hair is sticking out like I wrestled the pillow in my sleep, so I smooth it down and head back across the hall to get dressed.

THIRTEEN

Tammy

SOMETIMES THINGS ARE HARD

IT'S a miracle I made it out of the house without embarrassing myself this morning by reaching down and caressing every inch I could reach of Sam's beautiful body again. Jesus, if I had seen him like that at eighteen, I really would have been ruined for other men. The scars on his back didn't bother me like I'm sure he thought they would. They weren't as bad as I expected, to be honest, but they obviously bother him. I wonder if that's why he grew his hair out.

As I drive the short distance to work, I try to settle my racing heart. I don't know what I'm doing, like, at all. Not with Sam, not with my plan to adopt Donny. Nothing makes sense, but there is a current of electricity buzzing through my whole body. The last time I felt this way was when I decided to get my master's degree. It's that little sign that this is the right thing to do. At least that is what I have always thought it meant. My master's degree ended up landing me my dream job as an archivist. Well, I thought it was my dream job. Now, I am not so sure. This buzz might be a warning.

I pull into the parking lot, and it hits me all over again that I won't be meeting Donny at the bus. My heart squeezes in my chest, and I take a moment to gather my courage to get out of my car.

"Miss Tammy!" A tiny voice calls to me as I cross the campus heading for my classroom.

I spin and watch Kathy dragging her brother toward the kindergarten class. He seems to go more willingly these days.

"Hi, good to see you, my friend. How are you?"

"Good! I lost a tooth, and the tooth fairy left me a dime! Can you believe it?" She grins and there is a sizable gap in her smile.

"That's great!" I wave goodbye and walk toward class, hoping that C. J. is alone in there. My skin is tight and itchy with excitement.

"I'm sorry you feel that way. We will miss having you here," C. J. says into the phone. "Yeah, sure, I can write something up." I step around in time to see her roll her eyes. She sees me and lifts her hand in a little wave. "Okay, yeah, it will be at the front office by the end of the day. Take care of yourself." She hangs up the phone and rubs her hands down her face.

"Georgia?" I ask, and she nods.

"Yep, she quit. It's just you and me, kid." She punches the air, pretending to knock me on the chin.

"How long till you can find a replacement?" I ask.

"Who knows? It's fine; with Donny gone, you can float more easily in class. Laura will enjoy having extra time with you, and Mandy might as well. I actually just spoke with Justin's teacher about having him in his regular classroom for longer periods. She wanted to wait till after Thanksgiving break because they are finishing up a project, but I bet it could work."

"Okay, well, you know I'm available however you need me." I pause and look around the room, trying again to gather courage.

"How did the rest of your day go yesterday? I know that was a hard day," she says with a sympathetic smile.

"It was, I got through it. Sam came over," I say without meaning to volunteer that little tidbit.

"Oh, really?" She opens her mouth to say something else, but her phone rings, saving me.

"Room 27, this is C. J. Yeah? Okay, sure, no, it's fine, we don't mind at all. She is probably happy to miss that appointment, anyway."

I stand listening to a one-sided conversation until I realize I can move, put my lunch and purse away, and start getting ready for the students.

I check Laura's bins after I stow my belongings and notice the last act of Georgia was to give Laura three alphabet matching tasks. Jesus.

I quickly swap those out for some more challenging options, then get to Mandy's desk and pull out her coloring book along with her math. She's pretty good at multitasking, and if she can color while she does her work, she tends to get more done.

Justin is a little trickier; he can do the work that his Gen Ed peers are doing, it just takes him longer. I stack a few options for him since it doesn't really matter if he does his writing first or his math.

When I am finished, I hear C. J. behind me turning on the cassette player. "Without Donny here, we can have this on." She nods over her shoulder to the music. Background noise was Donny's mortal enemy.

"That's true." I glance down at my watch, then chew on my lip a bit before taking a deep breath. "Can I talk to you about something before the kids get here?"

"Oh God, you aren't quitting, are you?" She slumps into a chair dramatically, making me laugh.

"No, nothing like that. I just, well, I was thinking about adopting Donny."

She blinks at me, then turns and looks around the room before leveling her gaze at me. "What? Tammy, are you serious?"

"Yes. I've never been more serious about anything." My heart swells, and I swipe at a tear that has decided to appear for no reason. "I can't let him go, C. J."

She lowers her head and blows out a breath. "Listen, I think you need to take a few days to really think this over. Right now you are in shock, you're missing him, I get it. Paul and I had more than one drink last night, and I shed a few tears about this, but—"

I cut her off. "It's not like that, C. J. I care about him. A lot. That isn't going to just go away. I can't stand the thought of him somewhere where people don't get him, don't appreciate him." I stop talking because I am holding back some pretty fierce tears.

C. J. sighs and rubs her hands down her face. "Okay, but Tammy, he's only seven. Adopting a kid like Donny isn't just a ten- or eleven-year commitment. It's a lifelong one. He may never be able to live on his own. He might need assistance with every aspect of his life for the rest of his life."

"So shouldn't that life be with someone who actually gives a fuck about him?" My voice is louder than I intended, and my gut immediately clenches. "Sorry," I mumble.

"It's okay. We will talk about this later; Laura will be on the bus this morning after all. Her doctor's appointment got rescheduled. Why don't you go wait for her?"

I nod and hurry out of the room, embarrassed about my outburst. Hard to impress upon C. J. that I will be a responsible and loving caregiver if I am melting down at the first sign of pushback. I get to the curb just as the bus is pulling up, and I reflexively reach for Donny's favorite thing in my apron. Tears sting my eyes, and I blink them away quickly.

"Good morning, Miss Tammy." Sam opens the door to the bus and stands to walk back to get Laura. I wait on the sidewalk and swipe again at my stupid, leaky eyes.

"Morning." I walk to the back of the bus and wait as he lowers the platform. I hear him saying something and Laura squealing in delight.

"And here we are, bottom floor. Please be careful of the piles of unicorn poop. They were let loose this morning and we just haven't had the chance to clean up." His voice is pitched high and is perhaps attempting a French accent. I roll my lips to hide my laugh.

Laura arches toward him, smiling with so much love in her eyes it makes my heart swell. He takes her washcloth and gently wipes her face. "Glad you decided to go to school today, Miss Laura. I'll catch you on the other side."

Sam straightens and gives me a heart-melting smile. "Hi."

"Hi, Sam." I step behind Laura's chair and start to move her off the ramp, but don't get very far.

"Oh, wait, here." Sam reaches down and releases the brake on her chair.

"Right, thanks." I find it hard to look at him for some reason. Things weren't weird when we both left my house this morning, but I am suddenly reminded of his very hard body pressed against mine, and God, the sounds he made, the way he touched me.

"Well, see you after school." He rubs the back of his neck and looks everywhere but at me. I guess he is feeling the same way in the light of day.

"Okay, Miss Laura, let's get you inside. I don't want to get unicorn poop on your wheels.

Laura bangs her cup on her chair and squeals in delight. I laugh along with her and wonder if we have the ability to make an animal/poop matching task for her. This kid has a great sense of humor.

The day goes by faster than I expect, probably because I am the only aide now. Mrs. J runs all the groups, but I work with each kid during their work with teacher time and reset their independent work as fast as I can while they're on breaks. Thankfully, the kids all seem to be pretty chill today, so that helps. It's not completely unmanageable with just me and Mrs. J when there are no behaviors, but if even one of our kiddos has a bad day, this will not work. I hope she is able to get at least a substitute tomorrow.

"Do you mind getting Laura back out to the bus, Tammy? I need to call Mandy's mom about the after-school program."

Mrs. J is leaning on the door to her office as the day winds down. She hasn't mentioned my outburst about Donny, and neither have I.

"Of course. I have all the tasks set up for tomorrow and I am soaking the Legos in soapy water."

"Ugh, thanks. That was so gross. Maybe we will keep those as a special treat instead of a free-time activity. That was a lot." She chuckles and gives me a weak smile. "Are you feeling better?"

"Yes, but I am still going to look into how to adopt him," I blurt out.

"I know. I won't stop you, Tammy. He'd be lucky to have you." She sighs and says, "It's a long road. His father is still alive and would have to give up his rights." Her eyes go wide, and she steps into her small office, and I hear her rummaging through her desk. When she returns, she has a card in her hand. "Here. I just remembered I had this. I ran into her a few weeks ago." She taps the card with her finger. "This is a social worker who has helped with our kids in the past. She is in Yuba City now, but she knows a lot about the system and she might be able to help you get started."

I take the card from her and put it in my pocket. "Thank you. I will take all the help I can get."

The bell rings, and all the kids rush to their spot in line. I walk over to Laura and lean down. "Ready? I think Mr. Tony got all the unicorn poop cleaned up."

I expect at least a small smile, but she just blinks at me. Tough crowd. "Okay, let's go see Mr. Sam."

The chaos of after-school pickup is always the same. Someone always parks in the bus-only loading zone because the sign that clearly says "bus only" doesn't apply to them. So the parent who has abandoned their car to go find their student makes it impossible for Sam to pull up to the curb where he can lower the ramp for Laura.

"Sorry, Laura. We have to wait." I lean down and smile at her. Her eyes dart around, and for a brief moment I wonder if she's looking for Donny. I know she is smart; she understands a lot of things that people say and do around her, so I take a chance. "I miss Donny too," I say quietly.

Her gaze locks on mine, and her eyes fill with tears. I reach down and grab her hand, giving it a squeeze. I won't fill her with hope that we will see him again, even if I want that to be true. "He's okay, honey. Maybe we can make a card for him and send it to his new school. Do you want to do that with me tomorrow?"

I wait for some kind of response but am met with only her silent tears. "I know, honey. I know."

"Hey there, what did you say to my friend? Why the sad tears, Miss Laura?" Sam kneels down in front of Laura's chair and wipes her face with her washcloth.

"We are both just missing Donny," I say.

Sam looks up at me, then at Laura. "Yeah, me too. Listen, as soon as that person pulls out, I'll move the bus and get you loaded up. I have a whole bunch of new knock-knock jokes for you." I watch him gently wipe a tear from her face before he stands and blows out a breath.

We stand together on either side of Laura in comfortable silence as we wait for the missing parent. Eventually, they walk out with three kids in tow, completely oblivious to the bus inches from their bumper. I want to say something, but considering my mental state, it's probably not a good idea.

"Okay, Laura, that"—Sam points to the car that is pulling away from the curb—"is my cue."

I wait while Sam pulls the bus forward so the ramp is accessible for Laura, then I push her chair towards the platform.

"Thanks for your help, Miss Tammy. I got it from here," Sam says kindly.

"Sure, right. Okay. Thanks, Sam. Bye, Laura, see you tomorrow." I give a little wave and walk back to class, my fingers tracing over the card in my pocket. I'll call the second I get home.

FOURTEEN

TINY? I PREFER COMPACT

I'M STUCK in a line of traffic on my commute home. That's not something I've had to deal with since moving back here. We don't have traffic or commutes. Well, unless there is a farmer driving down the highway with his huge ass tractor, taking up the lanes like he owns the whole damn thing. That happens more than it should.

I roll down the window on my Jeep and try to see around the cars as the line starts to move forward a little bit. I'm only about a block from where I'm staying, so I almost just park the Jeep and walk, but I am able to get close enough to safely drive on the shoulder and get around the line.

I pull into the small gravel parking lot of Mario's and wave at my friend who is standing with his hands on his hips. His bright green long-sleeved shirt is stained right across his belly, and I wonder if all his shirts look like that, or if he has only this one and I happen to catch him every time he wears it.

"What's with all the traffic, Mario?" I ask as I climb out of my Jeep.

"Hola, mi amigo, cómo estás?" he asks without answering my

question. It's his polite way of reminding me it's rude to ask questions without saying hello first.

"Hola Mario, bien, y tú?" I say with a little shake of my head, a smile spreading easily across my face.

"Bien, bien." He nods his head, as he crosses his big arms across his chest.

"Qué pasó?" I ask, nodding to the road.

He shrugs. "Some idiot crashed about a mile up the road. I came out because I heard him hitting shit as far back as here." He uses his chin to point to the line of mailboxes across the road from us.

"Oh, damn." I sigh. "I'll help you put them back up."

He shakes his head. "Nah, I need to get a whole new post. I have the concrete here, but look at that! He snapped it off like a fucking toothpick, man. Good thing I wasn't out there getting my mail."

"No kidding. Jesus, did he hit another car up there?" I stand on my toes like I am suddenly going to be able to see past the line of traffic.

"I don't know. I heard an ambulance and a fire truck." He shrugs, narrowing his eyes at me. "Your Jeep did not stay here last night."

"Um, no. No, it didn't. I stayed with a friend."

A big, slow smile spreads across his face as he nods. "I remember having those kinds of friends."

"It's not like that. Do you remember Tammy Little?" I say, feeling very protective of her. I don't want him to think I would take advantage of her.

"Oh, shit, really? Yeah, of course, her father was a good man. God rest his soul." Kissing his fingertips, Mario crosses himself and looks toward the sky.

"Yes, he was. Tammy said she sold the rice fields."

"Sí. I heard that, pero the new owner wants to use my guys still." He shrugs again, "At least on the fields by the house. I think the North family bought those. I have a few guys coming up next week to meet with them and see what they need for the season."

I nod. Mario is an amazing guy. He's probably only ten years older than me, but he has been working in this area since he was about twelve. He coordinates getting the migrant farmworkers from Mexico here and ensures they are well cared for. The little studio I am currently staying at is part of the temporary housing for the workers in the summer. I know he'd let me stay if I wanted to, but I really do need to find a more permanent solution. Mario's wife is an amazing cook, but I miss having a real kitchen of my own. Staying at Tammy's last night made me realize that even more.

When I came to town with only my duffel bag, these little cottages were perfect. I didn't think I'd stay as long as I have, to be honest. I didn't think I'd get a job and find a way to be happy here again.

We stand out front bullshitting a little more as the line of cars on Highway 99 inches along past us. Mario has never pushed me for information about my time in the military, or about my father. He supplied Ford Nuts with at least a hundred workers during harvest. I know whatever my dad did to screw everything up; it hurt Mario and his men. He's never held that against me.

"I better head inside and rest my leg." I pat him on the back. "Come get me when you fix those mailboxes. I want to help."

"Sí. Claro." He smiles, but I know he won't tell me. He will fix it himself, like he does most things. I swear the man could build a house from the ground up without any help, and it would probably only take him a week.

I flip the light switch on as soon as I open the door. The single bulb in the center of the room flickers on, casting a warm glow. This isn't a terrible place, really. It has everything I need: a chair, a bed, a small sort of kitchen, and a bathroom the size of a phone booth. I flip the TV on just to have some background noise.

"The crash has caused Highway 99 to be shut down in both directions. The CHP is turning people around while they wait for the tow truck that can handle the semi. At this time, the only reported injury is that of the driver of the Toyota."

My head whips around. Did they say Toyota? Would Tammy

have been on that road? I step in front of the television and wait for Linda Watkins-Bennet to finish her report. She has nothing else to add to that story; however, she launches into a very informative piece about some kind of pumpkin soup that was a hit in her family.

Fuck.

I glance at the clock and try to do the math. Tammy gets out of school at two. She probably goes straight home, but hell, she could have gone into Gridley or something after work. It's well past five now. No, it was probably someone else. I mean, Tammy wouldn't have hit mailboxes and just kept going, right?

I look over at the phone on my counter and see the machine flashing red. Damn it. I take a deep breath and press play.

"Hey, Sam, it's me again. Listen, I really need my birth certificate. If you won't go to the house for me, just please tell me, so I can hire someone who will. I don't want to fly all the way out there to deal with this. The house finally sold, and escrow closes soon. Please—" the machine cuts her off, and I blow out a breath.

Fuck.

I pick up the phone and instead of dialing my sister, like I should, I call Tammy's house.

"Hi, you've reached the Littles. We can't come to the phone right now, so please leave a message at the beep and we will return your call as soon as we can."

I hang up and look at the clock again. There are probably a thousand places she could be.

She's fine.

I pace back and forth, listening to the newscaster talk about other fun Thanksgiving meals that you can prepare. I dial Tammy's again; this time the machine picks up faster, giving the same message. Slamming the phone down, I rub my face with my hands.

Fuck.

Stop.

She's fine.

A man's voice on the news catches my attention, so I step over to the TV again, hands on my hips waiting. A field reporter has his microphone held up to an officer. "As soon as the tow truck can get the semi upright, we will be able to open at least one lane. Thankfully, he had just dumped his load and was empty at the time of the crash."

"That is lucky, and the driver of the semi wasn't injured?" the reporter asks.

"No, he's a little banged up, but he declined medical aid. The driver of the red Toyota that caused the crash is in the hospital and will be booked for DUI once he is released. He had moderate injuries."

I blow out a long breath and close my eyes. Jesus Christ.

He.

Red Toyota.

My stomach is all twisted up and I'm breathing as if I just ran a mile. I sink down onto my recliner and rest my elbows on my knees, letting my head hang. I focus on my breathing and my heart rate, hoping both slow the fuck down.

I guess there is no question now whether I have feelings for Tammy. I mean, I knew the moment I saw her again that the crush I had ten years ago was going to reignite. After last night, my hands and lips all over her, the way she touched me, kissed me. There is no denying now; I am an inferno.

I'm not sure how long I sit there, but when I finally lift my head, the tight band across my chest has loosened. I take a deep breath and slump back into the chair. Watching the swing of headlights into the parking lot out front, I take a moment to see if they keep going. I hear a car shut off and a door slam before a familiar female voice says, "Here, let me help you! I almost hit you, Mario!"

Well, shit. I rush out the door and watch as Tammy helps Mario drag the mangled set of four mailboxes closer to the cabins. She wipes her brow and slaps him on the arm.

"Thank God you always wear those awful neon green shirts.

Why are you doing this in the dark?" she asks. She hasn't noticed me, and I think about ducking back inside before she does.

"Lo siento, mi amiga, I was trying to move it before Sam tried to help me." Mario nods towards me with what can only be described as a shit-eating grin.

Tammy's head whips towards me, her mouth dropping open a little.

"Sam? What are you—?" She stops, and I watch her gaze drift to my Jeep and the light spilling out from the open door of the little cottage where I have been staying.

I nod in silent answer to her question and step closer. "I would have helped, even told him to come and get me." I shoot a glare at Mario, who is just smiling at us like a damn fool. He turns and heads to his house, which is set back a little from where the cabins are.

"So you're staying here?" Tammy asks, leaning to look past me again at my cottage.

"Yeah, it, um has everything a guy could need, plus Mario's wife Linda's cooking." I shrug.

"But they're so tiny," she says, and I see the immediate regret that flashes across her face. She's not judging me, or these cabins, but she's worried about how that sounded.

I shrug and smile, hoping she knows I didn't take offense. "What are you up to?"

"I was just coming back from Yuba City. I had the chance to speak with a social worker about Donny. She gave me a bunch of information about how to start the process of adopting him." Her face is absolutely lit up, and I notice that she is bouncing a little on her feet.

"Wow, that's good. How did you find her?"

"C. J. Mrs. J. She used to work with her, and she said if anyone would know the process, it would be Melinda. Boy, was she right. I feel like I just read an entire dissertation on fostering and adopting. My brain is overloaded, but I'm so excited, Sam. This could actually happen. Melinda thinks I have a good chance to at least be his foster mom."

"What can I do to help?" I ask without hesitation. The thought that I could get to see Donny again, and maybe even get to know him better, warms the center of my chest.

Tammy glances over at the open door to my cabin, then back at me. "Well, for starters, can I use your bathroom? I might actually wet my pants."

I laugh realizing the bouncing wasn't just excitement about Donny. "Sure, come on in." I wave her ahead and she walks quickly through the door, finding the obvious bathroom door easily.

I shut my front door and stuff my hands into my pockets, looking around nervously. My place is tiny, but it's clean. The bed is made; the small kitchen counter is clear of dishes and clutter. I have a stack of mail on a folding metal TV tray, but that's the only thing that might be seen as messy. I step over and straighten the stack, glancing through the letters as I do. My sister, my therapist at the VA, and a few letters from friends who are overseas. They all have that yellow stripe of paper at the bottom indicating the mail was forwarded here from my old address. A gentle reminder that I need to tell these people I have moved. I set the stack down just as Tammy emerges from the bathroom.

"Thank you. I thought my bladder was going to burst when I was in Live Oak, then I almost hit Mario as he dragged that mess across the road. It's really a miracle that I didn't embarrass myself." She waves at her crotch, and my gaze follows her hand like a fool.

I snap my focus back up to her face. "Right, yeah, we don't want that. You feel better now?"

"So much." She looks around and smiles. "I've always wanted to see these on the inside. This is so cozy!"

"Yeah, it's been great." Suddenly the room is warmer, the air thicker. I take in a breath to try and steady myself. Fuck, why am I so nervous?

"Melinda said Donny is doing okay. He has adjusted as much as he can to things. He had a bad first day at school, but he'll figure it out. It helps that he likes the foster family he's with, so that's something. I don't feel that panic rush like I have to fix this tomorrow, you know?"

"How does she have all this information about him?" I motion for the recliner then sit on the bed next to Tammy.

"Oh, she knows everything. Seriously, that woman—Sam, she is incredible." She relaxes a little into the chair, like the weight of the day is catching up to her. I wish I could cook her a meal, but my hot plate and microwave aren't exactly chef-worthy. I have Hungry Man TV dinners and that's about it.

"Georgia quit," she says with a sigh.

"Oh, shit, really? Why?" I lean forward a little. She pulls me in without even trying. I wonder if she knows how much she means to me, how I haven't stopped thinking about last night. I wish I could tell how she felt about us and what happened. With all that is going on with Donny, it seems like that is her focus.

"She didn't like that Mrs. J told her not to baby Laura." She shakes her head and twists her lips a little, as if she's trying to find the right words. "I think she meant well, to be honest, but she just didn't get our kiddos. She thought they were all like, I don't know, babies isn't the right word, but that's how she treated everyone. I mean, I bet she thought she was being loving and grandmotherly, but it just came across wrong. Plus she never got the hang of setting up the work for the kids."

I ask more questions, realizing I have no idea what kind of work special education students do in class. I watch Tammy's face closely as she talks about the tasks they do and how they try to tailor the work for each kid's goals. If their IEP—I had to ask what that was—calls for them to learn their letters or numbers, there are a million ways to do that. The individualized education plan doesn't say how to teach them but does define goals and offers modifications. I'm not sure if I am more fascinated by the information or with the way Tammy is telling me.

She twisted towards me slightly, and our knees keep bumping because when Tammy talks, she does so with her whole body. "So, for example, Donny had a goal to match like items and identify things by size, small to big or big to small."

I hold up my hand because I would assume he could do something like that easily. "Wait, really?"

"Yeah, it's interesting because I think he knows things like that, but he's a little stinker and tries to make it harder than it is. Like, put all the things with wheels in this box, and he would add a pizza cutter or a rolling pin, you know? He takes it so literally and pushes the envelope, but part of getting him to do the simple tasks is getting him to follow the instructions."

"Oh, like in high school when they gave us that paper that had all the instructions, but you had to read the whole thing first or you'd totally screw it up?"

Her face lights up, "Exactly! Donny gets ahead of himself often, and that is what we were really working on."

"You really love your job, don't you?" I ask, wanting her to keep talking. Forever, here in this small space, like I am all that matters.

She leans forward to answer me, but instead I hear a very loud rumble of her stomach. She puts her hand over her stomach and laughs. "Sorry, I guess I need to eat."

"I have TV dinners!" I say a little too loudly.

"Hungry Man?" Her eyes light up.

"Of course, like there is any other option." I roll my eyes and stand, wiping my very sweaty hands on my jeans. "I think there's fried chicken or Salisbury steak, but I might have the fish stick one too."

"Any of those will be fine, if you're sure?"

"I'm sure." I walk the two steps to my tiny kitchen and pull the Swanson's Hungry Man dinners from a shrinking icebox. I need to defrost the damn thing before it closes off completely.

"Fish sticks or Salisbury steak?" I hold up the boxes and I can tell she's studying my face to see which one I want more. "Tammy, these are all my favorites; I honestly don't care."

"Okay, I'll take the fish. I haven't had fish sticks since I was a little kid. My dad used to love them, so we would eat them all the time, well, every Friday. It was his attempt at teaching me the Catholic ways of fish on Fridays." She stops and laughs at her own memories before she continues. "Dad was a twice-a-year Catholic, and by the time I got to high school, we didn't even go that often."

"Still, must've been nice to have some kind of faith. Did he find comfort in that at the end?" I ask, then wish I could take it back. What the hell am I doing?

"Yeah, maybe a little. I think he felt like he had lived a good and righteous life. He was injured in Vietnam before he even fired his gun, so I think he felt he was right with God." The last part of that sentence trails off, and I watch her face crumple.

"Oh my God, Sam. I didn't mean to imply. I don't think that of you, if you had to, you know . . . oh God." She buries her face in her hands, and I set the frozen meals on top of the microwave and cross to her.

"Hey, it's okay." I rest my hands on her shoulders, giving her a gentle squeeze until she looks up at me. Her eyes are shiny with unshed tears, and when one spills over, I catch it with my thumb, gently wiping it away.

Her breath hitches as she looks up at me. I'm frozen here, one hand on her shoulder, the other cupping her face. It's intimate and intense, and I don't know how to stop. I lean down a little as if my body needs her heat, her lips so full and soft. I let my thumb slide down her cheek because I need to touch those lips again. I move my other hand up from her shoulder to her face and dip my head, watching my thumb as it traces across her plump lower lip. My gaze at war with her eyes and lips, unsure what is more important.

"Sam, you got another letter from your sister. You need to answer her." The sound of Mario's voice reverberates off the small, narrow space, forcing us apart like the wake of a boat. "Oh, Dios mío. Lo siento. I'm sorry, man," Mario says as I step back away from Tammy.

Her head turns towards him quickly, and she sucks in a breath, her hand going to cover her racing heart. At least I hope I made it race. Mine is about to beat out of my chest right now.

"Hi, no, it's okay. Did you get the mailboxes moved okay?" she asks, even though she helped him do just that. She is just as rattled as I am.

He smirks at her, then tosses me a thick envelope from Gwen. "Did she call you? I gave her your number when she called the house."

That explains a lot. I wondered, but since I had been avoiding her, I hadn't worried too much about it. "Yeah, she called. Thanks, I will call her or answer this."

"You'd better." He gives me a pointed look, then turns and leaves, like he didn't just interrupt something.

"Want me to make dinner so you can read that?" Tammy asks. She's already at the microwave, opening the first TV dinner. She has her back to me, and I know the moment, whatever it was, has passed. I'm not sure how to get back to where we were last night. Do I just grab her and kiss her like it's a normal thing we do? I wish I could get out of my own head about this, but it's Tammy. I know there's a part of me that never got over her.

"Sure, yeah, thanks." I sit in the recliner and open the thick envelope from Gwen. The letter on top is in her handwriting and is direct and short.

Sam,

I am sorry. I know this whole thing has been harder on you than me. I left when it was just getting bad. Actually, was it ever good?

I wish I lived closer and could just get it myself,

but I can't. If I don't hear from you by Thanksgiving, I will hire someone. I hope you are well.
Love,
Gwen

I FLIP through the other papers, and it's just a copy of the offer that was made on the house and the proposal for the neighborhood that will be built once the house is torn down. Huh. I guess I can understand why she wants me to go. It's not like there will be another family moving in who will get the box she wants.

The ding of the microwave catches my attention. Tammy has one of the dinners on what little counter space I have, and the other on top of the microwave. This place is really only meant for one, and up until this minute I was okay with that.

I stand and walk to her, taking the steak dinner and grabbing two forks from the holder by the sink. "Thanks, I'm sorry I don't have a table. I usually just eat in my chair."

"No worries! I sat on my bed in my dorm room and ate more meals than I care to admit. I'll sit there, you take your chair."

Before I can object, she climbs onto my bed and sits with her legs crossed, her fish stick dinner placed in front of her. I open the small fridge and take out two sodas before sitting in my chair. I offer her one, and she gives me a small smile, our eyes meeting for the first time since I almost kissed her. This shouldn't be so hard; I should bring up last night. I should just ask her if she had fun, or if she wants to go on a date or something.

"What did your sister have to say?" she asks.

I sigh and lean back in my recliner, pulling the footrest up. My hip is immediately grateful for the new position. "She wants me to go to the house. She said her birth certificate is there, and she wants it before they tear the place down."

"They are tearing it down?" Tammy sounds surprised, which means she has never driven down the long gravel driveway. You can't see the place from the road.

"Well, yeah. I haven't seen it, but I heard that my parents' last fight was pretty epic, with not just the police but the fire department showing up. The bottom floor has fire damage, and I'm sure animals moved in after that since I bet they didn't bother to board it up. I can't imagine it's salvageable."

She picks up a fish stick and blows on it gently as she waits to see if I have more to add. I don't, it's fucking embarrassing how they acted. When I left, they just got worse. I don't know how you can ever grow to hate someone you once loved enough to marry and have children with.

"I'll go with you."

I shake my head, but since I just took a bite, I can't protest with my words. I chew quickly and swallow hard. "No. Thank you, but no."

"Yeah, I'm going with you. We aren't discussing this. Tomorrow. After school. I'll meet you at the yard."

"I work until four o'clock," I say as if this will deter her or something.

"Cool, that will give me time to go home and change into my grubby jeans and work boots." She takes another bite of her fish sticks. I glance down at her tray and wonder if she is the type to eat one thing at a time or if she will take bites from everything. I wait and smile when she reaches for a French fry.

"You'd really want to go with me?"

"Sam, you saw me at my worst yesterday. I owe you. Plus, and you can't tell anyone this." She points her fork at me.

I hold up my hands in surrender. "I won't."

She smiles and says, "I have a weird thing about old homes."

"Why should that be a secret? A lot of people like older homes."

"You didn't let me finish. I should have said, I have a thing about your old home."

I bark out a laugh. "Okay, I need an explanation on that."

She rolls her eyes. "I kind of had a huge crush on you our senior year, and I used to picture what your house looked like. I know where it is; I mean, we all did, but no matter how many times I drove past, I couldn't see beyond that little bend in the driveway. Your parents made it very hard to stalk you."

I shake my head. "No way."

"I did! I drove past your house all the time. I thought maybe I'd catch you out at your mailbox, and I could slow my truck down and say something cool like 'come here often?' or—" she stops when I start laughing. "Or something better. I mean, let's be honest, it's a good thing I never saw you."

"You are such a liar!"

"Sam! I am not lying. You had that big blue mailbox with like that little orange newspaper tube below it. For a little while, there were flowers planted around the base of the box. I'm pretty sure they were daisies. And there was a little ring of rocks that was painted yellow!"

"Oh shit, I forgot about that. Wow, I guess you were a frequent traveler of Jasper Ave."

She shrugs, then goes back to eating her dinner, seemingly happy that I finally believed her.

FIFTEEN

Tammy

ALMOST KISS ME AND I CONFESS

IF MARIO HADN'T BARGED in, I am positive Sam would have kissed me again. I'm not sure what happened when we went our separate ways for work, but I'm nervous, and he seems really nervous. I wonder if he regrets what we did? I'd love to see where this could go, if I'm being honest. I was brave last night, so I know I can do it. I should tell him. If he's not interested, I can stuff my feelings back in the same box where they lived my senior year. I don't want to think about how the pain from learning our date was a dare also lives in that box.

He laughs and says, "You did not have a crush on me, Tammy. That's absolutely ridiculous."

I raise an eyebrow at him. Is he really that dense, or is he being modest? Or hell, is this him letting me down easy, like there's no way a nerd like you thought she had a chance with me. That seems to be the most plausible one. I take a breath in and hold in for a beat, trying to decide how to navigate out of the mess I just made for myself.

"Okay. You can go with me tomorrow. I'll come pick you up after I get off work."

My head spins a little at the change of subject, but I rally quickly, blowing out the breath I had held and giving him my best smile.

"Good. I'm glad that my stern Miss Tammy voice worked on you. Filing that away for future use." I wink at him, and he makes a noise in his throat that I don't recognize. It's like a sigh but more growly.

We finish eating and it hits me that I need to get home and get ready for my day tomorrow. I left for Yuba City right after school, and I have to deal with all my normal after-work stuff now.

"Thanks for dinner, Sam. I look forward to seeing your house tomorrow." I wiggle my eyebrows at him, but he rolls his eyes.

"Okay, weirdo. See you tomorrow."

I duck out quickly, not wanting an awkward moment where I'm waiting for a hug or kiss.

The fog has lifted since yesterday, and I am able to make it back home without any issues. Once inside, I groan at the stack of dishes in the sink and the load of laundry I know I need to do.

I ignore the flashing light on my answering machine and get to work on my chores.

The next morning my alarm doesn't have the chance to wake me up; instead, the sound of a torrential downpour has the honor.

I sit up in my bed and rub my eyes. Holy hell. The wind and rain are waging quite the war outside, and even though the sun isn't up, I walk to my window and pull the curtains back. Normally I have a view of the backyard, but it's so dark I can barely make out the huge oak tree. Without leaves, I can't tell how windy it is, but the rain hitting my window gives me a little clue. I grab my clothes and head for the shower. Rainy day recess is always a challenge, and I am sure we won't be stepping foot outside at all today.

While I make a quick breakfast, I turn on the small black-and-white TV my dad kept in the kitchen. It only gets three channels, but that's all he needed to get the morning weather. I turn the dial to 12 and wait for the picture to come into focus.

"Get those jackets and rain boots ready if you have to leave the house today. We are looking at the start of a pretty significant storm here in the north state, with heavy winds, rain, and possibly even hail." The local weatherman, Anthony Watts, says while standing outside the newsroom. He's under an umbrella that is whipping around and rain is smacking him on the side of the face.

I shake my head, wondering why they do that. Do they think we won't believe them? I crack two eggs into the pan and give them a quick stir before adding salt and pepper. I have one normal piece of bread left and the heel. My dad loved the heel. Or at least, he said he did. Maybe he was only being nice, offering to take the weird thick end so I wouldn't have to. I put both in the toaster and got the butter out of the fridge as the power flickered off, then came back on.

Since I have been back, we've only lost power once, but when I was growing up, it seemed like it happened all the time. There is a box of half-melted candles in the cupboard and a box of matches, flashlights, and some extra batteries. There is also a battery-powered radio if I need it. Things my dad always took care of, just like he took care of me. It occurs to me I will have to do all of that for Donny. I will have to be all that my father was.

For the first time since I had the idea to adopt him, a tiny sense of doubt creeps in. Can I do this? Can I do what he did?

The toast pops, and I grab it and rush to the pan on the stove, flipping my eggs before they burn. I butter the toast and slide the scrambled eggs onto the plate. I realize I haven't started coffee, so I quickly get that going then sit at my little table and wonder how many more breakfasts I'll have alone. What will it be like to see Donny here? Not just at the table, but in this house? Will he like it? Will he feel safe here?

I glance around my house, trying to see it through his eyes, but it's almost impossible. I can guess a few things, like the cracks in the vinyl cushions on these chairs. If I'm wearing shorts, the jagged edges feel sharp on my legs, and that won't do. I grab the pad of yellow lined paper that lives on the edge of the table and pick up the pen. I write Things to Fix across the top and underline it three times.

Lists make me happy, so I jot down a few things as I eat. The lights flicker a little bit more but stay on. I finish my breakfast and make a quick lunch to take to work before filling a Stanley thermos with coffee. I'm going to need it.

Rainy days at elementary school are an interesting thing. In some ways they are easier, with no transitions to outside recess, no playground monitoring fights about who gets the swing next, or consoling tears and scraped knees. But with no time outside to burn off the energy, these kids are like ticking time bombs.

Laura didn't come to school today, so there was no Sam, no bus. It was a little surprising to me how much I missed that, those five or so minutes of seeing him in the morning, hearing his voice as he jokes around with Laura. Knowing I'd see him at the end of my day also made the day go better somehow. Today dragged on and on. The power flickered a bit and there was a moment of hope that we would get sent home, but that didn't happen.

"Tammy, there's a phone call for you," Mrs. J calls from her office.

"I'll be right back. Keep working on that. You almost got it, okay?" I give Mandy's arm a little squeeze and head to the small closet area where C. J. has been camping out all day. We're down a few students, so she is catching up on paperwork.

She smiles as she hands me the phone, her eyebrows raised to her hairline. "I'll step out and help Mandy so you can have a moment."

"Okay." I wait for her to leave, pressing my hand to my chest. I am pretty sure it is Sam calling to cancel.

"Hello?"

"Hey, Tammy, it's me, Sam. Sorry to bother you at work, but I wanted to let you know we have to cancel today. The rain is not letting up, and I don't want to deal with that place in this weather."

I try to hide my disappointment. "Oh, sure. I understand that. Okay, well, thanks for letting me know. Maybe I'll see you tomorrow?" My stomach clenches at the desperation I can hear in my voice. Did he notice? God, why am I so lame? I sink into C. J.'s chair and gently bang my head on the desk.

"Yeah, maybe. Mike said Laura's parents think she might be out all week. Trouble with some sores on her legs. They are going to U.C. Davis to check it out."

"Oh, right. Okay. Well, then, I guess I'll see you around. Thanks for calling, Sam." I hang up before he can say anything else because I'm afraid of what else I might say. My eyes are stinging like I am going to cry, God, I'm so stupid. My mind flashes back to the Monday after our date in high school. Sam wouldn't even look at me in class. When I grabbed his arm on the way to the next period, he acted like I had struck him, jerking his arm out of my grasp.

"Can't talk now, Tammy. See you around," he had said. That was the last thing he said to me until ten years later, when he showed up as the bus driver.

I force myself to act normally as I walk back out into the classroom. We only have about fifteen minutes left until the bell rings, which I am now dreading. How could my stupid heart have thought today was going to work out? No one should be out in this weather, not even a lovesick idiot who was hoping to finally see Sam Ford's bedroom.

Laura is, in fact, out for the rest of the week. The doctors at Davis wanted her to be out of her chair for a while to let the pressure sores heal, so she's been home. The week before Thanksgiving is all half-days, so Laura's parents let her come to see how she does.

I kind of thought I'd hear from Sam, or run into him at the store or the pizza place, but it's like he disappeared. Or he's avoiding me, which is a much more likely scenario. The rain kept up the whole week, so maybe that is why he went radio silent. That's possible, I guess, but that insecure teenager inside me is convinced he has met someone else and is happily engaged. Jesus.

When Bus 43 rolls up on Monday and the door swings open, I plaster on my best fake smile.

"Hello, Tammy!" Mike calls through the door before he steps to the back of the bus where Laura is. I hurry to the back and wait as he lowers the ramp. "Here you go, Miss Laura! I hope you have a great day, and I'll see you in just a few hours!"

I wait as he unhooks her chair and gets her onto the sidewalk. "Thanks, Mike. I appreciate it." I am forcing myself to be strong and not ask where Sam is. It's none of my business, after all.

"So you didn't get the flu?" Mike asks as I bend down to say hi to Laura.

"What's that?"

"That flu that ripped through here last week. Took Sam out on Wednesday, and he still sounded like crap today. I told him to stay the heck away from the yard. I don't want to get sick before break. The wife and I are going to Mexico for a little sunshine."

"Oh, that will be fun! Um, no, I didn't get it. I guess I got lucky." I gave him a little smile and pushed Laura towards the classroom.

"So that's what happened!" I say to her as we walk along. "Laura, don't fall for a boy; it's not worth it." I lean over and wink at her, and she gives me a big smile. "I missed you, kiddo. I'm glad you're back. We have a whole bunch of new things for you to try out today. Let's see what ones you like, okay?"

MINIMUM DAYS ARE THE BEST; they start, and you blink and they are over. As I push Laura back out to the bus, I breathe in the crisp fall air. Someone is burning leaves since it's finally a burn day and it gives the entire area a delicious smoky smell. Like a thousand times before, I think about Sam, sick and alone in his tiny little cabin. Does he have enough food? I should take him some soup and ginger ale and at least check on him? Yes. That's what a friend would do, and I think we are still friends, at least. Maybe that's all that is in the cards, and with all I have on my plate right now that should be enough.

I spent all last week making phone calls and signing up for the required classes to be eligible to be a foster parent. My list of things to fix now takes up three full pages, things like moving into Dad's old room and giving Donny mine. I'd rather he had a view of the back of the property. I love the idea of him staring at the same oak tree that I did. The wide, gnarled branches that seem to stretch out at impossible angles. At dusk, it looks even more magical. I picture us collecting acorns in the old Longaberger basket, like my dad and I did for years.

I decide to go home and make a pot of chicken soup instead of buying some canned crap. If you are taking someone soup, it should be the good kind, with homemade noodles and big chunks of chicken. My dad taught me how to make simple egg noodles that require two teaspoons of salt, two eggs, and enough flour to make dough. I knead the mixture and quickly roll it out on the wooden butcher block, then cut the flattened dough into thin strips. It swells up as it cooks because it pulls in all the chicken broth, making these fat, delicious noodles that will ruin you for store-bought ones. Once the chicken is cooked through, I toss the noodles in and cover the pot.

I know it's dumb, but since I am going over there, I might as well try to look my best. While the soup finishes up, I run upstairs and change into a nice sweater and a better pair of jeans. I never wear these to work because they are the lightest blue denim and I am sure they would get stained. It's silly, but I love the big label on the back of the waistband. Bongo. Made me laugh the first time I tried a pair on, because I thought they made my butt look a bit like a big drum. I was never into fashion in high school, not that I really could have been. We were comfortable with money when it came to things we needed, but I would have never asked my dad to drive me to Sacramento to get Guess jeans or those crazy Esprit pants that had paint splatters all over them. When I lived in D.C. though, and had my own money to spend, and stores that were cool and stylish, I discovered I liked to shop.

One last look in the mirror and a quick change to my hair, and I was as ready as I was ever going to be. I transferred the soup to a smaller container and grabbed a bowl and big spoon for him, just in case. His kitchen is so small at the cabin, I can't be sure what he has.

The drive takes only a few minutes, and when I pull into the lot, Linda, Mario's wife, is just coming out of Sam's place. I yank the emergency brake up and watch as she crosses herself, then wipes her hand across her brow before she sees me. Her eyes don't match the fake smile she plasters on as she walks towards my car.

"Hola, Tammy, cómo estás?"

"Hola, Linda, bien, y tú?"

She glances over her shoulder at Sam's door, then back to me. "I'm okay. Are you here to see Sam?"

"Yes, Mike said he was sick. I brought him soup." I nod toward my passenger seat.

"Good. I hope you can get him to eat. He is in a mood." She rolls her eyes as she says that last part, and I force a smile. My stomach is suddenly unsure about this swoop-in-and-play-caretaker thing I was about to attempt.

Linda waves over her shoulder as she walks off towards her house, so I reach back into my car and grab the bag with the homemade chicken soup. I pause before knocking, taking a deep breath to steady myself. I can't say for sure why I feel such unease, but I know something isn't right. I tap lightly on the door and hear a grumble in reply. I can't really make out what he has said though, so I knock again, this time a little louder.

"I said I'm not hungry! Dios mío, Linda, give it a rest, would ya?" Sam yanked the door open, clearly expecting Linda to still be on his porch.

"Sorry, it's me." I stumble back a little, which causes Sam to glare at me. I straighten. "It's me, not Linda. I brought you soup."

"Oh. Well, like I said, I'm not hungry." He walks away but doesn't close his door. He isn't wearing a shirt, just some faded plaid pajama pants and thick grey socks. The lights are on in the cabin, so I have another chance to see the scars that cover the left side of Sam's back as he inches his way to the bed. He slumps down and starts to cough so violently that I think he might throw up. I set the bag down and rush to him. I place one hand gently on his back, just between his shoulders, as he struggles to get a full breath. He flinches at my touch, but I keep my hand there.

"Do you want water?" I ask.

"No. Wait, maybe." He pauses and coughs again, then leans back, adjusting himself further onto the bed. I quickly grab his pillow and shove it behind him as he collapses onto it.

"Jesus, you sound awful, Sam."

"Thanks."

I spin and grab a glass that is on the counter and rinse it out a few times before filling it up. I hand it to him and watch as he struggles to bring it to his lips.

Fuck. He's really sick.

"Sam, I think you need to go to the doctor."

"No. No doctors."

"But—"

"No!" he says more forcefully, then falls into a coughing fit again.

"Okay, okay. No doctors. Okay." I sink down to my knees next to his bed and put my hand on his leg. He doesn't feel warm, so that is good.

His chest rattles as his coughing stops, and I take the glass from him and set it back on the counter. I feel a pang of sadness at how long he has been here by himself like this, while I wallowed in my self-pity about him not liking me.

I turn and grab a duffel bag that is shoved in the corner, then go to his dresser and pull out a few pairs of underwear, some shirts, and two pairs of sweats. I can only find one other pair of socks, so I add those to the bag. I spot his wallet on the counter. I toss that in and grab his keys, stuffing them in my pocket before looking around for his shoes.

"Here," I say, bending down again at the edge of the bed. I guide his leg down and put his shoe on one foot, then pull the other leg off the bed, trying to do the same.

"Stop. What are you doing?" he snaps.

"Putting your shoes on. You are coming to my house, and there are still puddles out there, so unless you want to walk in wet socks, you'll cooperate."

"I'm not a fucking baby. I can put on my own shoes."

"Great. Have at it." I stand up and sling his duffel bag over my shoulder, grabbing the bag with my homemade soup as I walk back out to my car. I set the bags in the back of my Toyota and go back for Sam, who is struggling to get his shoes on.

I bend and help him without making a comment, then step back and hold out my hand. "Let's go."

He looks up at me with a mix of gratitude and disdain, and if I wasn't so worried about him, I probably would have thought it was funny.

"Why can't I just stay here?"

"Because I think you've been alone long enough." I hand him a T-shirt that was on his bed and wait for him to slip it on.

SIXTEEN

ANGER HATES COMPANY

MY HEAD FEELS like it's underwater, and my chest is harboring the embers of hell. I don't have a fever anymore, but the body aches haven't stopped. I can't remember the last full meal I ate, let alone having drunk any water. That is until Tammy showed up and forced me to drink some.

Well, okay, forced isn't the right word, but even in my current state I couldn't say no to her. She hasn't spoken or looked at me since she dumped me in the front seat of her car, and I am currently staring out the window like a petulant child.

I smell. My hair has the texture of peanut butter, and I think my teeth are wearing tiny little sweaters. Of course Tammy smells like apples or that fucking awesome Snuggle fabric softener, or heaven, fuck, I don't know. I can't think straight because that's the only reason I am allowing her to drag me to her house.

"There is an extra toothbrush at the house. I think you'll feel a lot better if you take a shower and get into some clean clothes." Her voice is soft but steady.

I grunt instead of answering her because that is all I can muster. So she can read my thoughts, or maybe the stink wafting off me is obvious in this compact car. When we pull up to the house, she turns and narrows her eyes at me.

"Wait here. You are the color of typewriter paper. I'm going to put the stuff in the house, then come back for you."

Another grunt, which she seems to accept as my answer. As she walks to the house with my duffel bag and another I don't recognize, I let my head fall against the cool glass of the side window. Fuck, my eyes hurt. The dull thud that has taken up residence in my brain seems a little better today. What day is it? Is it the weekend? Is that why Tammy came to my house?

"Okay. Let's go, big guy." Tammy yanks open the door, surprising me. I grab at her so I won't fall out of the damn car, and she mumbles an apology.

I stand and move my feet like Bambi taking his first steps on that frozen pond. Tammy holds me under my arm and on my elbow like a pro, leading me to the house and then together we creep up the stairs. When we reach the top, I feel like Sylvester Stallone in Rocky. If I had any energy, I'd turn around and raise my arms above my head in victory.

She leads me through the house to the bathroom at the back, near what her father used as an office. She has a towel and a toothbrush still in the box on the counter, along with a new tube of toothpaste.

She parks me against the wall and pulls the shower door open, then turns the water on. I'm thankful it's a shower stall and not a tub, since I really don't think I could lift my leg over anything right now.

I notice the shower chair that must have been her dad's, and I wish I had the energy to complain. I want to yell that I don't need it. I want her to take it away. But my pounding head and aching body don't have that kind of strength.

"Do you need help?"

"No." The word erupts from me but I don't even believe myself. I close my eyes and tip my head back, letting it fall against the wall.

"Right. Okay, lift your arms."

She tugs my shirt off, and in one swift movement pulls my

pajama pants and underwear down. She bends and slips each leg past my foot. Without looking at me, she leads me to the chair in the shower.

"Sit."

I comply, even though inside I'm screaming against the care she is trying to give me. I flinch at the cold plastic as my ass hits the shower chair, but relief at sitting wins out. She pulls the shower head off and points the water away from me, testing the temperature.

"Tip your head back a little, Sam."

I close my eyes and sigh as the first blast of hot water hits my scalp and slides down my body. She moves quickly, grabbing my hair and getting it all wet. She hands me the showerhead while she puts shampoo in her hand. While she lathers my hair, I moan louder than I mean to, but she doesn't react. She's gentle but efficient, and I realize she did this for her father. She taps my wrist so I'll give her back the showerhead, and she puts one hand across my forehead as she rinses my hair, preventing the soap from getting in my eyes.

The dull throb of a headache I've had for days seems to slide off me along with the soap, and I take a deep breath in relief. That unfortunately causes another round of hacking and coughing that even I can admit sounds terrible. She holds the shower head so the water runs down my back, and her other hand is placed gently on my shoulder, a calm, steady presence.

When I finally stop, she hands me a bar of soap and asks if I need help washing my body. I know this may sound dumb, but it's the first time I am really aware that I'm sitting here buck naked in front of her.

"No. I got it."

"Okay. I am going to hang this back up. Let me know if you need help; I'll be right here." She puts the showerhead back in the holder, then steps back and closes the door to the shower, giving me privacy to wash myself. I have to grit my teeth to fight off the VA Hospital memories that are trying to sneak in. I put the bar of green soap to my nose and breathe deep. There was no Irish Spring at the VA. That helps.

The shower chair has two padded armrests that I use to push myself to a standing position so I can wash all of me. It's heavenly to be covered in soap instead of my own sticky sweat. I finally finish and sit back down while I have another coughing fit.

"Ready," I croak out, and Tammy is there, holding a towel out for me, averting her eyes like a trained nurse. She reaches past me and turns the water off as I wrap the towel around my waist. She guides me out of the shower and has another towel ready for my back and chest. Then she steps on a wooden stool and dries my hair.

"I have a robe for you. It was Dad's, so it might fit. I think you guys were about the same height." She's holding out a blue terry cloth robe while looking at the floor.

"Thanks." I try to think of something else to say, but as soon as I slip my arms into the sleeves, she leaves me alone in the bathroom.

I take advantage of my privacy to take a piss, then I wash my hands and brush my teeth. God, I thought the shower felt good. There is nothing better than having clean teeth.

I step out of the bathroom and find Tammy leaning against the wall with a comb in her hand. It's pink and wide-toothed like I've seen in the bathroom of a few girls I've dated.

"It's all I have. If you want to come sit, I can comb out your hair before it dries." She turns and walks toward the living room, so I follow. She has a sheet and a pillow laid out on the couch with the softest-looking blanket I have ever seen resting on the arm.

"SIT, and I'll get that combed out."

I do as she asks and fight off another moan. I love people touching my hair. At the VA, it was the only grooming activity I was okay with. I'm a whore for a scalp massage, and as my hair grew long, I realized I would also do anything for someone to comb or brush my hair.

"Okay. All done. Here are your clothes. I'm going to go into the kitchen and warm up that soup I made for you. If you need help, just call." She turns and leaves, so I get dressed as quickly as I can manage. I sink onto the couch as she emerges with a small bowl that is steaming hot. I don't know if I have the energy to eat, but my stomach is growling for the first time in days, so I should try.

"There are saltines if you want crackers with it, or you can eat it plain. It's chicken noodle. Homemade. My dad's recipe. Cures everything but cancer." She's chewing on the inside of her lip and is fidgeting like I've never seen her do before. It makes me feel a little like I am having an out-of-body experience. The normal, not sick version of me would ask her if she was okay.

"Thanks." I take the bowl and spoon from her and crack the smallest smile as I hold up the giant utensil. "Do you ever use a normal size spoon?"

"No. I like the big ones. If I'm going to put something in my mouth, I want it to be worth it. Why take a million little bites of something?"

There are so many things I could say to that, instead, I give her my best attempt at a smile and took a bite.

Another errant moan escapes my lips, and I glance up at her. "Are these homemade noodles?"

"Yeah. I made them."

"They are fucking delicious."

She lets out a long breath and says, "Okay, good. I have a few phone calls to make, so when you're done you can set the bowl there. I hope it's okay that I fixed you a bed down here on the couch. I didn't think you'd be up to climbing the stairs."

"This is fine, Tammy."

"Right. Okay, good." She stares at me for a minute like she wants to say something else, but she turns and leaves instead.

I finish all the soup and have to stop myself from licking the bowl clean. I set it on the coffee table like she asked and lean back on the couch. The sheet is cool and clean and feels so much better than the sweat-soaked bed I've been in for the last few days. I grab the blanket she left me and roll to my side, covering myself. I close my eyes and fall asleep immediately.

"YOU'VE BEEN ALONE LONG ENOUGH. I AM HERE NOW." SOFT WORDS AND EVEN SOFTER FINGERS TRAIL THROUGH MY HAIR, STROKING AND MASSAGING AS THEY GO. I SIGH AND TRY TO SIT UP BUT CAN'T, SO I LEAN INTO HER TOUCH INSTEAD.

MY MOM'S VOICE IN THE DISTANCE IS CALLING ME, AND IT MAKES NO SENSE. WHY IS SHE HERE? "SAM, YOU'LL BE LATE FOR SCHOOL! YOUR LUNCH IS ON THE COUNTER."

I LOOK IN THE MIRROR TO MAKE SURE I DON'T HAVE ANY NEW ZITS AND RUN MY HAND OVER MY SHORT HAIR. NO BASEBALL CAP TODAY. I DON'T WANT HAT HEAD FOR MY DATE WITH TAMMY TONIGHT, AND THERE WON'T BE TIME TO COME BACK HERE AND SHOWER BEFORE I PICK HER UP. OF COURSE, MY DAD NEEDS ME OUT AT THE PACKING PLANT RIGHT AFTER SCHOOL. HE NEVER NEEDS MY HELP, BUT THE ONE DAY I HAVE PLANS, HE DOES.

"COMING!" I YELL AS I BARREL DOWN THE STAIRS, LANDING ON THE LAST STEP WITH ALL MY WEIGHT.

"YOU BREAK THAT STEP, YOU REPLACE IT." SHE POINTS A LONG FINGER AT MY FEET. HER NAILS ARE BRIGHT RED AND PERFECTLY MANICURED, LIKE A GOOD, WEALTHY FARMER'S WIFE. "WHAT TIME WILL YOU BE BACK?"

THE SMELL OF THE CIGARETTE SHE HAS HIDDEN BEHIND HER BACK BETRAYS HER. THAT'S WHY SHE WANTS ME GONE. I'M NOT LATE FOR SCHOOL, BUT SHE'S LATE FOR HER NICOTINE HIT. I ACT LIKE I DON'T SEE THE SMOKE RISING BEHIND HER.

"I'VE GOT PLANS TONIGHT, SO PROBABLY CURFEW."

"WHATEVER, YOU STAY OUT AS LONG AS YOU WANT. YOU'RE EIGHTEEN. JUST DON'T DRINK AND DRIVE." SHE WAVES A HAND TO MOVE THE SMOKE, THEN ACTS LIKE SHE'S SWATTING AWAY A FLY.

"RIGHT. OKAY. SEE YA." I GRAB MY LUNCH AND MY KEYS AND STEP OUT INTO THE HEAT OF THE VALLEY. EXCEPT IT'S TOO HOT. I LOOK DOWN AS I WALK TO MY TRUCK AND NOTICE MY BOOTS AND FATIGUES. I'M SINKING IN THE SAND, IT'S FUCKING EVERYWHERE.

STUCK IN MY SHORT HAIR, MY EYES AND EARS ASSAULTED WITH THE TINY GRAINS, YOU CAN'T ESCAPE IT SO EVENTUALLY YOU STOP TRYING. I TOSS MY LUNCH ON THE SEAT OF THE LIGHT EQUIPMENT TRANSPORTER THE ARMY HAS FOR ME.

WHEN I GLANCE BACK OVER MY SHOULDER, I DON'T SEE MY HOUSE, JUST THE TENT WHERE WE HAVE BEEN GETTING BRIEFED FOR THE DAY. I KNOW I HAVE SOMEWHERE TO BE, BUT I CAN'T REMEMBER WHAT THEY TOLD ME. FUCK, SHOULD I GO BACK AND ASK?

THE WIND PICKS UP, AND IT'S LIKE A BLAST FROM AN OVEN AS IT BLOWS SAND ALL OVER, MAKING VISIBILITY DROP. I CAN HEAR THE RUSTLING OF PAPERS ON THE SEAT NEXT TO ME, SO I TURN AND SEE THE MAP AND THE ORDERS. RIGHT. THEY WROTE IT DOWN FOR ME. I AM TO LEAD A CONVOY INTO TOWN, GET SUPPLIES, AND MEET WITH OUR LOCAL INTERPRETERS. WHEN I TURN THE KEY AND THE ENGINE ROARS TO LIFE, IT SOUNDS WRONG. I CAN HEAR A HIGH-PITCHED WHINE OR SOMETHING. I COCK MY HEAD, PUTTING MY EAR CLOSER TO THE DASH, AND THAT'S WHEN I SEE HER.

TAMMY SMILING AT ME FROM HER PORCH. CUTOFF JEAN SHORTS THAT HUG HER BEAUTIFUL CURVES. SHE HAS ON A TIGHT BLUE TANK TOP WITH THE PINK FLOYD LOGO STRETCHED ACROSS THE SWELL OF HER BREASTS. DIRTY WHITE KEDS WITH NO SOCKS COVER HER FEET, AND I SEE HER TOEING THE TOP STEP LIKE SHE'S NERVOUS. SHE WAVES AT ME LIKE SHE WANTS ME TO COME UP. I WILL, OF COURSE, BECAUSE THAT'S WHAT YOU DO ON A FIRST DATE. YOU MEET THE FATHER AND TELL HIM YOUR PLAN TO RESPECT HIS ONLY DAUGHTER. TO TREAT HER LIKE THE PRINCESS SHE IS WHILE ALSO SHOWING HER A GOOD TIME. I WAVE AND SMILE AT HER, MY STOMACH FLIPPING OVER ITSELF AS I STEP OUT OF THE L.E.T. JUST AS EVERYTHING EXPLODES INTO A MILLION PIECES.

"NO! No! No, no, fuck no! Tammy! Tammy! No!" I'm screaming, but no one can hear me and I'm trapped, something is wrapped around my arms and twisting around my legs. A sharp pain in my hip makes me freeze, and I suck in a sharp breath as a warm, soft hand caresses my face.

"Hey, hey, it's okay. I'm here. Sam, it's okay. Stop, Sam, I'm here."

A voice that sounds a million miles away snaps into focus as the terror fades, slipping back into my subconscious like the retreating tide. I squeeze my eyes shut tighter and pray it stays where it has lived for years, undisturbed.

My eyes open and she is there, one hand on each side of my face, thumbs gently wiping away tears I didn't know I had shed.

"You're okay. You are safe. You're with me. You aren't alone, Sam. I'm here."

My whole body slumps back onto the couch, and I reach out, pulling Tammy down with me. My arms wrap around her, protective and strong. She doesn't fight me, just settles in with her fingers tracing gentle patterns on my face, my neck and my arms. I sense the wave of calm washing over me like her being near me is the balm to my fractured soul.

"Bad dream?" she asks after a while. She tucks into me, resting her head on my chest, legs tangled with mine, fingers continuing their soft journey along my arm.

"I guess," I mumble. I never remember my dreams, not in any helpful detail at least. Little snippets and sound bites sometimes surface, but even that is rare. I haven't actually had a nightmare since I've been back in my hometown.

"I think it was about my house?" I say, like she will be able to validate this. "My mom was in it, but that's all I remember." That's not entirely true, but I don't mention that this time I'm pretty sure there was no tank in my dream.

"Oh, maybe because we are going there?" Her voice is soft and her breath is warm against my chest.

"Yeah, probably."

She pulls up a little, looking down at me, concern etched on her face. I want to rub my thumb over her brow and smooth out the worry that doesn't belong there.

"I can go for you. Just tell me where your sister said her stuff is. I'm good at finding things, so I bet I can handle it."

"No," I start, but then shove her up and turn so I can cough. She climbs off me and rushes into the kitchen, returning with a glass of water.

"Here, drink this. Do you want some more soup or a sandwich, or something else? I have a roast in the oven for dinner, but it still has about an hour."

I shake my head and pull in a ragged breath, not wanting to attempt actual words. Fuck, I haven't been this sick in a long time.

"Okay. Try to close your eyes and rest. You sound awful. I think after I get off work tomorrow we should go to a walk-in clinic in Chico or something. You need to—"

"I'm not going to the doctor," I snap, expecting that to be the end of it.

Tammy steps closer to me and leans down, pointing her finger at me, anger flaring in her eyes. "The fuck you aren't! This is not up for debate; I'm not going to sit here and watch you die. Did that once with my dad, and I'm not doing it again. Stop being such a fucking baby."

She spins on her heel and stomps off toward the hall. I hear her heavy footsteps as she climbs the stairs, then I flinch as she slams her door.

Well, damn. I guess I deserved that. I sink back onto the couch and roll onto my back. My hip and leg are killing me, and if I hadn't been such an asshole, I could have asked Tammy for some Tylenol or something. I probably owe her an apology. I groan and sit up, swinging my legs to the floor. It takes considerable effort, but I manage to stand and walk to the staircase. Looking up, I count how many steps I have to climb before I can throw myself at Tammy's feet and apologize. Let's be honest, by the time I get to the top I'll just collapse at her feet.

I make it without dying, surprisingly without any need to cough. I guess having an apology as motivation is enough to pull me forward. Her door is closed, but I'm sure she's crying. Damn it.

I knock lightly, then push the door open. She is sitting on her bed, legs crossed, and she wipes at her face as I step closer. I see she's got a long blue string of some kind and she's fiddling with it, rubbing it between her fingers.

"I'll go. I know I need to," I croak out, my voice sounding hoarse and strained.

She nods and looks down at her hands. Fuck. I hate seeing her upset. "Tammy, I'm sorry. I'm not good at this." I scrub my hand down my face. "I've been an ass."

She twists the string around her finger, then unwraps it, then does it again. It never occurred to me she wouldn't accept my apology, but she won't look at me. I watch her play with the string a little longer, then finally she looks up.

"Can I ask you a question?"

"Sure, yeah," I stammer.

"Why did you kiss me at the end of our date?"

That is so far from what I thought she was going to ask I have to blink a few times to make sure I'm actually standing here. What if I never made it up the stairs?

"Huh?" I squint, trying to catch up.

"That kiss at the end of our date senior year? Why did you do that?"

I blow out a breath and run my hand over my hair, pushing it back out of my face. I wish I had my baseball cap. I hate it when my hair flops into my face. Looking at her, I shake my head, still trying to catch up.

"I wanted to?" I finally say, but it comes out like a question when it most definitely wasn't something I questioned at the time.

"Are you sure? You don't sound sure."

"Why are you asking me that? I wanted to kiss you. I had a great time and I, hell, I wanted to kiss you all night." I move to her bed and sit next to her.

"Was it a dare?" she asks so quietly I almost don't hear her.

"A dare? No. Why would you think that?" I want to scoot closer and grab her hand, but she's wrapping that string around her finger again.

She blows out a breath and finally looks at me. "Curtis was talking about it in class. He said he dared you to take me on a date and kiss me."

"What? No, I didn't even talk to him about our date. I didn't tell anyone we were going out."

"Oh, right. Sure, I mean why would you tell people?"

I groan because how is this happening? "Tammy. It wasn't like that."

"Right, okay." She starts with the damn string again, so I grab her hand.

"Stop. Look at me and give me a second to explain, would you?"

She turns her face towards me and lets her gaze rest somewhere on my face, but not on my eyes. I reach and tip her chin up a little with my index finger.

"I didn't want to jinx it."

Now she looks confused. "What? Jinx what, our date?"

"Well, yeah. I wanted to ask you out for a long time, and when I finally got up the nerve and then you said yes—" I stop and brush my hair out of my face again. "I didn't want to jinx it," I say with a little more confidence.

She's shaking her head like she doesn't believe me, so I say, "Just wait. I can prove it."

SEVENTEEN

Tammy

TRUTH AND CLARITY

THE NEXT DAY, as soon as I got done with work, I took Sam to a walk-in clinic in Chico. After a chest X-ray, they gave him a breathing treatment, and he was sent home with antibiotics and an inhaler. He felt better and could make it up the stairs, so he slept in my dad's old room, and by Friday he was so much better.

"Right after I get off work, I'll come here and we can go straight over," I tell Sam at breakfast. It's weird how quickly we've adjusted to him being here. I've almost asked him to just move in officially more than once, but I've chickened out each time.

"I'll be here. Since I can't leave or anything. Do you think we can go get my Jeep today?"

I laugh. "Yeah, sorry. I really didn't mean to kidnap you."

"Did you see me put up a fight?" he asks, and I almost point out that he was a complete ass the first day, but there is no need for that. The time we have spent together has made us both a little more comfortable, whatever weirdness we felt after our hook-up has faded.

The day passes at a snail's pace, even with it being a half day. Laura is out sick—hopefully, not with the bug that took Sam out—and Mandy left yesterday for LA to visit family. That left just the boys, so for our last day before break we played games and walked the track, then did some work to get them settled.

I'm nervous about going to Sam's house. C. J. said she drove there out of curiosity when she heard about the big fight his parents had. I guess windows were broken out and one corner of the house had been lit on fire. Since it had been raining and the siding was wet, it didn't get very far, but the damage is obvious.

Sam and I have talked a little about what his relationship with his parents was like, but I can tell there is so much more to the story. Where I have a thousand memories of my dad helping me with school projects, or my truck Big Red, or taking me fishing, Sam has none of that. He has memories of screaming fights and broken dishes. He remembers crying and yelling and doors slamming, not warm hugs and supportive words.

It kind of makes going out to his old house feel more oppressive than when I first agreed to go. I'm not saying I don't want to help, because I do. I just feel like a selfish part of me wishes I didn't know all of that about him. God, I sound like an ass, but the Sam in my memory, the Sam in science class, and more importantly, the Sam who took me on the best date of my life, didn't deserve to have that kind of home life. Not that anyone does, but it hurts my heart to know what he went through. It hurts to know that he dealt with that all alone, too. Maybe what I am feeling is guilt. How could I have spoken to him every day in class and not known what he went home to? Did anyone know?

"Can you hand me the glue?" C. J.'s request rips me from my thoughts.

"Sorry, yeah, here." I slide the bottle of Elmer's glue to her, bypassing Will, who has his fingers outstretched and ready for the interception.

"Nice try, dude. Mrs. J will put some on your plate, and you can use that Q-tip like we talked about. Get enough on there to keep the leaf in place. You picked some great ones for your turkey."

Will beams at me and says, "Thank you, Miss Tammy. I'm going to give it to my grandma. She loves turkeys since she married one."

I fight off a laugh and raise my eyebrows. "She married a turkey?"

"That's what she calls Grandpa." He shrugs, and C. J. snorts.

"Can you start on their bags, Tammy? I think I can handle the turkey craft, since Will is almost done."

"Sure." I push back from the table and grab the paper grocery bags that C. J. brought in. Each kid has a ton of papers and artwork to take home, as well as school pictures that finally arrived from the printer. It broke my heart to see the class photo from the first week. Donny was right up front wearing his tank top and knitted blue-and-white ski hat. He wasn't smiling or anything, but I could tell by his eyes that he was happy. God, I miss him so much. I wish he had taken pictures so I could have stolen one for my fridge. Although that's just sad and a little creepy. I remember trying to wrangle all the kids into the library on picture day. They saw the wooden stool and backdrop and, as a group, decided to have the biggest meltdown in the history of Room 27. I chuckle at Will's picture as I slide it into his bag. He was the only one happy to pose for the photographer. His smile is so big you can't even make out his eyes, and he's holding up his favorite toy from class, a Superman doll.

Donny was supposed to go next, but when I moved him around in front of the backdrop, he panicked and bolted right out the door. It was pure chaos after that.

Justin has been in his general education class for most of the day for a while now, so I don't have much to put in his bag, and I realize he won't be coming by here after the bell rings.

"Can I run this over to Justin's class?"

"Yep, good idea."

My little errand eats up what little was left of our day, and when I get back to class Mrs. J has everyone lined up at the door, bags in hand and backpacks on. We all walk out together, then I rush back to grab my purse.

I nearly run face-first into C. J. on the way back into the classroom.

"Whoa! Where's the fire, kiddo?"

"I, um, I'm going to take Sam to get his Jeep, then we are going to his old house for something his sister wants before they level the place."

"Sounds interesting. I won't keep you. Remember, the invitation stands if you want to come for Thanksgiving. Paul and I would love to have you. Hell, bring Sam too."

"Thanks, I'll talk to him. I'm not sure if he has plans," I say, trying to be polite, but I really just want to run all the way to the parking lot.

When I get to my house, Sam is standing on the front porch, and I squint to verify what I'm seeing. Jesus.

I pull to a stop and slowly climb out of my car, stopping in the open door frame. Resting my arms on the car, I let out a whistle, which causes Sam to duck his head. I can see his smile from here, though.

"You look good in that," I yell to him.

He walks down the stairs toward me, and I see the unease as he pulls on the coat. "I can take it off if you don't want me to wear it. I just realized I didn't have anything really warm here."

"No, I like it on you. The hat too. I forgot that was there." I nod towards his head, and he smiles again.

"Yeah, my hair was driving me fucking nuts. I mean, I prefer my Giants hat obviously, but a John Deere trucker hat is almost as good."

He gets to my car and turns his head to cough a little. It's so much better than it was, but I hate that he still has it. I wonder if I will ever be able to hear that chest-rattling cough without thinking of my father's last few days. Seeing Sam in Dad's Carhartt jacket warms a place in my heart that I had hidden.

"Ready?" I ask, and he nods.

"Let's just get this over with before I change my mind." He opens the passenger door and climbs into my Toyota.

I can tell he is nervous, so I fill the car with endless chatter. His old house is only about fifteen minutes from mine, so it's not like we have time to really get into anything too deep. I tell him about the leaf turkeys the kids made and about C. J.'s offer for us to come for Thanksgiving.

"That was nice," he says as I turn off the main road and onto his gravel driveway.

What once was perfectly manicured landscaping now more closely resembling a wild field. Huge oleander bushes take up the driveway, forcing me to skirt along the edge.

"Shit, we should have brought my Jeep. Be careful of that pothole and watch the edge there. I think that is where the drainage ditch was." He motions over my shoulder to a tall patch of grass.

"Thanks." I slow down even more, and we crawl along bouncing as my little car navigates the ruts and valleys of the driveway. Finally, I make the curve, and we both gasp at the sight of his childhood home.

"Wow, Sam. This place is enormous!" I say and look over at him. His jaw is clenched and his eyes are narrowed. I watch him force a swallow.

When I pull my car to a stop in front of the house, he blows out a breath. I turn the car off and wait, expecting him to get out, but he doesn't move. I gently place my hand on his leg, and for a moment, we stare quietly at the ruined home.

All the windows and doors on the bottom floor are broken or damaged. One side of the porch is black from a fire, the smoke stains creeping up to the second floor in only a few places. It's clear the fire was put out quickly. There are broken pots with dead plants strewn all over, probably more than what we can see thanks to the front lawn now being a waist-high pile of weeds. The path leading to the front door is littered with broken jars and soggy boxes, as if someone threw the contents of the kitchen out into the yard.

"Come on. Let's go around to the back." Sam finally gets out of the car, and I follow him around the massive home, being careful not to step on anything as we go.

"Shit. I didn't think it would still be intact." Sam nods toward a wooden staircase that leads from the back patio up to a small deck.

"That's my sister's room. Come on." Sam bends and picks up a rock from the ground and tucks it into the coat pocket.

We slowly climb the stairs that I'm sure were once very sturdy and now seem more like a staircase in a funhouse. Sam looks back at me often to make sure I'm okay. When we reach the little landing, Sam takes another deep breath and reaches for the door. It turns easily and opens with just a little nudge. The room is dark, but Sam doesn't hesitate. He just reaches back for my hand and pulls me through.

"Hang on." He drops my hand and crosses to the window, pulling down on the roller shade. Instead of making it snap up, the whole thing rips away from the wall, causing Sam to jump back.

He chuckles a little and says, "Well, that works, too. Let me open the door to the hallway and get some more light in here." He crosses the room, stepping on clothes and papers that are strewn about, and once the bedroom door is pushed open, the entire room comes into view.

It's a mess. I have seen movies where someone gets robbed and their house is in disarray, like the bad guys had to flip even small objects over to find the loot. This is worse. Pictures on the wall have been broken and hang crooked or are smashed on the ground. The bed has been tipped up, and the stuffing from the box spring is pulled loose and strung out into the hall.

"Did your parents do this?" I ask, trying to keep my voice calm.

"Nah, this is probably a mix of wildlife and looters. Mario said once the place sold, the new owner hired security, and they ran off a few squatters." He pauses and fishes around inside Dad's jacket, pulling out a flashlight. "Hope it's okay that I borrowed this."

"Oh, sure, that's fine." He walks over to the closet, which I am sure had beautiful white shutter doors at some point. Now it is twisted, broken slats clinging to a frame that looks like it was a target for demolition derby cars.

He flicks on his flashlight and looks up, aiming the light in the same direction. He stretches his arm up and fumbles around until he comes away with a thin metal rod that has a hook on one end. I step closer to see what he's holding.

"I told her it wasn't going to be there, or that someone would have found her little hidden door, but she was right; it's still here." He points up, and I see wooden slats and nothing else.

"Is there a door or something?"

"Yep. See that little metal piece hanging down?"

I squint, and he shifts the light a little to the left. "Oh! Yes."

He takes the rod and hooks the metal loop. It takes a few tugs for the door to swing free, and when it does, we are both showered with dust and debris.

Sam steps back and covers his mouth, coughing, and I do the same. "Holy shit. I didn't think that through." He wheezes and coughs some more. I'm in the same boat, so I can't be much help to him. Eventually, we regain our composure, and he looks up into the black space. Even with the flashlight, we can't make anything out.

"I had planned on standing on her desk chair, but that seems out of the question now." He nods toward the broken chair by what must have been a desk before it became a pile of wood. "Not sure how to get up there."

"Want to check the other rooms for something?" I ask.

"Nah, I'm sure they are all like this. Come here, I have an idea."

He pats his leg and squats down a little, and I cock an eyebrow at him. "You want to boost me up into a scary black hole?"

"I'll give you the flashlight. Gwen said the metal lockbox is right by the door."

I give him a wary look, but really, I will not say no now that we have come this far. "Okay. don't drop me."

"I would never." He smirks.

"Didn't you say that in the orchard? I distinctly remember being dropped, Sam." I put my hands on my hips, and he laughs. It seems like he remembers our date as well as I do.

"Okay, but you made me laugh. That wasn't my fault."

I shake my head and walk over to him, placing my hand on his shoulder and my foot on his thigh. He hands me the flashlight, and I push up, grabbing the opening of the small cutout. I feel the box before I see it and grab it before making the mistake of swinging the light through the darkened space. The scream that peels free scares Sam and whatever the fuck owned the beady little eyes that glinted off the flashlight. He pulls me down, and we dart out of the closet.

"What the hell, Tammy? What happened?"

"I don't know, something was looking at me. There were eyes, Sam, beady, evil eyes."

"It was probably a raccoon. Jesus, I think I might have had a little heart attack." Sam rubs his chest, but he's smiling at me.

"At least I got it," I say, holding up the metal box.

"Good. Now come with me so I can show you something."

I follow Sam out into the house. The hallway is dark, but we can see fairly well. We pass a bathroom and a small room that might at one point have been a library. There are empty wooden shelves and what was once probably a beanbag.

Sam pushes a door open and steps inside. I follow him, shining the light around the room. There isn't as much in here. His bed is stripped bare but still on the frame. The chair at his desk is tilted to the side because two of the legs are broken. His desk is built in, so it's still intact. There are no personal effects, no pictures or books, or even clothes like in his sister's room. A poster of a baseball player hangs on the wall, like Sam probably had it as a teen.

"Who's that?" I ask.

Sam clutches his chest and acts offended. "I can't believe you don't know who that is, Tammy." He shakes his head at me. "I'm disappointed in you."

"My baseball knowledge is limited to the boys who played for Bower High School. Sorry." I shrug and he laughs.

"That's Bob Knepper. He was a pitcher for the Giants in the early eighties."

"Ah, yes, well, I was going to say that, but you didn't give me a chance." I hold my head up, sticking my chin out.

"Right," Sam rolls his eyes, then rolls his shoulders. "Are you ready to learn something about me?"

"Oh, right, your proof or whatever."

He crosses to his closet, which is completely missing the doors. The rod is also gone, and the carpet has been pulled back, and it looks like something has been harvesting it for bedding. He waves me over.

"Come here and give me the flashlight."

I cross to him and hand it to him, then step next to him. He turns the light on and shines it on the wall. "There you go."

I squint and lean closer, then my eyes go wide. What on earth? That can't be.

"I did that the day I decided to ask you out. I was trying to give myself the confidence to do it, I guess." He shrugs and smiles, but it doesn't quite reach his eyes.

I reach out and let my finger trace over the faded heart that surrounds our initials. It's right next to a doodle of the Giants logo and a crude drawing of the Van Halen V with the lines jutting out from the top. I don't know what to say, since none of this makes sense to me. I mean, I knew Sam liked me as a friend. I knew that part wasn't an act, but when Curtis said he dared Sam to ask me out and to kiss me, I must have decided the whole thing was fake. I squeeze my eyes shut and try to remember the day I heard Curtis talking about it, but I get only flashes of things that are deeply clouded by the insecurity I had.

"So when you said Curtis dared me to kiss you, that just wasn't true at all. I don't know why that asshole was even talking about us, but I hope you understand I took you out because I wanted to, I kissed you because I wanted to."

I turn and look at Sam. Seeing the pain etched in his face reminds me of that Monday after our date, when he pushed past me like he hated me.

"Okay," I say tentatively. "But what happened after our date?

What happened that made you act the way you did on Monday? I thought we were starting something. I thought—"

Sam cuts me off by grabbing my hand and leading me out of the closet, out of his room and down the hall to a wide, grand staircase. The railings have been broken out, and the carpet runner is ripped and stained. This entire house reminds me of a cross between *Gone with the Wind* and *Nightmare on Elm Street*.

"Careful, this last step is broken." Sam says as he steps over it, then helps me do the same.

I turn and scan the room, trying to take in the destruction while my brain tries to picture it how it was when Sam lived here. We are in a grand entryway. Deep dark wood panels line the walls, and remnants of dark green curtains hang in tatters. There is a room to the left that must have been an office. There are books and papers scattered across the floor, and at odds to all of that is a plaque mounted to the wall that says, "Farmer of the Year—Wilton Ford 1980". Right next to the plaque buried deep in the wood is a hatchet.

"That is what happened." Sam points to where I am already looking. He rubs his hand over his face and says, "That's what I came home to after our date. To be honest, I wasn't sure it would still be here, but I guess the house held on to that little family secret."

"I don't understand, Sam."

"DID you ever watch the movie *The War of the Roses?*"

I shake my head. "I didn't watch the movie, but I read the book."

That makes him smile a little. "Of course you did. Well, my parents were worse. They fought all the time. Not just yelling, like actual physical fights. After I dropped you off, I came home and found my mother chasing Dad with that. He ducked as she threw it at him. You can tell how much force was behind that throw by how deep it's buried. My dad just laughed and picked up a heavy paperweight off his desk and went after her. I turned around and got in my truck and left. Sunday night I came back because I knew I had to finish the week at school. I had to get my diploma."

I step closer to him, wanting to wrap him in my arms, but I can see the panic on his face as I reach out. I drop my hands and step back a little.

"God, Sam, I'm so sorry. Where did you go? You should have come back to my house—my dad would have let you stay. My dad would have helped."

"I know. Craig was great. I couldn't, I didn't want you to know. I was embarrassed, especially after I got to see what your house was like."

"So where did you stay?" I ask, afraid of what his answer will be. My heart is breaking for him.

"My truck the first night. On Saturday, I drove over to Jeff's house. He let me stay with him. His family was cool, not in the farmer circle so they didn't know anything and wouldn't spread rumors."

The farmers in Bower were a gossipy bunch. I remember my dad leaning on his tractor, telling all sorts of stories about people one or two fields over. I give Sam a small smile. "I'm glad you found a place where you felt safe. That must have been so scary."

He shrugs. "By that time I was pretty numb to it all, but I made up my mind while I lay in my truck in the middle of one of our orchards that I was leaving. Jeff's dad was retired military, so he told me how to enlist, and that's what I was in a hurry to do after school on Monday. I drove to Sacramento and signed up for the Army, and the day after we graduated, I left for boot camp. I swore I'd never come back here."

"I wish I had known." But if I had known about the horrible life that Sam endured, it wouldn't have changed anything for him. I wouldn't have stopped him from leaving.

"Let's get out of here." Sam grabs my hand, and we make our way through the rubble down to my car. He still has the metal box from his sister's attic in his hand, and he sets it on the floorboard before he climbs in.

"Want me to take you to your place?"

"Yeah, I need to deal with this stuff." He motions to the floor where the box sits between his feet.

"Okay, I can stay?"

"No, that's okay, Tammy. You've done enough. Thanks for going with me. That wasn't . . ." He pauses and takes a breath. "That wasn't as bad with you there."

"I'm glad."

We drive in silence to his place, and I am working up the courage to ask him to get the rest of his stuff and just move in with me. I think he needs to be around someone. I think I could help him, and if I am being honest with myself, I really enjoy having him around. I like that there is someone else in my home. I want to know if something could happen between us again or if that was a onetime fluke.

"So listen," Sam huffs out like he's been holding those two words in for a while. I turn into the parking lot for the cabins and put my car in park, turning to him.

"I can't stay here much longer because the workers are coming and Mario—"

I cut him off. "Move in with me. Get your stuff and just come and live with me."

"Yeah? Tammy, are you sure? I was just going to ask if I could crash there until I find a place long-term."

"I'm sure. I was going to ask but didn't want to freak you out. Sam, we get along great, and I hate being in that big house all by myself."

"I can pay rent and help with the utilities and whatnot." He pauses and rubs his hand over his face. "Are you sure, Tammy?"

"Yes. I've never been more sure about something, Sam. Move in."

"Okay, well, let me gather the rest of my stuff, then go talk to Mario and Linda. I, uh, I'll be at your house by dinnertime, I'm sure. Want me to bring a pizza or something?"

"You'll be home around dinnertime. Yes. Pizza sounds amazing." I grab his arm gently and ask, "Are you okay?"

"Yeah, sure. Just overwhelmed, I think. Can I leave this box in here? I'll call my sister and maybe we can mail it or whatever tomorrow?"

"That sounds good. I can help you with that." I want to add that I will help him with everything, but I don't want to smother him. Not emotionally, at least. I haven't been able to stop thinking about the way he felt against me, his lips and hands on every inch of my body. The way his blue eyes held my gaze, like he wanted to be in that moment forever. It's entirely possible the remnants of too much tequila that day have clouded my perception since nothing has happened since then.

I guess if we're under one roof, we'll find out if this can be more than a friendship, finally.

EIGHTEEN

TIME FOR A CHANGE

AS SOON AS I get inside my little cabin, which has been my refuge, my home for the past six months, I sink to my knees and let the pain wash over me. I don't bother fighting the tears; no one is here to see them. I need to let them out so I don't drown. I cry for the destruction that was my childhood, not just the physical house where it occurred, but the absolute wreckage that my parents caused to my life. What they made me miss out on, what they drove me towards. I wouldn't have joined the military if it hadn't been for them, wouldn't have been deployed or hurt. Trying to escape the pain of their parenting led me to a different kind of pain. One that has physical proof of what I went through.

The tears fall without shame because it is time. It is far past the time to recognize I will never get those years back. I will never walk into my mother's kitchen to the smell of freshly baked cookies after school. I'll never have a heart-to-heart with my dad about the ways of the world and how to win a good girl's heart.

For fuck's sake, I'm twenty-eight, and I realize, as I step through the doorway to my childhood bedroom, that I've been waiting for those things. I've been holding a part of my heart for them in hopes that my parents would rise to the occasion and acknowledge I needed their love and care. That Gwen and I were more important than the feuds that carried them through life.

Seeing the physical destruction of the house was like someone had taken a picture of my soul and placed it for the world to see. The scattered debris, the marred wood and the ravaged interior mirrored so perfectly what I've been holding onto all these years.

The therapists at the VA wanted to focus on my accident and the resulting memory loss. They acted like that was my only trauma, or the only one that mattered. That being thrown through metal and into fire was the thing that made me shake and turn away from the comforting hands of the nurses. It was an assumption that was, I'm sure, for most people, a correct one. For me, it was so much more than my accident. The Army was my escape, my salvation, until it couldn't be. I realized when I woke up in the hospital that I wouldn't be able to stay in the military in the same capacity. That pain was worse than what the IED caused.

I didn't have to agree to come back here. I could've stayed at Fort Irwin, but when it was time to reenlist or walk away, I listened to my therapist and left. He thought being here would help my short-term memory problems and in some ways he was right. I've been holding onto things a little easier, remembering little things that used to slip from my grasp.

I wipe my face and huff out a breath, trying to regain some composure. I need to call Gwen. She will be happy that I found the box. Part of me is relieved that it was there, because that means she won't bother me anymore. I wish I didn't feel that way about my own family, but I do.

I stand slowly and wince at the pain in my hip, rubbing at it to loosen it up. The bed I've been sleeping on is a thousand times better than the shitty mattress here, but the hip pain has been bothering me since I got sick.

I dial Gwen's number and pray for the answering machine.

"Hello? Sam? Did you find it?" she says as soon as she picks up.

"Yeah. I got it. The box was up there like you said, still locked and everything."

She lets out a relieved breath. "Thank God. Okay, I'm coming into town after all. I should be there tomorrow."

"WHAT THE FUCK? If you were coming, why the hell did you make me drive out there to get it?"

"I'm sorry, Sam, I wasn't sure, and I couldn't chance it. I fly into Sacramento in the morning and then have a few meetings, but I'll drive up after. Will you be at Mario's cabins?"

"No, I'm moving in with a friend. I'm packing up right now. Mario is expecting his workers next week, so I can't stay here."

"Right, okay, so where can I find you?"

"Do you remember the Little Farm?"

"Sure yeah. Rice farmers out on County Road W?"

"Yeah. I'll be there."

"Great. See you probably around four. Thanks again, Sam."

She hung up before I could respond, but it's for the best since I wanted to say something rude. That isn't productive, and I guess I should wait until I see her in person. I try to picture her and struggle. She had brown, curly hair when I saw her last. It was cut short, but the fringe hung in her eyes. I have my father's blue eyes while Gwen takes more after our mother. I wonder if she has the same rage and anger that our mom had, or fuck, probably still has. Where did that guy say she was? India? I know he said my father is in Colusa. That is not far enough away, but I'm betting he won't show his face here in Bower, not after the way people grow quiet when he is mentioned. I need to get all the details; perhaps it would give me some closure.

I spent the next hour taking my stuff out to my Jeep and then cleaning the cabin. I strip the bedding and take it over to the washroom, where I run into Linda. She offers to finish up the wash and tells me not to worry about cleaning.

I'm glad I had already finished that, because I am sure she

would've stopped me if she had caught me. She's a good woman, strong and sure of herself. She and Mario met in high school and got married very young. I wonder—if I had stayed, if I had a normal family, would Tammy and I have had a similar life?

I never wanted to take over nut farming. I never wanted to be like my father, but Tammy's dad, Craig, was a good man. I would've probably enjoyed helping him with the rice. Tammy would've been able to catch his cancer if she had been here. If I had given her a reason to stay, would she have? Or was she as eager to leave this small patch of earth as much as I was?

I shake off the what-ifs that are starting to surround me like an insurmountable wall, and I climb into my Jeep to go get some pizza before going to my new home.

It's already dark when I pull into the wide gravel driveway that sits to the side of Tammy's house. All the lights are on, pouring yellow joy out in every direction, and I sit for a minute taking it all in. It hits me square in the chest like a fastball that got past my glove. I fight to take a deep breath and settle the racing heart that only a moment ago was calm. Holy crap. This is what I want. I mean, eventually, I want a home like this. Right? Who wouldn't? This big, beautiful home that has memories and love wrapped in every board, every curtain. A place where you can come and feel like you belong before you even step foot on the porch. I want that for Donny, too. I bet if Tammy and I work together, we can bring him here sooner. I mean, there is no way probably for Thanksgiving, but what if we could have him for Christmas?

That thought spurs me, and I grab the pizza box from my passenger seat and walk up to the house. I hold my hand up to knock, but then decide to just walk in. I catch Tammy's back retreating down the hall, her arms full of laundry. She turns slightly when she hears the door, and her face lights up at the sight of me.

"Sam, hi!" She shifts the basket a little, then says, "I'll be right there. I just need to start a load real quick."

I nod and walk to the kitchen where I see the small table is already set. A bottle of red wine sits beside two glasses on the counter. I grab the corkscrew and get to work. I set the full glasses down on the table just as Tammy rounds the corner into the kitchen.

"Well, that answers my question of would you like wine with your pizza?"

"The answer is usually no, but tonight, yes seems like the right answer," I say, wondering if I should explain that I don't usually drink. Since I've been hanging out with her though I've had tequila, a few beers and now wine, apparently. I don't have a problem with alcohol; I guess I just always worried I would develop one if I drank too often. I like the numb sensation a little too much.

"I usually have a glass of wine at night, but you don't have to join me if you'd prefer something else. I have soda and milk and, of course, the good ol' water that flows from the sink." She smiles at me in such a relaxed, easy way that my heart forgets all the years between us. I want so badly to touch her again, to feel her in my arms, tight against my body.

"Wine sounds nice. I have only had it a few times; I know I like red"—I nod towards the full glasses on the table, then add—"but I won't be joining you if you open a bottle of white. That shit tastes like hairspray."

She laughs and walks to the table, pulling out her chair. She sits, so I bring the pizza box over and lift the lid so she can take a slice or two. I put three on my plate, then return the box to the counter before joining her at the table.

"Did you get everything packed?" she asks as she lifts her wine-glass to her lips. My gaze is following her mouth as she takes a drink of her wine, but I can't look away.

I look up into her eyes and nod. "Can I take you out?"

She grabbed a piece of pizza and is now holding it halfway to her mouth, and she freezes. "What did you say?"

My eyes go wide because what the hell did I just say? Did I really just ask her out the second we sat down for dinner? I would think when it occurred to me to do this the right way, I'd be cooler about it.

Like, as we lounged on the couch after dinner. I clear my throat and say, "I would like to take you out. On a date."

"Like to dinner? Or a movie?" she asks, her voice pitched a little higher.

"Sure, yeah. I promise not to drive you through the orchards and convince you to do the dance from the 'Thriller' music video, but yeah. I want to take you on a date."

"It would be like an actual date?" she asks with one eyebrow raised. I nod, and she grabs her wine glass and takes a big gulp.

"Yes, a real, proper date."

"Our first date? Of, like, many? Like, what is the plan, Sam?" She swallows nervously.

"Well, no, technically it would be our second first date. But then, yes, the first of many, I hope." I sound more confident than I feel. My hands are sweaty, so I wipe them down my jeans, then reach for my own wine glass and take a big gulp as well. I don't know if I should tell her that before I got the flu, I was going to ask her out, and now that I am going to live with her—she cuts through my thoughts.

"But we are roommates now, won't that be weird?"

"No," I say, but fuck yes, it will be weird. Like, I can't come pick her up. What do I do? Knock on her bedroom door and lead her downstairs? Jesus, I really didn't think this through.

"Okay."

"Okay? You'll go out with me?"

"Yes. I would love to." She points her pizza at me and adds, "But if you don't have fun or whatever, you can't make this weird. I don't want to lose you as a friend, Sam."

I blow out a breath, feeling my chest loosen a bit, then nod and smile. "Don't worry about that, Tammy."

She takes a bite of her pizza, eyeing me suspiciously. I eat and try not to act like I just changed everything between us. After a few minutes, I see her relax a little.

"So, when is this big date?"

"Day after tomorrow? Sunday? I figured we could go into Chico, get burgers at The Bear, or if you want fancy, we could go to Basque Norte, or R Fish and Company. If you don't like any of those suggestions, there are a couple of other options like Sicilian Cafe or—"

She laughs and holds up her hand. "Sam, stop. Bear burgers sound perfect, just like the first time, well, except now we can get beer."

I smile and let my shoulders relax. "Okay, yeah, that sounds great. I'll pick you up at five?" I wiggle my eyebrows at her, and she laughs.

We finish the entire pizza and take our wine into the living room, settling easily onto opposite ends of the couch. I feel lighter since asking Tammy out, even if it could have gone the other way; she could have said no. What if the wild night we shared was a onetime thing? She seemed pretty nervous the next day; to be fair, I was a wreck thinking I had ruined things.

"So my sister Gwen is coming tomorrow to get the box."

"Oh, really? I have my CPR class in the morning, but I should be done a little after noon. Do you need me to be here or is she meeting you somewhere else?"

"No, I told her to come here. She said she would be here around four. I hope that's okay."

"Of course it is. I can be gone if you want to talk to her alone?"

"No, I would actually like it if you were here. I, um, I don't really know my sister that well. She moved out when I was twelve, and even when she was around, it's not like we hung out or anything. She was always off with friends. We are six years apart in age but like a million miles apart compared to most brothers and sisters."

"Oh, sure, I can stay. To be honest, I didn't know you even had a sister. You never talked about her." Tammy is tracing her finger over the top of her wineglass lazily, and I wish she were sitting closer so I could chase that finger with my own.

"Yeah, well, I don't think I ever really felt like I had one. There was one year that we were kind of normal siblings; she was thirteen and I was just about to turn seven. There was a thing." I shake my head, trying to remember but come up short. "All I remember was that my mom was working with my dad, but I don't remember why, because that was the only summer that happened. Anyway, Gwen was in charge of me during the day, and we had a great time. We went fishing and swimming at Rambo Bridge. We played in the orchards and rode around on one of the tractors. I remember setting up a whole mess of those green army guys along the canal by the almonds, and she built a little wooden house-like thing for the men."

"That sounds like fun." Tammy smiles at me, then finishes her wine and sets the glass on the coffee table before leaning back into the couch. She turns, so she is facing me and with her knees pulled up into her chest, she sighs. "I always wanted a brother or sister."

"Yeah," I tilt my wineglass back, finishing the last few swallows, then stand and take our glasses into the kitchen.

"We can clean up tomorrow," she calls, but I can't help myself. Knowing there are dishes in the sink makes me restless. Plus, I don't really want to talk about Gwen anymore. I don't want to think about the time I spent in the hospital where not one single member of my family came to see me, sent a card or dialed the phone. I know they were notified. All three of my family members were on the list, all with equal importance, and all three let me know exactly how important I was to them.

I finish quicker than I want and return to the couch where Tammy has a blanket pulled over her lap, her white-socked feet sticking out. She gives me a sweet smile, and I want so badly to dip down and kiss her, but I don't. I want to get this right. I want to treat her the way she deserves, not maul her like I did before.

"So, what does your sister do for work?" Tammy asks. It's a simple question, but I don't have an answer for her.

I shrug. "Not really sure. We haven't really talked in the last fifteen years. I got a Christmas card once when I was still in Georgia, but she didn't see the need to tell me about her life. It was just signed, 'Love, Gwen.'"

"That's awful, Sam. I'm sorry."

I sit and pull her feet into my lap, needing a way to touch her that won't send me climbing over her and pressing every inch of my body to hers.

"It's okay. You can't miss what you never had, you know? It's not like we had a falling-out or anything. I guess we will find out tomorrow when she gets here. I'll make a point of asking her."

"I wonder if she has any kids? I mean, you could be an uncle right now and not even know it," Tammy says, and I hate how sad her voice sounds.

I give her foot a little squeeze, then ask, "What time do you usually turn in? I should unload my Jeep, at least the stuff I'll need in the morning."

"Oh, I can help." She pulls her legs down as the washing machine buzzes down the hall.

"You finish up with that; I got it. I don't have very much to bring in. Where do you want me?"

"I guess Dad's old room? We can see if that works for you, or I can get a better bed for the guest room upstairs. Right now there is a twin that I swear will collapse if you try to lie on it."

"His room is fine, if you are sure."

"I'm sure. I am really excited about you being here, Sam." She pauses and looks away for a second before adding, "And for our date on Sunday."

"Me too."

THE WHOLE NEXT MORNING, while Tammy is in her class, I make myself useful around the house. I clean the kitchen and bathrooms, taking the liberty to remove the shower chair from the downstairs shower. I make trips with the chair and a few boxes that Tammy had by the back door to the garage. It's bigger than most standard garages, with a tall roof that can accommodate a rice harvester. That's gone, of course, but Tammy's truck, Big Red, sits on one side with the hood up and a mat resting over the edge, like Craig had been working on her. I found a home for the shower chair and the boxes of books that Tammy wanted to keep but wasn't sure they deserved prime real estate on the bookshelf in the office. I love her enthusiasm for literature but don't quite understand the hierarchy of her personal library.

I walk over to the truck and lean down to see all the spark plugs are removed and the carburetor hangs loose. The air filter is missing too, so I glance around the garage and spot a box with a new one on the wood counter that runs along the back of the whole place. There is about a year's worth of dust covering it. I wonder what happened the day he was out here to make him stop like this. Tammy must not have come out here. Maybe it was too much for her to see, or maybe she was too busy taking him to doctor's appointments. I can understand how this wouldn't be a priority.

I wonder if she would let me fix her up? Get Big Red running again? Damn, I wish I had time to have her ready for our date. That would be incredible.

My thoughts are interrupted by the sound of tires on gravel. Instead of going out the small side door, I pull the chain to open the bay door at the front. Tammy stops, and I watch her legs turn towards the garage; the door slowly revealing her whole body to me. She is wearing dark Wrangler jeans and a pair of lace-up Justin boots. Tammy has never really dressed like a farmer's kid, but she also didn't follow the trends like the other girls did. She's always had her own style, and I, for one, am a big fan. I smile when I see her oversized Bower Elementary sweatshirt.

"Wow, I haven't seen her since my first day here. I'm surprised the tires aren't more flat," Tammy says as she strides towards me.

"She just needs a little love and she'll be good as new."

"Yeah, I kept meaning to come out here. If I remember correctly, Dad was in the middle of switching out the spark plugs and the air filter?"

"Yep, looks like he was going to flush the carburetor or something because that is half off."

Tammy hangs her head a little at that. "Yeah, that was the day he called me. I guess even after everything the doctor had told him, it took him feeling too weak to remove a carburetor to reach out and ask me to come home."

I'm not sure how to respond, so I point to the shower chair and the boxes. "I brought those out here; I hope that's okay?"

"That's perfect. I'll put those books in his little office. I'm sure I don't need a book on the history of rice farming in the north state, but I just am not ready to let those go."

"How was the class?" I ask.

"Easy. I've taken a CPR class before, so it was just the refresher course. I have to start the foster parent training sessions next week. I guess they do some role-playing and talk about trauma and things like that. I'm glad because, like, I understand Donny, you know? But I don't know how to help him sort through what happened. I hope they can teach me what I am supposed to say. How I handle things."

"I can't think of a better person to help him, Tammy. Do you think it will be a problem that I live here now too? Should I come to the classes too?" I ask because I don't want to mess this up for either of them.

"That might be required. I'll call and find out. They're doing a criminal background check on me; I bet yours would be easy with all your military stuff. I had to have one when I was working at the archives, but they have to do one here in California. There will be a home visit too, a safety check, you know?"

"That makes sense. It's kind of weird to me that people can just have a kid, be a shitty parent and then a good person comes along and has to jump through all these hoops to take care of the child. I'm glad they do it, but fuck, everyone should have to pass those kinds of standards."

"I agree." She stops and looks around the big empty garage. "Do you think they will see this space as a danger to Donny? All the tools and sharp things?"

"It's a garage. Most people have them. I mean, it's probably good the big rice harvester isn't in here anymore, but I don't think this will be a problem."

"Okay, yeah." Tammy rubs her hands down her jeans nervously.

"Have you had lunch yet?" I ask, hoping to distract her.

"Nope, I bet that's why I'm freaking out. I'm hungry."

I follow her into the house after I close the garage bay door, thinking about how different this will all be when Donny lives here too.

NINETEEN

Tammy

LIES THAT BREAK YOU

SAM and I make peanut butter and jelly sandwiches and talk about nothing important. I insist on cleaning up the mess we made, since I can tell he spent the morning doing that. The whole kitchen is sparkling clean and smells like Pine-Sol. He must be a nervous cleaner like I am.

Standing at the window, finishing up the dishes, I notice a black sedan drive slowly past the house. The brake lights come on, then the reverse lights as it backs up and stops directly in front of the bay window where I'm standing.

I tuck my hair behind my ear and wait, expecting someone to get out. Instead, the car pulls away slowly and continues down the road, disappearing from my view. That was odd.

"Sam? What kind of car your sister is driving?" I yell.

"No idea, she said she was renting a car. Why?" Sam appears behind me, holding a TV guide that is at least two years old.

"It's probably nothing; there was a black sedan a moment ago. Thought it was her, but it pulled away."

Sam glances down at his watch, and his brow furrows. "She said she would be here around four, and it's only a little past three. Maybe someone was lost."

"That's probably right." I point to his hand. "I don't think you are going to find anything to watch using that. It's from a few years ago."

He turns the cover so I can see it and says, "I was just reading up about Billy Ray Cyrus. I don't want to have an achy-breaky heart, so I need to be prepared."

We make our way to the living room and settle into the couch to watch a rerun of *Columbo,* arguing about when he actually figures it out. I always thought he knew the second he met the bad guy, but Sam thinks he is really slowly gathering evidence.

The light tapping on the door makes me jump, and Sam laughs. "Easy there, tiger. It's just Gwen, not a murderer."

I swat at him as I stand and adjust my sweatshirt. Maybe I should have changed? I'm reaching for the door when I feel Sam's hand on my back, so I turn and smile up at him. He nods, letting me know he's ready.

I open the door expecting what, I'm not too sure, but not what I see. There is a tall, thin woman with brown, curly hair cut into a short bob. She has barely any makeup on, but it doesn't matter. She is breathtaking, with perfect skin and big, full lips. She's wearing a navy-blue suit with low black heels and a crisp white shirt that is buttoned almost to the top. Her blazer is open and with her hand tucked in her pocket, my eyes are drawn immediately to the badge at her hip. She catches my gaze and pulls her hand free, letting the coat slide back over the shield.

"Tammy Little?"

"That's me." I clear my throat. "You must be Gwen. You look like Sam." I step aside because Sam is standing behind me, and while I'm sure she can see him over my head, I don't want this to make this more awkward than it already is.

"Hi, Sam. Long time no see." She folds her hands together in front of her and shifts on her feet a little. She looks as nervous as I am, and this isn't even about me.

"Hey. Come on in," Sam says as he steps away from the door.

I notice she doesn't have a purse or anything with her, and before I close the door, I see the same black sedan that stopped earlier out front. There is a person in the driver's seat, but I can't see their face.

"My partner is going to wait out there," Gwen says as I stare out the open door.

"Oh, right. Okay." I shut the door and stand like I'm unsure how to welcome someone into my house. Thankfully they don't seem to need me.

"You found the box?" Gwen says, addressing Sam.

"Yeah, it was right where you said it would be." He crosses to the TV cabinet and grabs the box. "It's locked, but it's one of those little locks; I'm sure you can—"

Sam stops when he sees that his sister is holding up her keys. "I have the key." She gives him a small smile.

"Oh, well, then, here you go."

"Thanks. Can I?" She motions to the couch, and I snap out of my stupor.

"Yes, can I get you anything? Water or a soda?"

"Water would be great, thanks, Tammy." She glances at me over her shoulder but quickly returns her focus to Sam.

I scurry off, grateful for something to do. When I come back, Gwen has the box open, and she's reading what must be her birth certificate.

"Who do you work for?" Sam asks, and I wonder if he saw the badge like I did.

"Department of Justice," she says without hesitation. She holds up the paper and says, "Thank you, Sam. I have a copy from Butte County, but I wanted the original, before the adoption."

"What? Adoption? What are you talking about, Gwen?"

"Wilton is not my biological father." She holds up her hands and says, "Sorry, he's your dad. We share our mother, but Wilton adopted me when he married Mom."

"Why didn't I know about this?" Sam sits next to her and jams his hand into his hair.

Gwen's voice pitches up a little as she squeezes her hands together. "I didn't know until I was almost out of the house. I found it by accident."

"Here's your water," I say dumbly.

"Thanks." Gwen takes it and drinks the whole thing before handing it back to me. I step over to the coffee table and set the glass down. I move to sit next to Sam on the couch. I wish I could touch him. Console him somehow, but his body is rigid and I can almost feel the anger radiating off him.

"So is that why you left and never looked back?" he asks.

"No." She pauses, then sighs. "Yeah, a little, I guess. I was furious that no one had told me. I tried to find my biological father, spent my first year of college determined that he was out there living this great life without me."

"Did you find him?" I ask.

"Yeah, eventually. He's up in Oregon. We talk a few times a year, nice man."

"I know the house sold, but I don't understand what happened to all the orchards. Mario said something happened, but the town doesn't blame me. Do you know what happened?" Sam asks, and I lean forward a little because I am also curious.

She looks at both of us, the confusion clear on her face. "You didn't hear?"

"No, everyone just assumes I know. I get vague comments, but I need the whole story, Gwen."

"Wow, okay. So Dad and Mom, to a lesser extent, broke the law. They violated the Clayton Act, to be exact the mergers and acquisitions portion."

"I don't understand what that means," I say, and Sam agrees.

She narrows her eyes at us, then asks, "You really didn't hear about this?"

We both shake our heads, so she continues. "He convinced

everyone to form a co-op. Made them all sign contracts that they would sell together at a fixed price, then behind their backs he cut his prices. He used aliases to sell the bulk of his nuts, holding back some so the other farmers wouldn't get suspicious. He was making three times what he reported. When the other farmers couldn't sell because of the price Wilton had set, he offered to buy them out. That part of his plan took years, of course, but he ended up with like, 300 more acres of walnut and almond trees by the time he was caught."

"That's awful," Sam croaks out.

"Yeah, the lawsuit required Wilton to refrain from the purchase of any stock or ownership of any nut farms for a total of ten years from the date of the court case. That's next year. In 1996 he will be eligible to make purchases, and from what I understand he's been sniffing around over in Colusa. I'm sure he's hoping the farmers over there won't remember him, or they weren't in the area when Ford Nuts caused the entire industry to collapse."

"Oh, my God," I mutter.

"Yeah, the industry has come back slowly, but not without problems. There are a lot of family farms that went under and never recovered. Mostly, what you have now is big corporate farms run by some locals who just wanted to work and stay here. It's sad, and now I want to make sure he doesn't try the same shit over in Colusa. I flew out here because I was finally able to meet with Hurt, Lyle, and Gordon. Those were the first three nut farmers who joined him. When I was in high school, I was best friends with Dawn Gordon, so she was able to help arrange the meeting. They obviously wouldn't have met with anyone in the Ford family without that connection." She laughs a little but stops when she glances at Sam.

"So, what about Mom? Like, she was involved?"

"Yes. I think some of their fights, at least when I was around, were about money. She loved to spend it and got mad when he wasn't making it fast enough."

"That sounds about right. I heard she is in India?" Sam says, and my eyes go wide. I hadn't heard that; of course, he never talks about his family.

"Yeah, she was last seen in Mumbai, but I have a source who thinks she might have gone inland. She's on the run. They were both convicted, but she somehow managed to slip away between the trial and the sentencing. Wilton served five years, out on good behavior two years early."

"Dad was in jail?" Sam sounds shocked and defeated all at once.

"Well, yeah. His crimes were pretty serious. Like I said, he decimated the nut industry in the north state. I think if they hadn't thrown him in jail, the farmers around here would have found their own justice."

"When?" Sam's voice is barely above a whisper, and the pained look on his face is breaking me apart.

"Let's see, he went in 1987, got out in '93 or the beginning of '94," Gwen says. She tucks the birth certificate into an inner pocket of her blazer. I'm sure she will make her exit soon, leaving Sam to deal with this on his own. Well, no, I won't let that happen. I'll be here for him.

"Well, I guess that explains why no one in this fucking family came to see me when I was injured. No phone calls, no cards." Sam stands up and stomps off to the kitchen, and I glance over at Gwen in time to see her wince.

"Shit, I've handled this all wrong," she mumbles. She looks up at me like I might have an idea how to fix it.

"He's upset" is all I can say, which is about as useful as pointing out the color of the sky.

"Right." Gwen stands and reaches into her coat, pulling out a business card. She sets it on the table. "I need to get back. Our flight back to D.C. is in a few hours."

"Sure, okay. You live in D.C.?" I ask her as she strides toward the door. I wonder if I ever passed her on the street or ate at the same restaurant as her not realizing who she was.

"Yes, for now. I have been working on some antitrust cases." She looks at her watch, then towards the kitchen where Sam disappeared.

"Do you have kids?" I blurt out because I want to know for some reason, like that information will help salvage this disaster.

She gives me a small smile and says, "No. My husband and I both work so much. It wouldn't be fair to anyone."

"Oh. Okay. Well, I just wondered." I mentally punch myself because that was the weirdest thing I could have asked her.

"Tell Sam he can call me anytime. I'm sorry to breeze in here, drop all this shit and just leave." She glances at her watch again then over my shoulder. "But I really have to go."

"Okay." I nod, wishing Sam would come back.

"Bye, Sam," she yells, but no reply is coming, and we both know it.

I open the door for her, and she lifts her hand in a little wave. "Thanks, Tammy."

I watch her walk to the car and wait until it drives off before I step back into the house. Sam is holding her business card, running his finger over her name.

"Gwen R. Davidson, Esq. So I guess she's married?" he asks before tossing the card back onto the table.

"Yeah, lives in D.C., no kids," I report, wishing there was more I could tell him, like if he had that information he'd have a closeness to his sister suddenly.

"At least I know why I lay in that hospital alone for twelve weeks."

I walk to him and grab his arm, immediately regretting it when he flinches. I watch as he closes his eyes, then blows out a long breath. While his eyes are still closed, he reaches for me, and I give him my hand. We stand like that for a minute while he takes deep breaths, using me as an anchor. Eventually he tugs me in, wrapping me in both arms. I rest my head on his chest and place my arms loosely around his waist.

"Tighter. I need to feel you." Sam's voice is low, commanding.

I move closer so we are touching chest to chest and pull him into me. He slumps a little, letting me support him. I could stay here all day. He feels so good pressed against me, his warm, hard body and strong arms. I start to lightly move my thumbs over his back as we shift a little. Sam is resting his head against mine, and he hums a little as his hands start to move as well.

"God, Tammy, I like being in your arms," Sam huffs out.

I look up into his beautiful blue eyes, and my breath catches. It's like it happens in slow motion and snapshot pictures as he lowers his face towards mine. His lips stop just before touching mine, as his hand moves up to cup my face. His breath is ragged, and I want to hang in this moment in time forever. He lightly brushes his lips over mine, and we both freeze.

"Can I?" he asks, and he's so close that his lips are touching mine as he does.

"Yes, please," I breathe out.

He places his lips so softly over mine that I think he is going to pull back, but he sighs and kisses me slowly. It's the most sensual kiss I have ever experienced, even better than the first time, and somehow better than the night we fooled around. It makes me wonder if I ever got over him? Hard to say at the moment, as my heart is trying to beat in time with his.

Before I am aware of what's happening, Sam is stepping back, his hands trailing up and down my arms. I lean forward, chasing his lips when he finally breaks the kiss so I stumble a little.

"Sorry. I wasn't going to do that again, till the end of our date."

"I don't mind." I step back into his space, look up at him, and smile. "I liked it. We don't have to wait."

He runs his hand through his hair and looks back to the couch before sitting down. "My head really isn't in the right place for this."

"Oh, sure, I understand. That was a lot with Gwen. Are you okay?"

"Not really. I mean, I guess it's nice to finally understand why my parents never came to see me or sent a card or fucking called when I got hurt, but fuck, I'm so—" Sam's voice trails off.

I sit next to him and lay my hand on his knee. "So . . . what, Sam? What are you feeling?"

"Embarrassed, frustrated. Mad at myself for coming back here," he says without looking at me. I let my hand slide off his leg and scoot back a little.

"Right, I can understand that," I say, trying like hell not to get too offended by that.

"How could Mario and Linda be so nice to me? My God, they acted like I was welcome and that the whole town would be happy to see me, but how can that be?"

"Has anyone treated you poorly since you've been back?" I ask, genuinely surprised by his take on this. He had nothing to do with what his father did.

"No, but now I'm sure it was just pity, or fuck, I don't know what."

"I don't think that Sam. I think people can recognize that Wilton and Diane did all that on their own. Plus you left, you weren't even in the country." I throw up my hands in frustration when I say the last part because Sam has stood up and is pacing now.

"Yeah, but I should have known something was up; I should have paid more attention. Fuck, that's why he never wanted my help at the processing plant. He was hiding all the shady shit he was doing."

"Maybe, but you were, what, eighteen when you left here? There wasn't anything you could have done, Sam."

"Okay. Yeah, sorry. I'm going to call it a night. I have a raging headache and I just need to lie down."

I glance at my watch; it's just after five. "Okay, want me to bring you something to eat in a little while?"

"Nah, I'm not hungry. I'll grab something if that changes." Sam turns and walks up the stairs. I sink back onto the couch and listen to the bedroom door close.

In just a short amount of time, it's like he slipped away from me, from what we could be. It feels like that Monday of senior year all over again.

TWENTY

ESCAPE IS NECESSARY

I WAIT until I hear Tammy's bedroom door close before I write the note. I can't fucking stay here in Bower. Not after what he did to this community. What was I thinking? Okay, yeah, this coming back thing wasn't really my idea, but I agreed. It made sense when Mr. Darby suggested it, and I guess a small part of me thought I'd be able to start fresh. Not with my parents, I knew I didn't want to see them, but with everything else. This was going to be a reset. It was never meant to be permanent. I sure as hell didn't expect to run into Tammy Little, and I shake my head to stop that thought and finish my note to her.

I write out a letter of resignation to the school district too, because that would be rude to just not show up after break. I'll drop that in the mail when I get to wherever the fuck I'm going.

I trace my thumb over my bottom lip and close my eyes, remembering the way Tammy felt against me. I shouldn't have kissed her. I knew as soon as my sister left I was going to leave Bower. I knew I couldn't stay, but I'm a selfish fucker and I wanted another kiss from her.

I pack my stuff back into the duffle bags and stack them by the door, knowing it will be a few hours before Tammy is asleep. I'm surprised she didn't knock again when she turned in for the night. She tried to bring me dinner, and I know I was an asshole to snap at her like I did, but fuck. I couldn't look at her; if I did, I'd be tempted to stay.

I watch the little red numbers on the clock turn to 2:00 a.m. and grab my bags and make my way down to my Jeep. I leave the note on the little table in her kitchen, pausing a moment to run my finger over the cracked vinyl on the chair. This home holds so much love, so many stories that will never be mine.

Pulling out onto County Road W, I leave my lights off, letting the ink-black night envelop my escape. I glance back only once to confirm the house is still dark before turning onto the road that leads back into Bower. I have no idea where I am going. For the first time since leaving here in '85, I have no plan. No rope to tether me, no team to support me.

I am in free fall as I turn the headlights on and illuminate the path to nowhere.

TWENTY-ONE

Tammy

BUT HE NEEDS ME

I CAN HEAR the phone ringing from somewhere far away. I grunt and roll over. The clock on my dresser lets me know I slept way later than I normally do. I glance over at the phone charger for the cordless and it's empty. Fuck. No telling where that damn thing is. I jump out of bed and trot down the stairs, grabbing the phone from the kitchen counter.

"Hello?"

"Tammy? Oh, good. I was worried you left town for break."

I blink a few times and rub my hand down my face, trying to place the voice on the phone. "No, I'm staying here. Who is this?"

"Sorry, it's me, Melinda. I was calling because I got word that Donny's foster home is getting ready to release him. They aren't able to keep him past this week. He will go to another foster home right after Thanksgiving. I've heard they are going to try to keep him in Gridley so he can go to the same school, but with his diagnosis it's hard to find placement."

"Shit," I whisper, my chest suddenly too tight to take a breath.

"Where are you in the process?" Melinda asks.

"Um, I've taken some of the classes. I finished my CPR and first aid. I'd have to check the schedule, I'm sorry. I just woke up and my brain isn't working yet. I'll take him if I can, no question. I just need to figure out how."

"I'll help you with that. I'm going to talk to my friend at the court-house first thing Monday morning and see if they can grant an emergency order allowing you to take custody on a temporary basis. That will allow him to be with you until you sort out all the rest of the paperwork."

"They haven't done the home visit yet," I tell her, finally remembering what I learned in the last class. That was something I was supposed to schedule this week.

"I can expedite that. They will want to make this easy for you since he will be hard to place. If you are willing to take him and we can show you are a safe option, it should go through quickly."

I turn and lean against the counter, blowing out a breath. "Okay, yeah. I'm excited for this to happen. I miss that little dude so much."

"You are one of the good ones, Tammy. I'll be working on this today and, of course, I'll hit the ground running on Monday. I'll call you if I hear anything. Do you have a pager?"

"No, should I get one? You can leave a message at the house; I don't plan on going anywhere, I just have plans for—" My voice trails off when I see a folded piece of paper on the table where I sit. I glance towards the stairs and suddenly the silence of the whole house swallows me. "I'll be around," I manage to say. Tears well in my eyes because I know what that letter says without reading it.

"Great. Okay, Tammy, you can do this. Tell me if you run across any problems. Do you have the safety checklist they gave you for the home inspection?"

I nod, then realize she can't see me, so I clear my throat and say, "Yeah, I have that. It's done. All the things have been checked off."

"Great. I'll call you Monday."

She hangs up, and I set the phone on the counter behind me, my gaze never leaving that stupid folded piece of paper. I want to grab it and rip it into a million pieces. I want to read it and understand. I want to shove it in the fireplace and never have to learn why he left.

I walk over and pick up the paper, pausing to listen to the house for any sign he might still be here. I could live in this moment between knowing and not. If I never read this, never look outside to see if his Jeep is still there, never check in Dad's old room for his sleeping form on the bed.

That's not sustainable, of course. I get that, and my heart needs to catch up. I open the letter and wipe my eyes so I can read.

Tammy,

I'm sorry. It's too much. Take care of yourself and Donny. You're going to be a great mom.
Sam

What the fuck? I read it again, like suddenly there will be a heart-felt reason why he snuck out in the middle of the night. There's not. What a fucking coward. I crumple the paper into a ball and toss it back on the table just as my phone rings again.

I stomp over to the counter and grab the cordless, both hoping and fearing it's Sam. I take a steadying breath before I answer.

"Hello?"

"Hey Tammy, it's me."

My shoulders slump and tears form quickly in my eyes. "Hi, C. J. What's up?"

"Melinda just called to tell me about what's going on with Donny, so I wanted to see if you needed anything?"

My eyes stinging with unshed tears dart around the kitchen. The crumpled note on the table is like a boulder in my gut. I swallow hard and straighten my shoulders. I can't waste time on him, not now. I need to be strong for Donny; he is what matters. He needs me.

"Can you come over, actually? I, um, just woke up when Melinda called, so I need to shower and stuff, can you come for lunch so we can talk? I think I know what to do, but I'd love your insight." I'm surprised my voice is as steady as it is, but the tears falling down my cheeks tell a different story.

"Sure, kiddo. I'll be there at noon."

She hangs up, and I set the phone back on the charger and head upstairs to take a shower, fighting like hell to hold it together.

"HEY THERE! I BROUGHT STUFF." C. J. stands on my porch, balancing a huge cardboard box that is overflowing with toys and books.

"How did you knock?" I say with a laugh. My long, hot shower helped get rid of the tears to some degree. I also opened Dad's room and stripped the bed to wash the sheets. I don't want to sleep in there with Sam's scent all over. It was good, and by good I mean terrible, but it's a start. I should have made him sleep on the shitty twin bed in the spare bedroom. I sigh and plaster on a smile.

"I set it down, but I considered just banging my head on the door."

I step aside for C. J. to step through, and she walks straight to the living room, setting the box down on the coffee table. I watch as she looks around, hands on her hips. She's looking like the foster agency people will, for things that might hurt Donny. I twist my hands together and take a deep breath.

"Tammy, this place is great. Donny will love it."

"I hope so. I have a bedroom down here, and three upstairs. I thought I'd move him into my old room and I'll be just across the hall in Dad's old room. Do you want to look up there before we have lunch?"

"Hell, yeah, I do. I'm already trying to figure a way to move me and Paul in here with you. I love all the old wood molding, and don't even get me started on these floors."

I glance around and try to see it through her eyes. It's just an old farmhouse, but it does have charm. I wave for her to follow me and give her a tour of the upstairs, then back down to the bottom floor where the kitchen, formal dining room, and small bedroom that is currently an office are. Of course, the laundry room is her favorite since it's almost as big as the kitchen. There's a table next to the washer and dryer where I used to fold clothes before putting them into the basket to carry upstairs.

"I think that might be a concern. Is there a way to lock it?" She points to the laundry chute.

I open it and lean forward, craning my neck to look up. The door upstairs is in the hallway and it has never closed properly, so the light is visible. Damn. This could be a problem.

"Yeah. I'll just nail it shut, top and bottom. I can carry my clothes downstairs like a peasant, I guess."

She laughs and says, "Well, be ready to do that if they don't like it. I wouldn't want you to do unnecessary things. Seems unfair that you'll be providing him a home that is a million times safer than his parents', but you'll be under the microscope."

I nod in agreement. "It does seem unfair, but ultimately I just want him to be here, and be safe and happy."

She tilts her head a little to the side and smiles at me. "I want that too, but we have a lot to talk about getting you ready for that. Ready for lunch?"

I make sandwiches because it's easy and I know C. J. doesn't expect a gourmet meal. We talk about a little of everything at first, but I can tell she's dancing around something. When she finishes her last bite, she levels her gaze at me.

"Can I ask you a tough question?" She cocks one eyebrow, and for some reason it made me sweat.

"Sure, yeah, of course." I wipe my hands on my jeans and try to maintain eye contact.

"Why Donny?"

"What? What do you mean?"

"Did you think about fostering or adopting before?"

"No, but—"

"So, never in your adult life did you consider this? Do you want to get married and have children of your own someday?"

I blink a few times, trying to buy myself a moment, because I don't know how to answer that. "Maybe." It's all I manage.

She tilts her head and repeats, "Maybe?"

I haven't met anyone I would consider marrying, with the exception of the asshole who snuck out in the middle of the night. So I can't really answer that part of her question. "I am not against marriage, and I guess if I met someone who wanted to . . ."

She raises her eyebrows even higher.

"I don't know." I hang my head, sure that is the wrong answer. To be honest, I haven't really thought about any of that. I dated in college, and of course while living in D.C. but none of it seemed permanent. Nothing felt like forever. I thought there was a future with Sam, but I was way off on that assessment, so now is probably not the time to answer that. Can I tell her that? No.

"I see." C. J. stands and takes her plate to the sink, then turns and leans against the counter.

"Having a kid like Donny will forever change your life."

I start to protest, but she holds up her hand and continues. "It will change everything, Tammy. Any future partner will see a package deal. That isn't a bad thing, and I get the feeling that you wouldn't want to be with someone who couldn't love a kid like Donny."

I nod, but I can't speak. My eyes are filling with tears, and I know if I say something, I will cry. She's against this. She's going to try to talk me out of it. But because she is a mind reader, she steps forward and returns to the table.

"I am not going to tell you not to do this, Tammy. I could tell from day one that you cared for Donny. I watched the two of you, and it warmed my heart. He trusts you, he connected with you, and that, as you know, is a challenge for him. I want you to understand that with Donny, you are dealing with more than just his autism diagnosis.

That kid has lifelong trauma associated with his parents. While I don't think they ever physically abused him, the things he saw and heard." She stops and shakes her head. "And I'm not even talking about the last weekend he had with his mother. God that poor kid."

"I understand all of this, C. J.," I say, sounding a little snippier than I intended.

"I know you do, honey, but back to my original question: Why Donny?"

"I um, I guess I felt a connection with him. He is super smart and funny, and I think that if he had a better home life, maybe he could be happier."

She nods and twists her hair with her finger, considering me, but she doesn't say anything, so I continue.

"He needs me," I say as another reason, but once it's out, I know that's what she was waiting for.

"There it is. That's the answer I knew you'd give. So, okay, that's true, by the way, no question there. But why did you come back to Bower?"

I stiffen, not liking at all where this is going. "Because my dad was sick," I say because I'll be damned if I fall into the trap she is trying to lay down.

"You might say he needed you."

I stand quickly and take my plate to the sink, letting it clatter against hers. "That is true. What are you getting at?"

"I am just remembering when you first started with us. Your dad made you get a job, so you weren't hovering over him all day. Isn't that what you told me?"

I nod and cross my arms over my chest.

"It was such a blessing the day you walked in my door, Tammy. You are a natural at this job. You are smart and kind, and most importantly, you get our kids. You can see what they need just like I do. I want you to have Donny and wrap him in all the love that you have in your heart, but I want to make sure you are doing it for the right reason."

"What would be the wrong reason to give a kid a good home?" I ask her angrily.

"Because you need to be needed," she says with an emphasis on the word need. She waits with that goddamn patient way she has, like I am going to have some kind of epiphany.

"Don't we all like that? Is that really so bad?"

"It's not bad, Tammy. I just have watched you collect stray ducks and I want to—"

"Stray ducks?" I shake my head in frustration.

"You came back for your dad, fell in love with Donny immediately, then there's Sam."

"There's no Sam," I yell. "He's gone. You don't have to worry about that because he left town. I'll probably never see him again, so that's one less stray duck for you to worry about." I grab the note Sam left me and smooth out the crumpled paper, handing it to C. J.

"Oh, well, damn. I'm sorry, Tammy."

"Nothing to be sorry about. I can't deal with his problems right now, anyway. I am focused on getting this right, not just for me but for Donny. Do I like the idea of him needing me? Yes, of course I do, but God, C. J., he deserves so much better than what he was dealt. If I can provide that, then why on God's green earth would I say no?"

"You shouldn't. What happened with Sam? I need you to explain a little because I thought he was happy here."

"His sister came to town and told him what his father did to the nut farmers. He didn't know, and for the record, neither did I. He was upset; embarrassed was the word he used. I thought it was something we would talk about today, but he left in the middle of the night. I found the note when I woke up to Melinda's call."

"He was here?"

"I had asked him to move in. Mario is getting the first wave of his workers, and Sam didn't want to be taking up a cabin. It's not like that, or whatever you're thinking. We, I," I stop and rub my hands over my face. "I wasn't trying to rescue Sam. I liked him. We were friends, and the only thing that was messed up about that was I was hoping we could be more than friends. I thought we were heading that way at least, but I was wrong."

"You've had quite a day," C. J. says on an exhale. "For what it's worth, I wouldn't have guessed that Sam would bail. I bet you are feeling pretty shitty right now."

I nod and glance out the window, trying to give myself a break from her scrutiny.

"What do you say we go through that box I brought and talk about what Donny's first day here in your home might look like?"

I release a breath and force a smile. "I'd love that."

BY THE TIME C. J. left, I was physically and emotionally wrecked. I poured myself a bowl of cereal for dinner and ate while I wrote out notes from the things we had talked about. I had a lot of phone calls to make in the morning.

C. J. was confident that Melinda could make this happen, so I could at least be a temporary foster home for Donny as soon as next week. She warned me about the hurdles I'd still have to face with his father for adoption. Even though he will be incarcerated until long after Donny turns eighteen, he still has parental rights, and he could decide not to relinquish his rights. She also surprised me when she suggested that I leave Donny at Gridley Elementary. I had planned on him being back at Bower Elementary with me, but her explanation made sense. Donny's had so many changes, and since Gridley is a little bit bigger, the services they can offer Donny are better. He has access to more therapy since they have a dedicated speech and occupational therapist, so he's been going three times a week instead of once a week. He's also seeing a counselor there who specializes in childhood trauma. C. J. said he really likes it, since it's mostly play. I love that she's been talking regularly with his new teacher. She said he is doing well in class, too. I don't want any of that to stop for him so I will totally drive him to and from school until we make long-term plans. She said we can see about adjusting my hours for a bit, but for the rest of the year, it might be a problem.

On my list for Monday is to get the paper and see if there are any jobs in Gridley that I could apply for. It would be a lot easier to drop Donny off and be there to pick him up after school if I were in the same town.

My eyes are blurring more often, so I set my pen and paper down and climb the stairs to go to bed. Tomorrow, in between everything else, I'm going to switch out my room so Donny can have it. I love the idea of him here; I just wish I could hit fast-forward on all the things that need to happen before that is a reality.

TWENTY-TWO

SMALL TOWNS ARE NOT ALL THE SAME

I DROVE from Tammy's house in Bower until my eyes were shutting on their own, which, as it turns out, wasn't that long. I think I only made it three hours. The old me would have just crawled in the back of my Jeep and slept a few hours, but this new broken version found a hotel.

Now as I sit in this small diner off Highway 395, I realize my plan to go back to Fort Irwin is stupid. There is nothing for me there. Most of the guys I knew are gone. I can't reenlist, so why the fuck would I go live near an army base?

"Getcha another cup, sweetheart?" the waitress asks, and I nod.

"Can I also get this number 3?" I tap the plastic-covered menu. The good kind, with pictures of all the food.

"Sure, you want bacon, sausage, or both?"

"Both, thanks." I hand her my menu and go back to staring out the window. There is snow on the ground here, not much but a light dusting. I've never lived in a place that had snow. I wonder what that would be like. Should I keep driving east? Although I know I don't want to live on the East coast, or in the South. I could go up north, like Idaho or North Dakota?

"Morning, Miss Poppy. I need a big cup of coffee this morning, darling," I hear a man say. He walks past me and sits in the booth next to mine, and the waitress slides right up to the table with the coffeepot.

"Mary giving you trouble again, Fred? I told you that woman was nothing but trouble." She makes a *tsk* noise as she pours his coffee.

"Nah, it's not her. My damn brother is coming for Thanksgiving and I gotta hide all the liquor and find a chair that won't split in two when he sits his fat ass down to dinner."

The waitress throws her head back and cackles while Fred slaps the table, overcome with his own laughter. Must be an inside joke.

When she regains herself, she wipes her eyes and pats him on the shoulder. "I'll get your French toast order in; you aren't getting any bacon, so don't even bother asking. That guy took the last of it." She points at me.

I hold up my hands in surrender. "Hey, no, it's okay if he wants it. I can just have the sausage."

"Thanks, son, but she's just messing with you. I can't have it on account of my ticker. Doc Taylor said bacon is off the menu unless I want to have another bypass surgery." He leans forward and winks at me.

"Right, okay, if you're sure."

He nods and gives me a big, easy smile. "Passing through on the way to visit family for the holidays?"

"No, nothing like that. I am passing through. I think."

The old man raises an eyebrow and cocks his head. "Are you lost or something?"

I want to say yes, in fact, I am really fucking lost, but I force a smile and say, "Needed a new start. Trying to figure out where that should be, I guess."

He rubs a gnarled hand over his chin and nods thoughtfully. "I can understand that. After World War Two, I got off the plane in Florida, bought a car and drove until it felt like I was home."

"Oh yeah? Where did you end up?" I ask, leaning forward a little, my arms resting on the table.

"Right here in Minden. Best town in the whole damn country, if you ask me. Good people, quiet living, and a quick drive up the road you can have a little excitement in Reno, if that's what you like." He winks again, and I smile.

"I grew up in a small town in California. Joined the Army to see the world. Now that I'm out, not sure what sounds like home," I say, but that seems like a lie as it leaves my mouth. Tammy's place felt like home.

"You see combat?" he asks, leaning back and taking a sip of his coffee. His expression has shifted, and I wonder why.

"Yes, sir. I was in Desert Shield. Injured, sent home but grateful to have served."

"Bullshit," he barks out. "No one is grateful to be injured. You don't have to blow smoke up my ass, son. I took a bullet to the leg in Berlin. Lost half my squad in that fight. To this day, I'll never understand why I got to go home, and they didn't."

I bow my head a little and say, "Yeah. I understand that." I look up at him and add, "Thank you. I guess I have my canned answers. Forgot who I was talking to. What branch were you in?"

"Air Force. Parachuted in with no problems, but got caught when we took a wrong turn. We were supposed to cut along the outside edge of town, but ended up in the damn middle of it. Got into a fight in the cemetery, of all places." He shakes his head, probably trying to clear the images I know are popping up behind his eyes.

"I read a lot about the ground fighting there. Must have been awful."

"All war is awful, son. There was an old quote that I heard once, went something like, war doesn't decide who is right, only who is left."

I nod. "I've read that and found it to be true."

Poppy returns with both of our breakfasts, but she sets my plate on Fred's table, and she gives me a little nod as she walks away.

"Okay if I join you?" I ask with a chuckle.

"It would be my pleasure."

"SO THEN POPPY'S husband Lyle comes down the hill, hair soaking wet, and he is fuming mad. I tell you what, I've never laughed so hard in all my life."

"Would you stop telling all my secrets, you're gonna get me in trouble if he comes out here." Poppy is leaning on the booth seat with one hand holding the coffee pot and the other resting on Fred's shoulder.

"You want more, honey?" She gestures with the pot towards my cup.

"No, I think I've had enough," I say. I honestly don't know how many cups I've had, but based on how my hip is hurting, I'd say I've been sitting here for hours. Fred is a great guy, funny as hell and probably close to ninety.

Poppy and her husband Lyle own this little diner that serves breakfast around the clock, and it seems the whole town comes here. It's like I stepped into a Norman Rockwell painting or something. Everyone who has come in here is kind, and they all seem to support each other based on the questions I heard people asking. Not just a generic "How's the wife?" Real, honest-to-God questions, like "How's Cindy's cancer treatment coming along?" and "What happened with the Bryson boy's college application?" Probably wouldn't hurt to stick around for a few days. It's not like I have a timeline to this escape of mine.

"Where you staying, Sam?" Fred asks as he reaches back for his wallet.

"Over at the Motel 6, I hadn't planned on staying more than one night. Got in around five this morning." I finally look at my watch and see I was right; I have been here for hours. I feel more refreshed from the lively conversation than I do from the few hours of sleep I had.

"Nice place. Reggie owns that, and he takes pride in his being the best in the state. I told him if he wanted to really be the best, he needed to put chocolates on the pillows." Another wink and smile from Fred, and I laugh.

"That explains the Hershey bar. I thought another guest had left it behind."

Fred howls with laughter, and I realize that is something I admire about him; laughter comes easily to him. I wonder how he battled his demons back enough to let the light shine through.

"Well, if you stick around a few days, you'll meet some of the best. I know I am partial, but as I said, this is a wonderful little town. We even have a good barber if you want to get rid of that mess of hair you're hiding under." He nods at me.

I reach back and smooth down what's sticking out from under my ball cap. "Maybe. I grew it out because of the burns, didn't like seeing them, or the looks from other people who saw them, you know?"

"But they are still there. You know that better than anyone, so why hide them?" Fred levels his gaze at me; his cloudy blue eyes seem to sharpen as he scrutinizes me.

I consider what he said and think about how when I decided to grow it out I thought I'd feel better, safer somehow. Do I? Not really, just annoyed at the care long hair requires. I wonder if letting the scars speak will be its own form of freedom?

"You know, I think you are right. Are you going to tell me to get rid of the earring next?"

"No, that's—what do you kids say? The bomb?"

I burst out laughing. "Yeah, I think that's a saying." I reach back for my wallet, but Fred waves me off.

"I got it, Sam. If you're still here tomorrow, you can return the favor. I'm here every day at two. It's the only break the little lady gets from me."

"I bet she doesn't feel that way." Even though I just met him, I am betting he is the light in everyone's life.

I spent the rest of the day driving around Minden and Gardnerville. It's a flat, high desert area with very few trees, but it's in the shadow of the Sierra Nevada mountains. Reno to the north, and on the other side of the mountains is South Lake Tahoe.

When I've passed the auto body shop for the third time, I decide to stop and go in. If I am going to stay here, I'll need a job, and I can't stomach the thought of working for a school district again. I don't want to drive other kids around; all I would think about is Donny and Laura. Hell, I even miss the cousins who fought constantly. Nope, I can't do that again. I never realized how much I liked kids.

I walk into the shop and spot a pair of legs sticking out from a '67 Mustang. There is another muscle car up on the lift and it looks like an Impala. I wait while the legs twist and move, then finally pull the owner free on the roller board.

"Jesus Christ. How long have you been standing there?"

I blink a few times, trying to school my expression. Those legs belong to a woman who looks to be only a few years older than me. She has white-blond hair that is shaved on the sides and a thick mess of curls on top. Grease is streaked across her face and neck. She has a few tattoos on her arms that I can't make out without getting a lot closer.

"Uh, sorry, I haven't been here long. I didn't want to startle you by calling out."

She grunts and pulls a rag from her back pocket, wiping it across her face, somehow making the grease worse. "That didn't really work out, did it?" She pulls herself up and sticks out her hand. "I'm Dylan. What can I do for you?"

"I was wondering if you were looking for a mechanic. I have a lot of experience."

"I work on mostly classic cars, you have experience in that?"

"A car is a car," I say, and immediately regret it. Based on the expression on her face, that is not what she wanted to hear.

"Get out." She points to the door, but the anger in her voice doesn't match the way her smile is taking over her face.

I smile back at her and take my ball cap off, running my hand through my hair. The motion must have pulled up my sleeve enough for her to see the tank tattoo I have on my right bicep.

"Army? Where'd you do bootcamp?"

"Georgia, both basic and armory."

"Same, except I didn't stay for armory. Went up to Missouri for electrician training." She stuffs her rag back into her pocket. She's about as tall as me and could probably bench-press me if she had to, so her military background doesn't surprise me one bit.

"When did you leave?" I ask because, of course, I wonder if she saw combat like me.

"As soon as I could. I think I had only about five years total. Met my husband in Missouri and we moved here to be close to his family about three years ago now."

"That's cool. Is he a mechanic as well?" I glance around the shop for another person.

"Nah, not his style. He owns the café with his parents."

"The place over by the Motel 6? I ate there today. Great food."

"Well, then you met my mother-in-law, Poppy. Salt of the earth, that woman, and the patience of a thousand saints."

I nod and smile because that doesn't surprise me at all. "That sounds about right. Well, Dylan, are you interested in having another mechanic around?"

She glances over her shoulder at the impala that is up on the lift, then back at me. "You want to prove you can change the oil and rotate the tires on that while I take this sweet Mustang out for a test drive?"

"I can do that."

"Great. I fucking hate both of those things. When I get back, we can talk more." I watch as she walks over to the open wooden door across from where she was working. She pulls it shut, then takes her keys out of her pocket and locks it up, then returns to me with her hand out. "Give me your keys and your name."

I dig my keys out of my pocket and hand them to her. "I'm Sam. Sam Ford."

"Great last name for a mechanic, Sam." She chuckles.

"Yeah, I got lots of shit about it in armory."

"I bet. There's a pair of coveralls on the hook there; I bet you can figure out how to use the lift, and all the tools you'll need are here." She waves her arms open wide, then narrows her gaze at me. "Don't steal my shit, Sam Ford."

I laugh and shake my head. "Don't worry, I won't."

"That's exactly what a thief would say, but okay. I'll be back soon, just need to make sure the clutch is working on this damn thing." She nods over her shoulder at the '67 powder-blue Mustang. It's a beauty, clean and ready for a showroom on the outside, but obviously it's not in perfect shape if it's here.

As soon as she pulls away, I grab the coveralls and get to work.

I'm just lowering the Impala down when I hear the Mustang. She parks it outside and comes in whistling.

"Clutch work as expected?" I ask.

"Smooth as silk. I bet Grandpa won't be letting the kids learn to drive on that anymore." She laughs. "How'd it go here? I see my toolbox is still in place and my compressor." She leans over and peers behind me. "You also didn't steal anything from the vending machine. Seems as if you can actually be trusted, Sam Ford."

"To be honest, I didn't see the vending machine, or I might have gone astray." I lean to take pressure off my hip and rub it a little. Most people don't notice these subtle things, but it seems Dylan is not most people.

"When did you get injured?" She crosses her arms over her chest, and I am again impressed with her muscle tone. I need to get back to the gym.

"Desert Shield, first wave. Before the real fighting started, actually. My tank unit was one of the first to discover the IED problem."

"Shit. Sorry." She turns and crosses to the closed office door, unlocking it and going inside.

Okay, I guess that's all there is to that conversation. It's different sharing with people who were in the military, I guess. When she doesn't return, I walk in and find her at her desk with a stack of papers. She looks up when she sees me.

"Have a seat, Sam. I'd like to talk about you coming to work for me."

I pull out the chair across from her and sit, realizing I am more nervous than when I interviewed for the job at the school yard. I wipe my hands on my jeans and let the jittery feeling I have come out by bouncing my right leg a little.

"I do actually need someone. Ricky has been bugging me for a while now to get some help in here, and with Hot August Nights coming up fast, I'm about to hit my busy season."

"What does that look like?" I ask.

"Mostly tune-ups, oil changes, cleaning the engine to make it look like they never drive the damn car, which most don't. Henry, with the '67 Mustang, is about the only local guy that drives his vintage cars like they are just off the lot. Maybe because he has so many?" She shrugs, then continues. "Sometimes we get a re-wire, or a major engine overhaul, but I try not to accept those as we get closer to August. If I had extra help, I'd be able to handle more, though."

She writes a number on the paper in front of her and circles another, then turns it and slides it over to me. "This is what I can pay you per hour. This is what I'll put into a retirement account, or we can talk about you joining the health plan, but I assume you use the VA?"

I nod and she continues, "Right now I don't have full-time hours available, but after Thanksgiving it will pick up. I usually close for a week at Christmas, but I guess if you wanted to keep things going on your own, we can talk about that."

I glance down at the numbers and try to keep my face neutral. It's twice what I was making at the school district.

"This could work." I tap the paper. "When would you want me to start?"

"Anytime. Tomorrow I am getting three cars in, all maintenance, nothing too bad." She pauses to move some papers out of the way so she can see the calendar on her desk. "But like I said, next week I hit the ground running."

I can see that every square is filled with names and phone numbers. It will be good to throw myself into something like this. "That sounds perfect, actually."

"Great, fill these out and make sure you put your phone number on there." She digs my keys out of her pocket and sets them next to the paperwork.

I nod even though I don't have a phone number or an address. Jesus, talk about putting the cart before the horse.

TWENTY-THREE

KNEES AND TOES

I SPENT THANKSGIVING WITH C. J. and Paul. From Monday until I walked in their door on Thursday afternoon, I was either on the phone or talking to someone in person about all things foster care. I had my home inspection, discussed all the things that could go wrong living on a busy county road, and assured the inspector that the garage would be locked unless I was with Donny. I was asked to seal the laundry chute, so I took care of that.

Thankfully, Paul is the cook in the family, because I needed C. J. to spend the whole time telling me what to expect today. I barely ate anything for breakfast; my stomach was just too upset. I pull up in front of the foster home that has cared for Donny for the past few weeks and take a deep breath. Here we go, whether I am ready or not.

A woman steps out onto the porch before I can even knock. She pulls the door shut behind her quietly and looks me up and down. I might have taken offense to that a few weeks ago, but all the scrutiny I have been under since starting the process has me a bit numb to it.

"Tammy, right?"

"Yes." I hold my hand out to her, and she shakes it with a firm grip.

"Nice to meet you. I understand that you have worked with Donny in the past?"

"Yes, I came on full time last year in January, so half of that year and when we started up again in August I was there."

"Okay, well, that's a bit of a leg up then. I understand you know about his situation, but he might seem different at home than he was at school. He's a rule follower at school, but tends to lose that thread once he's home."

I nod and say a silent thanks to C. J., who had warned me about that. It's like they use up all their good behavior at school and are exhausted by the time they get home.

"What are you seeing specifically, so I can be prepared?" I ask.

She sighs and tucks her hair behind her ear. "Well, he has those three fingers shoved in his mouth most of the time. At night after bath, he has started to rock and whine. I have been giving him a slinky, one of the plastic ones, and that has helped. He throws himself on the ground when he doesn't get what he wants, which is frustrating for everyone. I have been giving him lots of space when he gets home from school, and that seems to help. He doesn't want to play with the other kids here, and he hit one of my foster kids yesterday, no idea why. He sleeps in a room with three other beds, and two of those have kids, so that has been a challenge for him. Will he have his own room?"

"Yes. Right across the hall from me."

"And it's just going to be you two?"

"Yes." I swallow, willing myself not to think about Sam.

"Okay. He knows you're coming. I told him Tammy from his old school was coming to get him."

"Good. Okay." I shove my hands in my pockets, not knowing what else to say or do. Does he understand that he's coming to live with me, or does he think I am taking him back to Room 27?

Finally, she reaches back and opens the door, motioning me to follow her. My breath catches when I see the little blue pom-pom sticking up over the back of the couch.

"Donny. Tammy is here," the woman says, louder than I was expecting, and I jump a little. I've noticed that with a few people, they think if someone doesn't talk, they must be hard of hearing. I bet that's why she's speaking loudly.

The hat starts to move, and then ten little fingers and two eyes appear. His whole head pops up, revealing his adorable face, eyes as wide as saucers, then he disappears.

"Dude, grab your stuff, let's go," I say, using the same level tone I always have with him. I wait, but the foster mom steps in and says his name loudly again. I reach out and gently touch her arm and shake my head, hoping she will let me handle this.

She does not.

"Donny! Can't you hear me? It's time to go. Tammy is here; don't make her wait any longer."

I walk over to the couch and hold out my hand to him.

"He doesn't like to be touched," the lady says. She has followed me, and I really wish she would just let me do what I need to do.

I nod and give her a smile, but I don't speak. I just wait, my hand extended. When she goes to move, I step in her path and hold my finger up, indicating I want her to give me a fucking minute. I hope that is what she gets from it at least.

It takes him a few minutes, but eventually he stands and removes his fingers from his mouth, sliding the middle one into my palm. Nothing on earth will ever feel better than that one sweet gesture of trust. I bend down and quietly say, "Time to go. Do you want pizza or tacos?" I hold up my fingers and wait.

"HE IS SUPER PICKY. I don't think he will eat either of those things. He has only had mac and cheese and cut-up hot dogs since he got here. He doesn't even like cereal," the woman says loudly from over my shoulder.

I wait.

Donny quickly bats at my first finger, and I smile. "Pizza. Thanks for letting me know." I turn to the foster mom and quietly ask, "Does he have a bag?"

"By the door." She has finally lowered her voice to match mine, and I want to jump in victory, but I don't. I just smile and nod at her as we walk toward the door.

"We say thank you, Donny," I prompt when we get outside, and he turns to her and repeats word for word what I've said, making her chuckle.

"Nice to know you can talk, kid. Hopefully, I won't see you again. I bet Tammy here is going to do a great job with you."

Donny steps behind me a little when she moves like she might hug him. I stick out my hand to her and she settles for a handshake.

I get him buckled in the back seat of my Toyota and toss his bag in the trunk. By the time I get in the driver's seat, I see he has his fingers in his mouth again, and he's staring out the window.

"Donny, we are going to my house now. I have pizza there," I tell him, not expecting any response. The drive over is quiet, and I vacillate between absolute terror and complete happiness. When we pull up, Donny waits for me to open his door. I hold out my hand and he offers me his finger. We walk together for the first time into our home.

I let go of his finger when I get the door unlocked. "You can look around, Donny. This is your home for now." C. J. made sure that I understood to use temporary terms with him so that I won't create hope, which, to be honest, broke my fucking heart. I want to tell him he's mine forever and that I will fight for him like his parents didn't.

I step aside and watch him shove his fingers in his mouth, then step closer to me. I wait.

When it doesn't seem like he's going to explore on his own, I bend down and hold up a finger. "I want Tammy to show me." Then hold up a second finger and say, "I can explore by myself." Then I wait again, hand down so he can reach it. He bats at my first finger, so I say, "Oh, you want Tammy to give you a tour. Okay, dude. This is the living room. We watch TV in here, or read books. Follow me. I'll show you the kitchen." I walk away and don't look back, hoping he follows.

AFTER THE HOUSE tour and lunch, I take Donny out to the backyard and show him the tire swing, which is an instant hit. He spends the next hour twisting and swinging. I worry a little that he will fight me when I tell him it's time to be all done with the swing, but he climbs right off. I show him the garage, and he seems to enjoy the big open space where the harvester had been parked. I could probably hang a tire swing in here for him so he could enjoy that during the rainy days. When it's time to go back in for dinner, Donny follows me quietly. I know this is too good to be true, his calm demeanor, but I forge ahead like this is just our life now.

"Time to wash hands. Kitchen sink or bathroom?" I ask, and he veers off to the kitchen. He climbs onto the little wooden stool I had used as a kid and holds his hands under the sink, waiting for me to turn on the water. I point to the cold side handle and say, "Turn on," then I pull it forward. Before he can get his hands wet, I push it to the off position, and he whines and thrust his hands under the faucet again.

"Donny's turn," I say, pointing to the faucet.

He blinks at me, and I wonder if I should just do it for him, but I hold out. Unfortunately, so does he.

I shrug and walk to the fridge to grab the hot dogs and pretend not to care that he is getting mad. He whines and stomps on the stool while I put the buns on the counter. He throws himself on the floor while I get the mustard out of the fridge. He kicks his feet and screams while I take out a pot. I calmly walk to the sink and fill the pot, blocking Donny from the water stream the whole time. He kicks me in the leg and I roll my lips together in a grimace, trying not to react.

"Donny can wash his hands. Turn on faucet," I say, then walk back to the stove and start to boil the water for the hot dogs. I hate them this way, but C. J. said she knows it's something that Donny will reliably eat, and I really want him to go to sleep with a full tummy his first night here. I sit at the table and watch him roll on the floor and kick, and yell. At one point he takes off his knit cap and bites the little blue puffball at the top, then he throws it across the room. A moment later he scrambles to get it, returning it to its permanent spot on top of his head.

I hear the water boiling, so I get up and add the hot dogs. I set the oven timer for five minutes and return to my chair. Donny is now lying perfectly still, arms at his sides, legs spread, and head tilted. He lets his tongue hang out like he's dead, and I fight off a giggle.

God, it's good to see him. He looks the same, except his hair is a little longer. I learned a lot about him and his parents getting ready to be a foster parent. His mom was a hairdresser for years in Yuba City, where she met Donny's father. He has held about as many different jobs as one could, but seemed to excel as a mechanic, although he couldn't ever keep a job for very long. They had moved to Bower when Bea was pregnant with Donny because of a job offer that never materialized. Once he was born, they both struggled to find any consistent work, and as Donny grew, so did the realization that there was something going on with him. He didn't speak and would spend hours fixated on random objects in the home, like the vacuum cleaner or the hair dryer. He showed no interest in playing with other kids in the apartment complex or in toys that were offered to him. Once he had the diagnosis of autism, his parents were able to get more financial assistance and for about a year it seemed like they were doing okay.

The timer on the oven goes off, and I glance over at Donny in time to see his eyes open wide. I continue to ignore him and fish the hot dogs from the pot. I put his on the cutting board and slice it thin, the way C. J. told me he liked them. I smile as I drizzle mustard on the bun, then put the pile of cut-up hotdog next to that on the plate. He's so wonderfully weird. I can see movement out of the corner of my eye, and my shoulders relax when I hear the faucet turn on.

I set the plate on the table, and Donny climbs into the chair and starts eating. My heart is full, but I know it's one battle down, three million more to go.

After dinner, we go into the living room, and I let Donny pick what he wants by showing him the books or the VHS tapes C. J. brought. He grabs the *Magic School Bus* video and says, "Knock-knock."

"Donny wants to watch this?" I ask, a little confused.

He nods, so I take the tape and get it started while he continues to rummage through the box of small toys I have for him. When I turn around, I see him sitting on the couch, tiny toy spatula in one hand and his favorite dinosaur lodged firmly in his mouth.

After watching Mrs. Frizzle's class explore Arnold's digestive system three times, I turn off the TV and announce it's time for bed.

"Do you remember where your room is, Donny?"

He stands and sets the spatula down but doesn't take the dinosaur out of his mouth.

"Do you want to take Dino to bed, yes or no?" I ask, without holding up my fingers.

"Yes," he says around the dinosaur.

"Great, let's show him how we can brush our teeth."

I decided not to tackle bath time on his first night with me, since I want him to feel comfortable before we cross that bridge, and I'm pleased to see he has no problem brushing his teeth. He even takes his hat off to comb his hair. It's neat to see the brief glimpses into the routines he must have had at home. I follow him into his room and point to the dresser.

"Donny's pajamas are in the bottom drawer. Donny can get dressed by himself. Tammy will be back."

I leave the room and go across the hall to my own room, shutting the door so I can get into my own pajamas. When I return I find him already in bed, hat on, Dino right next to him on the pillow.

"Donny is all set for bed. Nice job, dude." I smile at him, then ask, "Does Donny want a bedtime story, yes or no?"

"No."

"Okay." I step forward and reach my hand out slowly to touch his arm, expecting him to jerk away. He doesn't; instead, he grabs my hand and puts it on his knee. "Knee," I say, and his eyes go wide. He grabs my hand and sits up, pushing my hand toward his foot. It takes me a second to get what he wants.

"Do you want Tammy to sing?"

"Sing, yes."

I smile and sit next to him so I can reach. I gently touch each part of him as I sing "Head, Shoulders, Knees and Toes." C. J. had been doing this with him to get him used to touch and to teach him body parts. I let my voice get softer with each verse, and I see his eyes fluttering shut after three rounds.

I wake up with the uneasy feeling that I'm being watched, and as I roll to my side and open my eyes, it takes everything inside me not to scream. Donny is standing at the side of the bed, silently watching me sleep. He steps closer when he sees I'm awake.

"Dude, you scared me." I sit up and rub my eyes. "Are you hungry?"

"Hungry, yes."

"Okay, let's get some breakfast." I want to ask him if he slept okay, if he had any nightmares, or if there is anything I can do to make him more comfortable, but those questions are too abstract; no yes-or-no concrete answers are available in his brain. I don't doubt they are there; it's just not easy for him to access them.

We spent the day inside due to the rain, but it's easy and quiet. Donny asked to watch "Knock-knock" again by handing me the *Magic School Bus* tape. I make a note to see if I can get other episodes so I don't lose my mind watching this one over and over.

The rest of the weekend is the same with the exception of my frequent reminders to Donny that he will go back to Gridley Elementary tomorrow and see Mrs. Erin. He puts up no fight to that and in general seems pretty relaxed. I don't want to live in fear of the tantrum that may or may not appear, so I take each day we are together with minimal issues as a win.

DECEMBER SNEAKS UP ON ME, and if it hadn't been a school day where we talk about the calendar, I might not have believed it. When Donny and I return home after school, I let him get the mail from the oversized box on County Road W. It has become one of his favorite things, and since Christmas is coming, the number of catalogs has increased.

Donny grabs the Sears Christmas Wish Book and drops the rest of the mail on the road as he takes off for the house. I laugh and bend to pick up the stack, my gaze snagging on a red envelope. The return address makes my stomach twist, and tears spring to my eyes.

Sam.

I should throw it away. He's only been gone about a week and a half, but to me it feels longer. So much has happened since he walked out on me. What could he possibly say? Do I even care?

Yes, of course I do, damn it.

I walk up to the house and kick off my shoes, leaving them on the porch next to Donny's. So far he's been pretty good about following the rules at home for me. Maybe the chaos of his other foster home was too much for him. It's pretty quiet and predictable here.

I sit next to him on the couch, and he scoots to the other side of the couch, so I say, "Donny needs space."

"Space, please," he responds.

"You got it, dude," I say with a sigh and put my feet up on the coffee table. I could play it cool and open all the other mail first but there is no one to impress here, so I rip open the red envelope, being careful to keep the return address intact so I can write him back and tell him to leave me alone.

Dear Tammy,

I spoke with Mike, and he told me you have Donny now. I am so happy for you, and I know you probably don't want to hear from me, but I just couldn't leave things the way I did.

I STOP and close the card, blowing out a breath. I glance over at Donny, who has taken off his socks and is rhythmically pinching each of his toes while he stares at the Lego page of the catalog.

I landed only a few hours from there; I know my leaving like that wasn't okay. I should have stayed, at least talked to you about what I was feeling, but I couldn't. I'm not proud of that.

I STARE at his neat writing and wonder if I should stop reading and just flush this down the toilet. I have a lot of wild desires that never seem to come true, though, so I read on.

I couldn't stay in Bower, not once I knew what my family had done to that place. To be honest, if I had known all of that, I would never have come back. For that reason alone, I am glad that I didn't have a clue what happened there. I am so grateful that I ran into you, Tammy, and I was really looking forward to taking you on our second first date. I imagine you are very angry with me, but I hope in time you can understand and forgive me.

I want to see you again. I want to see Donny too. I think about him all the time. I hope Laura is doing well. If it wouldn't cause too much drama, tell the kids I say hello. I'll write again. I know you won't understand this, but I didn't leave you, just Bower.
Love,
Sam

I CLOSE the card and huff out a breath, then open it and read it all over again.

What?

He thinks what? We will just be pen pals? Like, is that what he wants? I read it again and groan, then stand up and take the card to the fireplace, wanting to toss it inside, but of course I don't. I read it again and fight off tears. Chicken shit didn't leave me his phone number because I would have called. To yell at him. Not tell him I do understand and oh my God I miss him so much, and whatever he needs . . . Jesus, I am pathetic. Thank God he didn't include his phone number.

TWENTY-FOUR

TRY AND TRY AGAIN (SAM)

Dear Tammy,

I always want to include Donny in that, but since you aren't writing me back, I am not sure if that would be cool.

I hope you guys had a good Christmas. As I said in my last letter, Dylan and her husband left for the week, so I had some time to myself here at the shop. Since they've been back, we have started to get busier, just like she had said we would. The car show that happens in August provides her with a lot of clients. I think I told you about that in one of my letters.

Someday I hope you'll come for a visit. I bet Big Red could handle the journey if you can get her fixed up. I shouldn't tell you this, but I think about her all the time too. I pictured finishing what your dad had started for you as a surprise, but left like a chicken shit before I could.

I SIGH and look around my small apartment. My hip decided for me that I needed a day off, and Dylan said I earned it, so I've been resting, watching television, and writing. I've sent letters to some friends that I had from basic that I had lost touch with, and unlike Tammy, they respond and seem happy to hear from me. I finally got my phone hooked up, so I plan on giving her that number in my letter today. I guess she could be enjoying these almost daily letters but not have time to respond in writing. I'm sure her life looks very different now.

When I first started writing, I didn't have a phone, but I was finally able to get one hooked up. Things move slowly here in Minden, but it's a good place. If you ever want to talk, I am usually home by six.

Take care, Tammy.
Love,
Sam

I WRITE my phone number under my name and stick the letter in an envelope, then walk down the stairs to the mailbox, hoping I'll make it for today's pickup.

Four days later as I am climbing the stairs to my apartment I hear the phone ring and almost trip as I rush to get inside to answer it.

"Hello?" I pant into the receiver and rub my shin where I smacked it on the cement stairs.

A very quiet voice says, "Hi, Sam."

I sink into my couch. "Hey, Miss Tammy. How are you?" I try to sound casual, but I doubt it worked.

"Fine. Okay, busy but fine." She clears her throat and asks, "How are you, Sam?"

"Better now. So you've been getting my letters. I wasn't sure."

"I got them. To be honest, I wasn't going to call because I'm mad at you, but—"

I wait, closing my eyes and letting my head hit the back of the couch. I'm afraid to even breathe deeply because I don't want to ruin this any more than I already have.

"Donny has this VHS tape he watches every day. Like constantly. The second we walk in the door, he goes straight to the TV and pushes in the tape."

"Okay," I say, not really understanding.

"Well, today at school, Laura's mom came to pick her up early for a doctor's appointment, and she mentioned how Laura misses you."

My chest starts to tighten, and I sit up, heaving out a sigh. "God, I miss her too. Please tell her I said hi, and that I hope she isn't causing too many problems for the new bus driver."

"Okay, sure. Um, Laura's mom said you used to tell the kids knock-knock jokes. Is that true?"

I chuckle and say, "Oh yeah. They were terrible. I was dropping Laura off at her house one day, and as I was lowering the ramp, Donny and I were going back and forth with his favorite one. Laura was grinning ear to ear and banging her cup. Her mom asked about it, and I had to admit my terrible jokes to an adult. Not my finest moment."

Without responding to my little story, she says, "So the video that Donny watches is an episode of *The Magic School Bus*."

"Huh, okay. I've never seen that." I'm totally confused but not about to interrupt her.

"He calls it Knock-knock. He's talking about you, Sam."

If I wasn't sitting down, I would've fallen over. "Holy shit. Really?"

"Really. I hadn't been able to figure out why he called it that, but it makes sense. In fact, the other day when we were driving to his school in Gridley, he saw a school bus and he said, without any prompting, 'knock-knock.' I almost crashed because it was the first time I heard him speak without it being an answer to something, or a demand for something, you know?"

I did know. I got a little thrill every time he would answer my stupid knock-knock with his own. I can't imagine what it would've felt like if he had said "Who's there?" I probably would've crashed the bus. I swallow down the lump that has formed in my throat.

"I'm honored he remembers me. If it's okay, would you tell him I said hello?"

"Yeah, I can. I called because I was wondering if you would talk to him on the phone? Not tonight. I need to prepare him. I don't think he has ever done that, or even had someone show him how to do that. I just think it might be nice for him. He doesn't make connections with people very easily, and he clearly misses you."

"Sure, of course. God, I would love that. I'll have to get some new knock-knock jokes ready. I always come home right after work, and on the weekends the only place I go is to the store, so just let me know when and I'll be available."

"Okay, thanks. Maybe Sunday?"

"Perfect. Tammy?"

The line is silent, and I worry for a minute that she's hung up, but then she clears her throat. "Yeah?"

"Has it been good having him there? Are you both okay?"

"Yes," she says, but she doesn't elaborate. I don't want to push my luck, so I don't ask any more questions.

"That's good. Hey, is it okay if I keep writing to you? You never answer, and it's okay, really, if you don't. I know that might seem a little weird, but it's been kind of nice for me. I like sharing my day with you that way, but I can stop if it's upsetting you."

I wait for what must be an hour before she responds quietly, "You don't have to stop."

"Okay. Well, thanks, Tammy. I'll be around all day on Sunday, so call anytime."

"Thanks, Sam. Have a good night."

The line clicks off, and I stand and run my hand over my short hair and down to my neck. I took Fred's advice and went back to having short hair. The first day I felt a little exposed, but when no one said anything or asked me questions, I got over my fear. I actually get more comments about my blue stone earring than anything else, well, and my Giants hat. I am the lone fan out here, but I'm okay with that. Mark Leiter is due for a good year, and I'm going to be the loudest one cheering him on when he gets it.

I toss and turn all night because I'm so excited about Tammy's call. Since I can't sleep, I decide to get up early and have breakfast at Poppy's Place. Fred and I sit together now without invitation or question. He gave me an approving smile when he saw my haircut, and damn if it didn't feel like getting praise from my CO in boot camp. All the time I was supposed to be healing, and really, I was just hiding. I hid behind my hair, my "I don't follow the rules" earring, and even my return to Bower. I thought I could slip back into my old world there and hide from all the pain, but really Bower is where it all started.

"Are you enjoying that view?" Fred's voice startles me out of my staring contest with the parking lot. I shake my head and laugh.

"Nah, I didn't get a lot of sleep last night. I think I'm going to be paying for that all day."

"Nightmares again?" he asks. We have shared some of our recurring dreams, different wars, but strangely the theme of what keeps us up at night is the same.

"No, remember that girl I was telling you about? She finally called me."

"Tammy, right? Did you find out how things are going with that young man?"

"I did. She has him, and it seems like it's going well."

I had already told him all about Donny and how he doesn't really talk, but he will respond or repeat what you say. I told him about his knit hat and his dinosaur and spatula. I talk about him and Tammy all the time.

"That's good news. Did you invite her and Donny to come visit?"

"No, but I will. She is going to call on Sunday and let me talk to Donny. He has been asking for me, well, in his own way at least."

"That has to feel good." Fred smiles at me, and I nod.

"It does. He's such a cute kid. I can't believe he even remembers me, actually. I was only in his life a few months. I didn't know that I made any kind of impression on him."

"Sam, I bet you make an impression on everyone you meet. You are a good man, and I'm not saying that just so you'll sneak me a bite of that bacon." He wiggles his eyebrows at me, making me laugh.

I break off a small piece and am reaching across the table to put it on his plate when a hand smacks it away.

"Not on your life, Mister. I will stop letting you have bacon if you pull that again." Poppy picks up the bacon and plops it back on my plate before filling both our coffees.

"Yes, ma'am. Sorry, ma'am," I say with all the sincerity I can muster.

She lightly smacks me on the back of the head as she walks away, making Fred howl with laughter.

"You got me into trouble. Did you see her walking this way when you asked for that bacon? You set me up," I say incredulously.

He just shrugs and scoops out a piece of melon from his fruit cup.

———

I WRITE two more letters to Tammy before Sunday telling her about Fred and the diner. I'm glad she said I didn't have to stop writing.

When the phone rings at eleven on Sunday morning, I answer it halfway through the first ring.

"Hello?"

"Hi, Sam, it's me. I have Donny here and he wants to say hello." Tammy must've held the phone away from her because her voice is farther away as she says, "Donny says 'Hi, Sam.'"

I wait, sucking in a breath and closing my eyes. Come on, little guy, you can do it.

"Donny says hi, Sam." A little voice barely audible comes through the line.

I respond immediately, "Knock-knock."

Tammy must have the phone out so she can listen too, because her soft voice says, "Like we practiced, what do you say?"

Donny says, "Knock-knock!" and Tammy laughs.

"No, Donny says 'Who's there?'" Tammy prompts, but I know he rarely gets that. I wait.

"Knock-knock," Donny says, again sounding frustrated.

"It's okay, little guy, I got this. Who's there?"

He falls in step and responds, "Who's there?"

I go with his favorite for the first one. "Tank."

"Tank tank tank tank."

I hear Tammy laughing, then some rustling, and then, "Is Donny done with the phone?"

I wait, laughing to myself, trying to picture what just happened.

"Sorry, he got so excited he ran off. Overall, it went better than I thought it would. Thanks for doing this, Sam."

"Anytime. I had a few new jokes for him, so if he wanders back to the phone, I can try again."

"No, I think he's done for the day; now he's watching *The Magic School Bus* for the millionth time." She says it with a little sigh that I feel straight in my gut.

I close my eyes and picture her tucking her legs beneath her on that big, comfortable couch. I can hear the cartoon Donny's watching in the background, and I imagine myself there, hand resting on her thigh. Fuck, what I wouldn't give to have them both with me.

"I really enjoyed hearing his voice again, Tammy. Thank you."

"It's pretty special, isn't it?" she says softly.

"How is everything going with fostering? Are you going to be able to adopt him like you wanted?"

"Um, yeah, I'm not sure. It's something I want, but we have a few more hurdles to jump through before that can happen. I can't really talk about it right now."

"Oh, sure, I understand. He's sitting right there. Well, I hope you can get some resolution on that soon. I'm here, you know, if you ever want to talk, or if you need anything."

That seems like the wrong thing to say, because she thanks me quickly and gets off the phone.

Damn.

I decide to take a walk to clear my head after all that. I'm not going to give up, even if it's like this for a while. At least she's letting me try.

TWENTY-FIVE

Tammy

DEAR SAM

I HAVE STARTED and thrown away no fewer than twenty letters. How is this so hard? He writes to me almost every day. Going to the mailbox has become my favorite thing. Donny loves it too. I bet Sam would start writing to Donny if I asked.

I stop, pen held midair and call out, "Donny, dude, come here, please."

He comes skidding around the corner on his socked feet. Today he is wearing an old pair of my dad's long socks that would come past his knees if they would stay up. He also has one of Dad's old T-shirts that hangs to his mid-thigh. He's choosing not to wear pants at home these days, but at least he agreed to underwear.

"Do you want to write a letter to Sam?" I hold up the pen and wait.

"Letter, yes," he says and scrambles onto the chair across from me. He sits on his knees and leans on the table with his elbows.

"Let me get another piece of paper. You can trace or write."

I grab a few more pieces of lined paper and write out a few simple sentences.

Hello, Sam.

I hope you are doing good. I like my new school. I don't like that I can't ride on your bus anymore.

I show it to Donny, and he grabs it and lines it up next to his paper and gets to work. His writing and reading have really taken off. I lean back and watch him working carefully to get all the words neatly on his page.

When he is done, I ask, "All done or more?"

"More," he says.

"Okay, what else should we tell Sam?"

Donny gets down from his chair and takes off across the house. I can hear him skidding and banging into things as he slides on the wooden floor. He comes back with his new dinosaur and the well-worn box for the VHS tape of *The Magic School Bus*. He taps the dinosaur first.

"You want to tell him you got a new dino?"

"New dino," he chirps back happily.

I write out a few lines and wait for Donny's approval. When he lines up the pages again, I take that as a yes.

When he's finished, I ask, "Want to tell him about *The Magic School Bus*?"

"Knock-knock. Yes."

I love that he still calls it that. I thought once we made the connection he would stop, but now I find myself calling school buses knock-knocks.

I write out a few more lines and slide it over to Donny. He takes it and gets to work copying the sentences. I wait, then ask, "All done?"

"All done," he says proudly.

"Well, when we finish a letter, we can sign our name at the bottom. We can write that in a few ways." I give him some options on my paper and wait as he reads them.

When he's done, he scrambles off with the dino and VHS box. I hear the video starting as I pull the paper over to read what he wrote.

Love your friend,
Donny.

Wow. That wasn't one of the choices I had given him. Damn, I love that kid so much.

I GET BACK to work on my letter to Sam. I can do this.

> Dear Sam,
>
> Donny and I wanted to write to you and tell you that we appreciate getting your letters every day. Donny has been reading them (after I do, of course), and I think he would love a letter addressed to him, if that wouldn't be too much trouble.

I FEEL like I could ask for anything and he would do it, especially if it was for Donny. I know some of my attraction to Sam is the way he was with Donny from day one. The care he took to get it right, most people can't seem to be bothered. Speaking of not being bothered . . .

> We are one step closer to a possible adoption. My attorney has drafted a letter for Donny's father to review and sign stating that he will relinquish all parental rights.
>
> Logically, I know he should sign, but I worry he won't. He's not even up for parole until after Donny turns eighteen, so if he hangs on to his rights, then I'll just continue to be the foster mom. That puts me in a tough spot, though, because I was thinking about leaving the area. I don't think that's something I can

do as a foster parent, and I have been afraid to ask

I PAUSE and think about leaving that out, but Sam needs to know I'm considering moving back to D.C. Even if I can't. If I adopt Donny, I know I don't want to stay here. There are things that I love about this house and this town, but thinking about a future with Donny makes me want a different setting. A fresh start for both of us.

We expect an answer soon, so I'll let you know when I hear. C. J. has been so helpful through all of this, and Donny has enjoyed going to her house for dinner. You'll appreciate this: when I told him we were going to dinner at C. J.'s house, he ran to the closet and pulled out a tie that I had saved of my dad's. He looked very dashing in his Power Ranger T-shirt and mallard-print tie.

The people that you talk about in your letters sound very nice. Fred is my favorite. I love that you have found a community there, Sam. I guess since I can say that now, my anger about you running away in the middle of the night has lessened. A bit. Not all the way. But some.

I stop there and wonder how to end my letter. Sam always writes love at the end of his, and maybe that's why Donny chose to add that to his, but it doesn't feel right for me to say that. I chew on my thumb and stare at the letter for a while before deciding to just sign my name. I put both letters in the same envelope and put a stamp on it. First thing tomorrow morning, before we head off to school, I'll let Donny put the letter in the mailbox.

IT'S hard to believe that it's almost spring break. Sam still writes to me every day, and he's taken to calling every Sunday. Somehow we never run out of things to talk about.

Donny's father is stalling signing the letter even though my attorney has gone multiple times to discuss it with him. I guess he asked for a visit with Donny but thankfully she was able to change his mind. I can't imagine what that would have done to the little dude. When the phone rings, I set my coffee down and grab the cordless off the counter.

"Hello?"

"He signed! You can go forward with the adoption," she yells into the phone.

I hold it away from my ear, then ask, "What? Seriously? Can you say that again?"

She laughs. "Sorry. I just got back from the jail and I was expecting him to put me off again, but he signed. I think they are moving him soon, so I'm glad I won't have to drive to Folsom to beg for the signature."

I glance into the living room where Donny is standing on the coffee table watching *Knock-knock*. He is swaying back and forth and has his tiny toy spatula in his hand. He starts jumping a little when the magic school bus shrinks, and I pray the table holds out.

"That is the best news ever. What do we do next and how long will it take?"

She goes over the steps that are required and lets me know the timeline. I am mentally trying to see if my plan to visit Sam will still work. Instead of guessing and worrying, I decide to just ask her.

"Can I take him over to Minden for spring break? Like do I need permission for that?"

"No, not just for a visit, and once the adoption is through, you can do whatever you want. Are you still considering moving out of the area?"

"Yes. I know the change will be hard for him short-term, but I just can't see raising him here."

"I understand that. Tammy, it has always been very clear to me that you have his whole heart in mind with the things you do. He's so lucky to have you."

"It's the other way around, actually. I feel like the luckiest person on earth when I'm with him. Thank you for calling to tell me, and for going so often to the jail to make this actually happen."

"You are welcome. I may frame a copy of the adoption certificate for my wall, because this win is probably the best I'll have for my entire career."

Once we finally hang up, I move into the living room to be near Donny. This amazing, life-changing thing just happened, and I can't really even talk to him about it. I don't know if he would understand.

He's happy here; I know that. His teacher in Gridley said he's growing by leaps and bounds in his classwork. He's reading at grade level now and absolutely loves to write. He only copies what someone else has written, but sometimes if I ask him a yes or no question about something, I am able to get a little glimpse of what he wants to write. He likes his routines, so we write to Sam every Wednesday after dinner. I have told Donny we will go see Sam when we can, but again, I'm not sure what he understands. That kind of vague concept doesn't seem to click with him.

I can't help but laugh as Donny wiggles his butt and waves his arms like he's on the Magic School Bus traveling through the intestines with the other kids. He isn't wearing his ski cap anymore, but he does have it on his bed, lying neatly on the pillow next to him. Just as I thought, he loves looking out the window at the huge oak tree in the backyard. I moved a chair over there so he could sit and pinch his toes while the branches tell him a story that's only for him.

He still has meltdowns, usually caused by my forgetting to warn him about a change or something new. I hope that during our visit with Sam I can scope out the area to see if it would be a good fit for us too. I'll take pictures and make a book for him so we can talk about it. I know it will be easier if he has an actual memory of a place.

When Mrs. Frizzle is done, he jumps down and runs to the VCR. I assume he is going to hit rewind, but instead he turns off the TV and comes to stand in front of me.

"What's up, dude?" I ask, my smile huge as I think, *he's mine.*

He grabs my hand and tugs so I stand up to follow him. We end up out in the garage, and I shouldn't be surprised. We have been working on Big Red together, and she is almost done. I had mentioned to Donny that we needed to clean her out, vacuum up the leaves that had collected on the floorboards and dig under the seat for any lost items. His eyes had gone big at that; I'm sure he was imagining all kinds of treasures.

Probably just a bunch of receipts and dirt or a stray work rag. I can't imagine anything he would find interesting, although he finds joy in odd things.

He runs to the cabinet and grabs a trash bag, then tugs the driver's-side door open and dives in, scrambling to the seat. He loves to honk the horn, so he does that first. "One honk," I remind him, and he chirps back, "honk honk," then lays on the horn. It sounds like a dying goose, but I don't have the faintest idea how to fix that.

"Okay, dude, why don't you see what's in that glove box." I point, and he moves over to that side of the truck and pushes the button, springing the door open.

I laugh as a million gas station receipts fall out. Jesus, Dad. There are some bigger pieces of paper wadded up in there as well, so I take those before Donny can put them in the trash in case they are important. I smooth out the first one—a letter from a doctor, dated about a year before Dad called me. It's encouraging him to come in for more testing and to start on some kind of chemotherapy. The doctor even says that with aggressive treatment they might be able to stop the progress of his cancer.

I don't bother reading the other ones; I just hand them to Donny to throw away. I've beaten myself up enough for not being here. I can't keep doing that, and leaving town will be a good way to break up those painful memories. I see Dad everywhere here; it's both comforting and agonizing.

Donny pulls out a big button from the glove box and turns it over to look at the front. I smile down at it. Most of the farmers here are Republicans, but not my dad. He loved Jimmy Carter, said farmers had to stick together.

"That's a button," I say, pointing to it.

"Button!" he says, then holds it out to me.

"Does Donny want to wear the button?"

"Wear, yes." He taps his shirt. Huh, I guess he knows what it is. I lean over and put it on his shirt, and he rubs the smooth surface, looking down at it. He seems to like it. Thanks, Dad.

We get the rest of the trash out of the glove box, then Donny crawls around on the floorboards and pulls things out from under the seats. He hands me a wadded-up blue piece of fabric, and I furrow my brow. That looks too small for Dad's shirt. I shake it out and realize what it is.

I wore this on my date with Sam. It's a blue tank top with the Pink Floyd logo across the chest. I loved this shirt so much. I wonder how it got in here. There's a little bit of grease at the bottom, but I bet I can get it out.

We take the now-full trash bag out to the can that sits just outside the garage and then go back to use the vacuum. I thought Donny would hate the loud noise the Shop-Vac makes, but it's the opposite. The kid would vacuum for hours if I let him. I step back and let him do the honors.

Once we are finished, I take a walk around the truck, running my hand along the frame. So many memories, both mine and Dad's, are trapped in this truck. I'm glad she's up and running again, and I imagine wherever Dad is, he's smiling about that too.

"Want to take her for a drive, Donny?"

His eyes go wide, and he jumps and flaps his hands, but he doesn't say anything.

"Drive, yes or no?" I ask.

He runs to the passenger side and flings the door open, climbing onto the seat and buckling himself in before I can even get to him. I laugh and say, "Okay. Drive, yes. Let's do this."

I sit behind the wheel and reach up to the visor, pulling it down and letting the keys fall into my hand. She starts right up and sounds like my childhood. I put my arm across the back of the seat and look out the window as I back her out of the garage for the first time in over ten years.

We pull out onto County Road W, and I reach over and roll down my window. Donny sees me and leans forward in his seat, straining to do the same thing. I almost pull over to help him, but his determination pays off, and soon we are both smiling as the cool spring air whips our hair around. I look over at him, and a tear slips free as I watch him tip his head back and close his eyes.

Later, once Donny has had his bath and his round of "Head, Shoulders, Knees, and Toes," I lean down and kiss him on the forehead.

"Night, little dude. Tammy loves you."

"Tammy loves you," he whispers back. I don't need him to say he loves me; hearing him affirm my love by repeating that is more than enough.

I go downstairs and grab the phone. I have been waiting to tell Sam about the adoption all day but felt like it was best to wait until Donny was down for the night. I take the phone into Dad's old office and sit at his desk. Donny likes to come in here and practice his writing; sometimes he insists on wearing a tie. It's amazing.

"Hello?"

"Hi, Sam."

I hear him sigh happily. "Hi, Miss Tammy. This is a pleasant surprise. I was going to call tomorrow."

"I know, I couldn't wait to tell you. It happened, Sam. He signed. I can adopt Donny." The last sentence comes out as a sob. I didn't realize it was going to make me cry to tell him, so I apologize.

"Oh, Tammy. Jesus, that is great news. God, I wish I was there to hug you right now. You must be so happy."

"I am," I say, nodding like an idiot as I wipe my face.

I explain that hopefully by the end of summer, Donny will be legally mine.

"That is so incredible. I'm sure you must feel a huge weight has been lifted."

"I do. Um, I was wondering if you are busy for spring break?"

"No more than usual. Dylan has us booked out until the car show in August, but it's just simple stuff. Why, what's up?"

"I want to come and see you."

TWENTY-SIX

DREAMS DO COME TRUE

"HERE?" I sink into my recliner, shocked at what she said.

She laughs. "Yes, Sam. I, um, I fixed Big Red and Donny and I would like to come for a visit." She pauses, then adds, "If that's okay?"

"Fuck, yeah, it's okay. Are you messing with me?" I ask because I can't believe this is finally going to happen.

"I wouldn't do that," she says incredulously.

"Right, no, of course not. God, that is such great news. I'll talk to Dylan tomorrow about getting a few days off. What are you thinking?"

"Well, I don't want to drive in the dark because I want Donny to see everything, you know? You said it's about three hours from here, right?"

"Yeah, easy drive."

"Okay, so maybe we would leave here Saturday morning and stay till Wednesday or Thursday? I'd want him to have a few days at the end of his week off to chill and get back into his routine, you know?"

"Sure, that makes sense. I can make that happen; I'm positive."

We talk about logistics since I have a one-bedroom apartment.

Donny isn't used to traveling, so she is being extra careful about the planning. If anyone can pull this off, it's her.

"I can't wait to see you. I miss you so much," I tell her, taking a chance.

"I miss you too, Sam. Guess what I found today?" Her voice is quiet and intimate, and my stomach tips a little.

"What did you find?"

"I don't know if you remember what I wore on our first date, but I found that Pink Floyd tank top."

"That sinfully tight, light blue one? Fuck, yeah, I remember it. I almost tripped walking up to your porch, seeing you in that. God, you looked so beautiful standing there. I wished I had a camera, although I relived that night so many times, it's like it's burned into my memory."

She laughs quietly, and I get that warm all-over feeling from the sound. I have been honest with her in my letters, detailing the first time I laid eyes on her in ninth grade and how over the years my crush grew. It occurs to me that she might not know something, though.

"Hey, did you know you were my first kiss?" I ask her.

"What?" She laughs again and says, "There is no way that is true, Sam."

"It is. I know you think I was popular and like all that and a bag of chips or whatever, but I had no idea how to talk to girls. You were the first one I asked out, and it took me three years to do that."

"God, Sam, what would I have done with that information as a teenager? I'm glad I didn't know. It would have gone straight to my head."

"Yeah, sure," I laugh out.

"You were mine, too. First kiss, that is. I felt it all the way to my toes."

I sigh, closing my eyes and remembering the moment our lips touched for the first time. "Me too."

We are quiet for a little, and finally I say, "Tammy, I can't wait to have you both here. I can't wait to have you in my arms again. Thank you for giving me another chance." I stop, and panic hits me like a slap in the face. "That's what this is, right? Do I get another chance?"

"I think so. Yes, Sam. I really fucking miss you. I should be thanking you for not giving up. Those endless letters, and now the calls—you wore me down."

That makes me laugh. "I am a determined guy when I know what I want."

I almost say when I'm in love, because that's what this is. I realized it a few weeks ago. She is it for me. I'll do whatever it takes to make this work. If she wants to move to D.C., well, I'll do that. If she wants to stay here, or find a place that is somewhere totally different, I am on board with all of it. As long as I can be with her and Donny.

His letters are piled up in a little basket by my door. I read them a lot. From the first one to the most recent, I can see the improvement in his handwriting. The last one was long because it was all about dinosaurs. I think some of it was copied right out of an encyclopedia, but that's okay. He wants me to know about the brontosauruses because he likes them, and well, that is an incredible honor.

AFTER ANOTHER HOUR, we finally get off the phone, and I toss and turn trying to fall asleep. Fred told me once that big news, good or bad, tends to trigger his nightmares, and that pattern rings true for me as well. When Tammy first called all those months ago, I had a horrible couple of nights, the bad dreams coming one after another. I remember more of the dreams when I wake up, which isn't great, actually. The visions of my friends injured and dying that I could see from the ditch where I lay are either real or what my subconscious has decided is real. I hope for the latter. The images are too horrific to be real.

This time, however, my dreams are of Tammy dancing and spinning in the orchards, taking bites of ice cream off a giant spoon, and pink painted toes on my dashboard.

The days until they arrive are long, slow, and painfully dull. Dylan had no problem giving me the days off, as long as I promised to bring Tammy and Donny by the shop so she could meet them. I can't wait. I'm going to take them to Poppy's place too, to introduce them to Fred. I've explained as best as I could about Donny and how to talk to him, what to expect in return. These people are so kind; I have no concerns about how it will go.

That doesn't make the butterflies stop swirling around my gut on Saturday as I stand in the parking lot waiting for them to arrive.

I hear Big Red before I see her, but when Tammy turns the corner and comes into view, my heart attempts to leap from my chest.

I want to wave my arms and jump up and down so she sees me, but I stuff my hands in my pockets instead. I watch as she parks her truck. Donny's knit cap and his eyes are visible just above the dashboard. He must've unbuckled his seat belt because I can see him better now. Tammy leans over and says something to him, holding up her fingers. He bats at the first one, and she nods. She gets out of the truck and gives me a little smile and a wave as she walks to me. The wind is light today, but it's enough to make her long brown hair dance around her beautiful face.

"Hi," I say, fighting the urge to grab her.

"Hey, Donny asked to wait in the truck for a minute. He wanted me to say hello first. I think he's nervous."

"Fuck." I breathe out. "Tell him I'm nervous too."

She laughs at that like I'm kidding. I step a little closer and hold my arms open, a silent invitation. She waits for only a minute, before she's stepping into me, letting me wrap my arms around her. I kiss the top of her head and rub my hands over her back as she holds me tight.

I dip my head a little so I can say quietly, "I'm so fucking glad you're here."

"Me too, Sam. You ready to go get Donny?"

I nod, and we step apart. He is watching us, and I smile and give him a little wave. Tammy told me how to act when I see him, but damn, is it a challenge not to just rip the door open and pull him into my arms.

I open the door to the truck and say, "Hey little dude, what's up?"

He searches my face, then looks at Tammy, confusion clear in his expression, and then it hits me. I have on my Giants hat, but it's still obvious to him I cut my hair. I don't think Tammy noticed, but damn Donny sure has. Tammy steps forward and says, "It's okay, Donny. It's Sam."

I look over at her and take off my hat, pointing to my short hair. Her eyes go wide and she laughs.

"Sam cut his hair. Just like Donny," she says with a laugh. "Hat, please." She holds out her hand, and to my surprise Donny takes his ski cap off and hands it to her. He has much shorter hair than the last time I saw him, and right in the front where he used to have bangs is a neat little short strip of hair.

"Guessing you did that yourself, huh, little dude?" I say, trying to keep my voice quiet and even.

Tammy laughs again and says, "Oh, yeah. We fixed it as best we could, didn't we, Donny? You look handsome."

Donny still looks unsure, and I wait as he scoots closer to me. He holds his hand up and touches my short hair, rubbing his hand over the sides. His little fingers dip down to my scars, and I hold still as he navigates them. He stops and reaches for my arm, shoving my T-shirt up to look at the tattoo. His fingers explore that as well. It must convince him that I am, in fact, the Sam he knows, because he stops and looks at us. Then he snaps his hand up in a perfect salute. I give him one back and fight the tears that are trying like hell to spill out.

"Ready to go in?" Tammy asks. She sounds like she's fighting them off too.

"Ready, yes," he says. I step back so he can climb out of the truck and marvel at how tall he is. He's filled out a little too. Tammy must be feeding him well. That thought does something to my heart, making it feel larger than it did a few moments ago.

There is a bag on the floor by his feet, so I grab that. He has his whole hand in Tammy's and I swallow. That's huge. God, she is doing so well with him.

"My suitcase is in the back if you can grab that too, Sam?" Tammy asks.

"Of course." Once I have it, I lead them up the cement stairs to my little apartment. Donny digs through his bag and grabs the *Magic School Bus* videotape that Tammy told me about. I borrowed a TV/VCR combo from Dylan so that Donny would be able to watch it. I show him how to turn it on, and he lies down in front of it and presses play.

"How was the drive over?" I ask quietly.

"Pretty good. You cut your hair," she says, then laughs a little. "I didn't even notice; I was so nervous."

"Nervous?"

"Well, yeah. I mean, this is kind of a big deal, you letting us come stay here. He's been practicing sleeping on the couch at home," she says in a whisper.

"God, really? That makes me . . . " I wipe my hand down my face and take a deep breath. "I'm so honored he's willing to try something new for me. Is that dumb?"

She shakes her head and wipes away a tear. "It's how I feel every single time we do something new, something I know will be hard for him. Sam, he's grown so much."

I reach out and pull her into me, and whisper in her ear, "You are doing a great job, Tammy."

We stand like that for a few minutes, just holding each other, hands lightly moving. If we were alone, I would take this a little further, but this week is about something else. It's about reconnecting with Donny and letting Tammy understand I am here for her and him. She may have forgiven me, but I doubt she trusts me. I haven't earned that yet, and I understand why.

Suddenly there is a little hand on my leg that moves up to my hip. I wait and pull away from Tammy just enough to see Donny trying to wedge himself between us.

"Hey there, little dude. What's up, man? Does Donny want a hug?" she asks.

"Hug, yes," he tells her and wiggles himself into our embrace.

I catch her gaze and mouth "wow."

She nods. "Donny likes hugs sometimes, but Donny needs to ask first." Tammy moves a little more so Donny is sandwiched between us.

"We learned Donny likes hugs when his occupational therapist in Gridley started doing deep pressure with him," she explains.

"What's that?" I ask.

"I'll show you," she says, then tips her head down to look at Donny, who is happily squashed between our bodies. "Donny want squeeze?"

"Squeeze squeeze squeeze." He chirps and wiggles a little.

"Okay. Turn, please," Tammy instructs, and he shifts so his nose is in my stomach. She looks up at me and says, "And now we hug tighter."

"For real? I'll squish him," I say with a laugh.

"Yes. He wants that." She pulls us together, and all the air leave my lungs. I take a breath, then hug her back as best as I can with a seven-year-old in the middle. She counts to ten, then releases, so I do the same.

"More," Donny says, and I smile.

"One more, then break," Tammy tells him. We pull our bodies together again, and she counts off to ten again.

"All done. Break time. Color or write?" she asks.

"Write," Donny says, then slips out from where we were standing. He spots my little table and climbs up onto the chair and waits.

Tammy goes to his bag and pulls out a spiral notebook and another book. She rummages around for something else, so I walk over to her to see if I can help.

"Oh, thank God. There it is. I thought I forgot his pencil." She holds up a #2 Ticonderoga and winks at me.

I glance down at the book she's holding and laugh. "Is he learning to repair Big Red?"

She shrugs and says, "I guess. He found it in the glove box and has been recopying it all week." She flips open the spiral notebook and shows me his perfectly neat handwriting. He has even copied the diagrams and illustrations that are in the book.

"This is incredible," I say, and she nods, then takes it over to Donny, setting it on the table next to him. He picks up his pencil and flips the book open to where he left off and gets right to work.

"Ten minutes, Donny." She checks her watch and then goes back to the living room where I have a couch and my recliner.

"So the hugging thing is new," I say quietly.

"He surprises me daily. I guess the occupational therapist is a big fan of Dr. Temple Grandin. She has autism and found that deep pressure helped her own anxiety. She wrote an entire book about her experiences as a person with autism. I have it on order from a bookstore in Sacramento. Hopefully, it will be at the house when we get back from our trip."

I immediately hate that she is talking about when she'll leave, but I don't mention it. "That sounds like an interesting book. It also sounds like a good thing that he ended up in Gridley."

"Yeah, they have more services, but I'm sure there is more we could be doing to help him. My first priority is to just give him time to heal. He's been going to therapy through the school, and the courts have helped facilitate it more often because we were able to show it was helping."

"I don't really understand how therapy works for him if he isn't talking." I lean in and wait for her answer.

"I don't really either. There is a sand tray, and he creates scenes with the plastic figures. It's funny they usually have those little toy dinosaurs, but it was obvious pretty quickly that those were more of a distraction. They use little people now. I get to see pictures of what he makes, and I don't always understand them. He has one that he does a lot, where all the little figures are at one end of the tray, all grouped together, and then he puts one far away from them. I've seen that at least ten times."

"That's heartbreaking," I say, but she shrugs.

"I think it's like a verbal kid telling you they feel alone or scared. All kids feel that way at some point, right?" she says, giving me a warm smile.

"Yeah, I sure as hell did."

We both glance over at Donny, who is up on his knees, concentrating very hard on his work. Tammy checks her watch and says, "Five more minutes."

"Why make him stop if he's enjoying it?" I ask.

"I will ask if he wants to have more time, but leaving him with open-ended tasks causes him stress. It's more of a check-in than a line in the sand. In C. J.'s class, we use timers or tasks that take a certain amount of time to help teach time management and reduce anxiety."

"That makes a lot of sense."

TWENTY-SEVEN

BACK WHERE WE BELONG

THE REST of the day went smoothly, including dinner and bedtime. I brought Donny's favorite pillow, and Sam did a great job with soft sheets and a blanket for the couch. Donny helped us make up his bed, so it could be how he wanted. He changed his mind about which side of the couch his pillow should be on about five times, but eventually settled in. Sam left us alone so I could have our nighttime rituals. One story and a few rounds of "Head, Shoulders, Knees and Toes."

Back at home, I have been leaving him to fall asleep on his own, but since we were in a new place, I stayed in the room until I knew he was out. I'm so proud of him. I don't think he's ever been farther than Gridley before, and he did so well on the drive over. He looked out the window, fascinated by the change of scenery. We stopped when we got up into the pine trees, and I let him get out and look at the trees up close. It was a nice little break for me, too.

I stand and glance down the hallway to Sam's room. His door is open and soft light is spilling out. He offered to put a nightlight out here for Donny, but I haven't seen him bothered by a dark room. To be honest, he's a great sleeper. That was one of the things that worried me most about our first few nights together. I was prepared to stay up with him and work through it, but he falls asleep easily and is conked out till morning.

The clock on the wall says it's a little past nine, and I realize I'm stalling. I've been standing here watching Donny sleep and staring down the hall towards Sam's bedroom. It's funny, I feel like I know Sam better since he moved away. He has shared so much with me through all his letters and our weekly phone calls. I'm afraid to admit that I am falling in love with him, because I am terrified of getting hurt again. That's not only about me anymore; I have Donny to consider. It seems he loves Sam almost as much as I do.

Sam's head pokes out the door, and I'm not sure if he can see me standing here in the dark, but it spurs me towards him. I don't want him to know how nervous I am, because he might realize my feelings for him have grown. He's proven himself to be a bit skittish, so I should keep that in mind.

"Hey, sorry, I wanted to make sure he was asleep," I say as I get closer.

"It's okay. Did he have any trouble?" Sam steps back into the room, and I follow him.

"None. He's pretty easy at night, but since this is his first trip, I was worried."

Sam smiles at me and I notice he has already gotten into a pair of plaid sleep pants and a plain grey T-shirt. Something so simple should not be that sexy, but on him, it is.

"The bathroom is all yours if you want to get ready for bed. I figured since we'd be in here, I'd be more comfortable in these. I have an inflatable mattress, but it will take up all this space, so I thought I'd wait until you are changed."

I cock my head at him, raising an eyebrow. "You are not sleeping on an air mattress with your bad hip," I say and he laughs.

"No, you're right. I'm not. You are." He gives me a big grin, and I am taken back to our senior year. His hair is like how he wore it then: short on the sides and a little longer on top and back. His eyes stand out even more with it like this, and right now they are absolutely dancing with joy.

"We are adults, Sam. I think we can share a bed. The last time I slept on an air mattress was at a sleepover in the eighth grade. Ginny something. God, what was her name?"

"Not Ginny Franco?"

I snap my fingers and point at him. "Yes, that was her. Ginny Franco. I wonder what that little Barbie-beheading freak is doing now."

Sam barks out a laugh, quickly slapping his hand over his mouth. "Sorry."

"It's okay. He's a pretty sound sleeper." I lift my suitcase onto the bed and fish out my pajamas. "Let me change so I can tell you how absolutely horrifying it was to spend an entire night with her and her sisters."

"I can hardly wait."

When I get out of the bathroom, Sam's in bed, leaning back against the wooden headboard. I smile at the other side of the bed, where he has turned down the covers for me. There's a glass of water on the nightstand next to a copy of *The Hitchhiker's Guide to the Galaxy*.

"Enjoying that?" I ask, pointing to the well-worn book.

"Yes, as much as I did the first four times I read it." He chuckles.

"Is this your side of the bed? I'm not picky, if you need to scoot over?"

"Nah, I sleep dead center when I'm alone, but I'm comfortable here."

He watches me climb in next to him as if I suddenly have no memory of how to use my own body. I get up on my knees, then sit awkwardly sideways, resting on my outstretched arm, I shift a little, trying to slide down. I flop onto my stomach and groan into the pillow.

"Are you okay over there?"

"No. I'm nervous," I mumble. I turn my head and peer at him

through my hair, which has flopped over onto my face. I usually pull it up to sleep, but I haven't done it yet. I have my scrunchie on my wrist, and as soon as I stop being weird about this, I can put my hair back.

"Nervous? Really? Why?" He reaches over and moves the hair so he can see me better. He takes the throw pillow that he was resting on and does a quick readjustment, sliding the pillow between his knees as he rolls towards me. He tucks one arm under his head and rests his other hand near me.

"Yeah, it feels like a really big deal that we're here, you know? That I'm here in bed with you." I swallow nervously.

"I have no plans to maul you, Tammy," he says.

"Well, that's not what a girl wants to hear," I tease, but he just gives me a small smile.

"It is a big deal that you are here. It's important to me, and I want to do this right. I won't screw this up again, Tammy."

"Oh" is all I can manage because the softness of his gaze and the sweet way he is speaking to me is making me feel like I'm dreaming.

"Do you know what I am usually doing right now?" he asks. He reaches for my hand and gives it a squeeze.

I adjust myself a little better, rolling to my side to mirror him. "No, what are you usually doing?"

"Every night before I read, I write to this really amazing woman and tell her about my day. She gets to learn all about the little things that happened, and sometimes I get brave and tell her things that are hard."

I squeeze his hand and want to say something, but I can tell this is important to him, so I wait.

"I have shared things with her that no one else knows. Things about my parents, my childhood. She gets pieces of me that I had buried, that I had run away from."

"She's a very lucky woman to get those letters," I whisper.

He leans over a bit and gives me a soft, sweet kiss, but pulls back before I can take it farther.

"I hope she feels that way."

"I do, Sam. I have loved getting your letters and, oh, my God. Donny absolutely lives for the mailbox. I swear writing to you sparked his love of copying things."

"He seems to enjoy the owner's manual." Sam laughs.

"Yeah, that's not all me. I guess his dad was a mechanic, so maybe it's a comfortable memory for him too. He helped me get Big Red ready for this trip. His favorite place on the property is the garage."

"Smart kid. I can't wait to show him where I work. I think he's going to love Dylan. She is so cool. Tomorrow we will go to Poppy's Place for breakfast, then over to Dylan's. If that's okay."

"Sounds perfect, Sam." I pause before asking, "What would you have written about today?"

He smiles, his eyes crinkling a little. "I would have said, 'Dear Tammy, today is a big day. Two people I care very deeply for are coming to see me. I know I will want to wrap them in my arms and never let them go, but I'm still trying to prove myself.'"

Tears start to form in my eyes as he continues.

"I spent the morning cleaning my house and pacing the walkway outside my door. I walked down to the parking lot a whole hour before they arrived because I didn't want to miss even one second of their time here."

"Sam," I whisper, and I wonder if he can hear the desperation in my voice. My heart has been cracked wide open.

He reaches up and wipes a tear away from my cheek with his thumb, letting it trail down to my mouth where he gently rubs across my lower lip. My whole body aches for him, so I scoot closer, needing his body against mine.

I stare into his beautiful blue eyes and know I am a goner. This man has my whole heart, and he probably always has. I lean in and kiss him because I get the feeling he won't. He's got some crazy idea that he still needs to prove he's a good man.

His lips are soft, and I know I could get addicted to this, being close to him physically as well as our newfound emotional connection. I moan as he swipes his tongue across my lower lip wanting access. I open easily for him, wanting more, craving the way he is growing more urgent. I love how his strong hand is gripping my face, sliding down to my neck pulling me closer.

Without realizing what's happening, I am suddenly on my back with Sam covering my whole body. The throw pillow he had been using was kicked free, and now the weight of him pressing into me sends jolts of electricity through my body as he continues to kiss me. It's like I'm flying to dizzying heights as his mouth moves over mine, a subtle thrust of his hips causing me to soar even higher.

We break apart and I pant out, "God, Sam, don't stop."

He grunts and thrusts against me again while kissing and sucking along my neck, and I hope and pray he rips this top right off me, but then as quickly as it started we stop and stare into each other's eyes for a second before glancing at the open door.

The only sound in the apartment is our heavy breathing, but this really should stop before we get too carried away.

"Jesus, I'm sorry. I have no self-control around you," he whispers in my ear, then pulls back and kisses me a few times before rolling off me. I instantly miss his weight but put my hand on my chest to settle my breathing.

"I feel the same way. I honestly didn't mean to escalate that, but you are a fantastic kisser," I tell him as I roll to my side. He gets up and grabs his pillow from the floor and returns to lying on his side, pillow between his knees.

"I'm good at a lot of things; I can't wait till I can show you." He wiggles his eyebrows at me, and I give him a playful shove.

***

"DONNY WILL GET to look at the menu and point to what he wants," I tell him as we drive over to Poppy's Place in the morning. Sam wanted to drive Big Red so I am perfectly happy between my two favorite guys. Donny is staring out the window at all the stores as we make our way over to the restaurant. I have taken him to the Pizza Palace back home, and he did really well, so I think this will be okay.

I need to redefine my idea of okay. That will help. I take a deep breath in and blow it out slowly, then hold my hand under the table so Donny can see it. I wiggle my first finger and say, "Donny can sit next to Sam in the booth." Then I wiggle my second finger and say, "Donny can sit next to Tammy on the chair."

He bats at my second finger, and Sam and I move over so Donny can climb out. Poppy is an angel sent from heaven, so she finds a chair and tucks it in at the end of the table. I have no idea why he hates the booth seat, but after screaming at the top of his lungs, then shoving all his fingers in his mouth, he darts under the table to hide and pinch my leg. That part is fun.

I watch as he climbs up into the red vinyl chair with its high, round back. He likes the metal arch; I know this because his hand is moving up and over it again and again. He's trying to calm down, and I'm so proud of him. Pretty damn impressed with everyone in this place, to be honest. We got a few stares at first, but one look from Fred and people went back to minding their own business.

"I recommend the fruit cup," Fred says as he folds his menu closed. He leans forward and whispers, "Do you think Poppy heard that?"

Sam laughs and shakes his head. "You are not getting my bacon."

"Bacon," Donny chirps happily. I reach over with a napkin to wipe his face, but he dodges me.

"Donny needs to wipe his face." I hand him the napkin. He rubs it all over his face, somehow missing his nose. I sigh and turn back to Fred. "Are you supposed to be eating healthy? I think Sam mentioned that to me."

"I am, but half the fun of coming here is seeing if I can sneak a little bite of bacon."

"Have you ever been successful?" I ask with a smile. He is just as delightful as Sam described.

"Not once, but mark my words, the day I get bacon"—Fred winks at me—"it will be a good day."

Poppy comes and gets our order and brings Donny a paper placemat and some crayons. He looks at her, then glances down at her apron, and I swear I can see the second he decides to steal from her. His eyes grow wide and a slight smile tugs at his lips. He darts out his hand and grabs the pencil she had sticking out of her pocket. In a flash he snapped the eraser off and tossed it over his shoulder without looking. I watch as it arcs up, then comes down right into someone's coffee.

Donny gets to work on the alphabet like he isn't a destructive little thief. Sam and I look at each other and burst out laughing. "I'll pay for their breakfast. Will you please go tell them I'm sorry?"

Poppy looks over her shoulder and laughs at the person who is looking around, trying to figure out what the heck just ruined their coffee. "Sure thing, sweetheart."

"At least I know he wasn't hiding them somewhere. I've never been lucky enough to see the eraser removal in action."

"Kid is quick, and what's he got against erasers, anyway?" Fred asks with a laugh.

"No idea."

Sam and Fred started telling me stories about when Sam first rolled into town, and even though I've heard Sam's version before, it's nice to listen to Fred share about how he looked out for him from the start. When Poppy returns with our food, she makes a comment on Donny's beautiful handwriting. He has about ten lines of alphabet perfectly spaced and totally straight, even though there are no lines on the paper. He amazes me.

"I'll set this aside so he can keep working."

"Okay, thank you," I tell Poppy, then to Donny I say, "Food is here. Eat or write."

Donny looks up at the plate, then back at his work, clearly unsure what is more important. It's hard to wait and not give him another option, but when I have, it just causes him more stress.

"Eat," Donny says. I pick up his paper and pass it to Sam, who places it neatly on my purse next to him. I slide the plate over and we all dig in. Sam was right; it is the best breakfast I've ever had.

I lean back and pat my stomach, full and happy. Sam and Fred are just finishing up as well, but Donny is fascinated by how the waffle is holding the syrup. He is dipping his finger into each little divot before he'll cut some off to eat. He hasn't touched his eggs or bacon yet, but I can always get those to go if Sam wants to leave.

As if he can read my mind, which I swear happens more than I think is a coincidence, Donny starts eating his eggs. He finishes those and grabs his bacon and holds it out to Fred.

"What do you have there, Donny?"

"Good day."

Fred furrows his brow as if he doesn't understand, but then he realizes what Donny means. "Oh, little man, you just made me so happy."

He looks around for Poppy and when he deems the coast is clear; he takes the bacon from Donny and winks at him. He stuffs it in his mouth and grabs the napkin to cover his mouth as he chews. The pure joy that is dancing across his face is something to behold.

TWENTY-EIGHT

PIECES OF THE PUZZLE

DYLAN'S LEGS sticking out from a black 1974 Dodge Charger are the first things we see when we walk into the shop. I glance over at Donny, who has his middle finger tucked neatly into Tammy's hand. His eyes are huge and dart from the cars to the toolboxes, but they land on the open manual on Dylan's workbench. Her library of repair manuals rivals that of an auto parts store.

Donny grabs Tammy's other hand and pulls her to the bench. He grabs her finger and uses it to point to the book.

"Donny wants to see the book. Donny can ask. Book, please."

"Book, please," he practically shouts.

Dylan pulls herself from the bottom of the car and sits up. "Oh, hey, guys, I didn't hear you come in."

"Hey, Dylan. This is Tammy and Donny, my uh, the people I was telling you about." Damn, that was smooth, Sam.

"Cool, nice to meet you." She stands up and walks towards them, but stops. I've told her about Donny and how he gets nervous around people, especially if he thinks they are going to touch him. During this visit, I've seen less of that though; he seems more relaxed and confident than I remember him being.

"Hi! Nice to meet you. Donny wants to know if he can look at your book."

"Sure, dude, totally. He can sit at the desk in my office if he wants." Dylan motions over her shoulder.

"Oh, sure, he can just walk right in?" I say, turning to Tammy. "When I first met her, she locked the door to the office and stole my car keys."

"You looked suspicious," she says with narrowed eyes. "It was all that long hair. You looked like a freethinker."

I laugh and notice Donny has the big book held to his chest like he has found the lost Dead Sea Scrolls. Tammy leads him over to the office and gets him set up with his notebook and pencil that he stole from Poppy. She comes back out and stands where she can keep an eye on him, but from what I can tell, he is in absolute heaven.

"He found a carburetor diagram, so he will be busy copying that for a while."

"That's neat that he likes that kind of thing," Dylan says. She has grease across her face again, and I have to wonder what she does under the cars she's working on. Is she motorboating the driveshaft or something?

"Yeah, this is new. He was just copying words, but when we fixed up Big Red together and he saw the repair manual, he found a new passion. I'm going to run with it as long as I can because it keeps him occupied and happy," Tammy says.

"I have a cousin who has autism," Dylan says. "He's my age and still lives with my aunt and uncle. I wish there were things like that for him. He has a lot of struggles."

"Yeah, they are learning a lot more about it, and there are some new therapies that seem promising, but everyone seems to be affected differently, so that is a challenge."

I stare back and forth between them as they talk as if they've been friends for years. Tammy leads Dylan out to check out Big Red, so I wander in the office where Donny is working.

I lean over his shoulder and watch as he draws. My hand immediately flies to my mouth, because holy shit, it's good. He keeps turning the book and looking at the picture from different angles, then makes small lines on his drawing before flipping the picture back upright. He has about half the diagram drawn, including the labeling lines the artist added. It's incredible considering he's only seven. Hell, I couldn't draw it that well.

He doesn't acknowledge me, and I decide not to interrupt him. I just quietly stand behind him, watching him work. Eventually, I hear Dylan's laugh as they walk back into the shop. I'm about to leave Donny when they come into the office.

"Wow, Donny. Nice work, dude," Tammy says, and I glance at Dylan, whose mouth is hanging open.

She glances over at me and mouths, "What the fuck?"

"He's very good at that, isn't he?"

"Donny, five more minutes or ten more?" Tammy holds her fingers down, but Donny pushes them out of the way. When she tries again, he smacks her hand and pulls the book and his papers away.

"Donny needs more time. Donny can ask. More time, please."

"More time, please," he yells.

"Gotcha, little dude. I get it. That's a pretty neat picture." Tammy nods to the doorway and walks out with both Dylan and me in tow.

"You have the patience of a saint," Dylan says once we are back out in the shop.

Tammy just shrugs. "I don't know if that's it or if it's just that I get him. I could see how excited he was about that picture, like in his mind, he was already figuring out how he was going to start. If he were better at using his words, he could have told me he just wanted to work until it was finished. Since he can't, I pay attention to the things he's telling me without words. Unfortunately, sometimes that involves him hitting me or pinching me. That's a fun new thing he's started."

"Is it okay if I think you're amazing?" Dylan asks, and Tammy smiles and nods.

"Sure, but Sam is really good with him, too. Did he tell you Donny saluted him the first day he met him?"

"That's adorable. No, no, he did not mention that." Dylan swats at me as she says that, so I move out of the way.

"He saw my tattoo, so I told him I was in the army. I wasn't sure if he knew what that meant, so I saluted him. He did it back before he took his seat. It was pretty cute."

"Oh, no! I was talking about when he was outside the bus. I had never seen him do anything like that; he just snapped to attention and held a perfect salute when Sam pulled up," Tammy says. I can hear the pride and amusement in her voice.

"Oh, yeah, that was pretty great."

We talk for a little while longer, and eventually Donny wanders out with his pencil tucked behind his ear.

"Is Donny all done?" Tammy asks.

"All done."

I glance down at his hands and see he doesn't have the picture.

"Where is your picture?" I ask, not expecting an answer.

Donny chirps, "All done."

I look at Tammy for an explanation, and she shrugs. "He probably doesn't want to keep it. Hang on."

She heads into the office to look for it as Donny notices Dylan's tattoos. He walks to her and puts his little hand on her arm. I try what Tammy does.

"Donny asks to touch. Can I touch?"

Donny looks over at me, then back at Dylan, then at me a little confused. He says, "Sam touch?"

I see my error and correct it quickly. "Can Donny touch?"

He looks at Dylan while rubbing over her arm with his fingers, "Can Donny touch?"

"Yes, go ahead." Dylan chuckles.

Tammy emerges from the office with the picture. "It was in the trash; I guess he didn't want it."

I hold out my hand, and she gives it to me. I glance over the whole thing and am shocked at how accurate and detailed it is.

"I want to keep this, if it's okay?" I ask Tammy.

"Sure, but don't make a big deal about it, though." She nods towards Donny.

"Got it." I set it on the workbench by my clipboard. When he and Tammy leave, I will hang it on my fridge at home so I can admire it in private.

The rest of the week flies by with no real problems, well, unless you count the fact that Tammy and are barely able to keep our hands to ourselves after Donny goes to bed. I stick to my promise that I'm going to do this the right way, so we don't have sex. We do a lot of other things, and every single one of them is the hottest experience of my life. I guess knowing we can't go farther makes us desperate. After the first night, Tammy felt comfortable closing the bedroom door, but she was still worried he might walk in on us. That is not an image I want to put in his head, so we kept it under the covers and clothes on. There is a lot that can be accomplished with those parameters, and we enjoyed all of them.

Even though I know they have to go, the day they pull away from my apartment feels like a cruel joke. When Tammy and Donny are here, everything feels right. It's as though the last piece of my puzzle has snapped into place. It seems like we are on the same page, so once the adoption is final, maybe she really will move out here.

Fred and I spend the rest of that day at his house shelling walnuts. I crack them and put them in a bowl next to his chair, and he scoops out the meat. His wife, Mary, makes spiced nuts and gives them out as gifts all year long.

"That little boy can just sneak into your heart, can't he?" Fred says after a few moments of silence.

"Yeah, he sure can."

"I wouldn't mind having him around here," Fred says as he flicks the nut out of the shell. His aim is perfect, and the pile of walnuts is getting bigger by the minute.

"You just want more bacon," I tease.

"That was a pleasant little surprise, I won't lie." Fred chuckles.

"I want them here, too. Tammy and I talked about it a little bit, but she still seems a little unsure. She knows she doesn't want to stay in Bower, but leaving one small town for another might not work for Donny. She was hoping to have more services for him."

"Makes sense. What about Carson City? You guys could live there and it wouldn't be a bad commute to work for Dylan."

"How far is it?" I ask. I haven't done a lot of exploring apart from the first day I was here.

"'Bout a half hour, straight shot up the highway. We could take a drive up there if you want. Give Mary a break?"

"Sounds like a plan." I shake my head at him, fighting off a laugh. He has always made it seem like he drives his wife crazy, but when I met her, I found the opposite to be true. She looks at him as if he hung the moon.

Later that night, when I sit down to write Tammy, I almost don't know where to start.

TWENTY-NINE

Tammy

FINALLY

Dear Tammy,

I miss you both so much. Two more months of school and then you guys can come back. I'm not sure when the adoption will be finalized, but I really want to show you a place about half an hour north of here. Fred and I went today, and it was perfect. It's a bigger town than here, so there will be more available to you and Donny. I'm not trying to pressure you, but they have a pretty nice library.

Fred couldn't stop talking about you and Donny, and I have a feeling when I go to work tomorrow that will be all Dylan will talk about. I'm going to hang the carburetor picture Donny made on my fridge at home. I can't believe how good he has gotten in such a short time. I will spend my life being amazed by him.

I FOLD the letter down and smile. We go back to work and school tomorrow, and I have already tucked a new notebook and three new pencils, without erasers, into Donny's backpack. I'm sure he will work for that if given the chance. I found his carrot, and I am going to dangle that as much as I can. I'll call the school in the morning and give them a heads-up. I'm ready to get back to our routine, but I miss Sam so much it hurts.

I always thought that was a dumb saying, but my chest actually hurts.

The sound of Donny jumping in the living room fills the house, and I can picture the scene playing out on the television. I take a sip of my coffee and flatten Sam's letter out to finish reading it.

> *I can't write too much more because I want this to go out today so you'll get it by Saturday. I've been going over how you said Donny seems to be doing better because he has a tribe now. I know you were talking about there and at his new school in Gridley, but I'd like a chance to build something like that for him here. I miss you both so much it hurts, and it's only been a few hours since you left.*
>
> *I'll call on Sunday, and we can talk more about this.*
>
> *Love,*
>
> *Sam*

WHEN SAM CALLS, Donny and I are just coming in from the backyard. I lean over him while he takes off his boots and grab the phone off the counter.

"Hello?"

"Hi, Tammy."

"Hey, Sam." Donny's head whips towards me and he tries to grab the phone. I had told him Sam was going to call soon, which was the only reason I was able to get him off the tire swing.

"Hang on! Donny waits. Ouch, no pinching. Donny waits." I

maneuver away from his damn pinchy fingers and tell Sam, "I think Donny wants to say hello."

He's laughing on the other end of the line, and I smile. "Donny says, hi, Sam."

"Hi, Tank," Donny says.

"Hey, little dude. Knock-knock."

"Knock-knock."

"Who's there?" Sam says.

"Who's there?" Donny jumps up and down and almost drops the phone.

"Olive."

"Olive," Donny repeats, almost out of breath with excitement.

"Olive you and I miss you," Sam says. My eyes instantly fill with tears as Donny repeats it. He drops the phone and runs off, bouncing off every wall as he goes.

I pick up the phone and wipe my eyes. "That was pretty sweet, Sam."

"Yeah, I figured out how to get him to say he loves me. I am pretty proud of myself." He laughs.

I peek around the corner to check on Donny and sigh when I see he has dug the new notebook out of his backpack and is copying the Christmas Wish Catalog we got months ago. It's falling apart, but he really likes to draw the pictures and write out the descriptions. I love that he does the little dots in a line and the price, just like in the ad.

"I'm proud of you too. That was a good one."

"Did you get my letter?" he asks.

"Yes, I did. Thank you for writing. I was going to answer it, but like you said, we were going to be talking today." I walk over and sit on the couch. I've noticed that Donny doesn't usually scoot away from me anymore. His little space bubble has shrunk, and while that might not seem like a big deal, it's huge.

"So, what do you think? Will you consider moving here?" I can hear the almost desperate tone in his voice, and it hurts me that he doesn't know how important he is to me, to us.

"Knock-knock, Sam," I say quietly.

He's quiet for a beat but says, "Who's there, Tammy?" and makes me chuckle.

"Olive."

I hear him suck in a breath. "Olive who?"

"I LOVE YOU. I miss you so much it hurts. I want to be wherever you are; I just didn't want to scare you away." I don't hear anything really on the line, so I say, "Sam?"

"Sorry, yeah, I'm here." He clears his throat and says, "I didn't think anything could top what Donny just said, but um, yeah. That topped it."

"So it's okay?"

"It's okay. It's better than okay. God, I wanted to tell you in person, but this is—you're sure? You love me?"

"We both do, Sam." I glance down at what Donny is drawing and smile. "I have another drawing for you. Donny is working on it right now."

"I can't wait to see it. I can't wait to see you. I know you just left but when can you come back?" He asks with a laugh.

"I have a lot to ask my attorney; I'm going to make a list of everything tonight. That has to be the first step. It can take up to six months for the adoption to be finalized, and I'd rather not wait that long to move. Ideally, I'd like to leave here right after school is out."

"That sounds amazing."

Sam tells me all about Carson City and the houses that he and Fred looked at. Of course, by the time I'm able to come, they might not be available. He also tells me all about the library, thinking that will be more of a draw than being with him. I will check to see if they are hiring, because I know I can't be in Donny's class at school. To be honest, he was the reason I loved my job so much. I miss having a job that involves research and doesn't involve anyone wiping their nose on me.

I notice Donny has finished with the picture and I make a mental note to remove it from the notebook before it goes to school with him tomorrow. He never wants to keep the pictures he draws. Sometimes I'll put them on the fridge because I like them, but he doesn't seem to care. I've found some in the trash can that I would have liked to save. It's like once it is done, he's no longer interested.

"Tammy?"

"Yeah, Sam?"

"I love you, too. And Donny. If he can understand that, will you tell him?"

I glance down at the perfect replica drawing of G. I. Joe complete with his Jeep and nod. "Yeah, he understands that, Sam, and I will tell him."

BY APRIL, my attorney had a signed letter from Donny's father giving me permission to move with Donny across state lines. She had to drive to the prison in Folsom more than once because the first time, he was not allowed visitors after trying to start a fight with some inmates in the yard. She said the second time took less than five minutes. I'd like to believe he knows I'll take good care of his son, and that's why he's agreeing to these things, but who knows.

"You all set for your trip?" C. J. asks.

I glance over at the door where my suitcase is waiting. "Yeah, I think so. I just need to make sure Donny understands—"

She cuts me off. "He does. He knows Paul and I are staying here with him; he knows you'll be back; he knows you love him."

I take a deep breath and walk to the back door off the kitchen so I can see him. Paul is hanging out with Donny on the swing. Something is very funny based on the fact that they are both laughing. C. J. puts a gentle hand on my shoulder.

"You're a good mom, Tammy. Part of being a good mom is knowing who to trust with your most precious treasures. The other part is taking care of yourself. Go."

I nod and wipe the tears from my eyes. "Okay, I know you're right. Thank you. I'll be home Sunday night."

"Yep, and that's not too long from now, so get moving." She swats me on the ass, and I jump.

"Okay, okay! I'm going."

I already said goodbye to Donny; she's right. There's no reason to go back out there and do it again; it would just confuse him. I walk down the steps and out to my truck, running through the route I'll be driving in my head. When I climb into Big Red, I lean on the steering wheel and glance up at the huge farmhouse. It's hard to understand after all these years, but I'm ready to move on. When I left for college, I was safe in knowing this would always be here, like an anchor for my life.

Coming back and nursing my father through the end of his life loosened the lines. I am not adrift. I am free.

Sam is waiting in the parking lot when I pull in, and I barely put the truck in park before he's tugging on the door handle.

"Hi."

"Hey there, handsome." I turn in my seat as he hits the button for the seatbelt. I open my legs a bit and he steps right in, cradling my face in his hands.

"Hi," he says again, this time softer, more reverent. He tucks a piece of my hair behind my ear. With me sitting in the truck, we are the same height. I lean a little, enjoying the warmth of his hand on my cheek. I let my eyes fall closed and sigh softly.

"I'm so glad to be here," I say, then open my eyes to find him gazing at me, his eyes searching mine. "I'm so glad to be with you."

He leans in and gently rubs his nose across mine before angling his head just a bit. His breath ghosts over me before his lips land on mine, like he's pausing to draw it out a little. To make me want him even more. I didn't think that was possible, to be honest, but as he takes his time kissing me slowly and thoroughly, I know there's a whole new level of want unfolding within me.

I put my hands on his forearms because he's still holding my face as he takes me apart, one kiss at a time. I don't know if I am holding him in place or making sure that he is real. My heart is going to beat out of my chest as he steps in even closer. He lets one hand trail down my cheek to my shoulder, where he tucks a finger under the strap of my tank top. He gently slides his finger back and forth across my skin as he dips lower each time. Our kiss has changed, turned a little more intense; frantic isn't really the right word, it's measured and deliberately moving us to a place we haven't explored yet.

With that thought, I pull back a little and look him in the eyes. He looks as wrecked as I am; his chest is heaving and his pupils are blown. He licks his lips and shakes his head a little, giving me a wide, sexy smile.

"How did I not notice this?" he says, tugging on my tank top a little.

"You seemed focused on other things," I say.

"Let's get inside so I can do what I wanted the first time I saw you in this tank top." He tugs on my hand, and I step out of the truck, waiting as he reaches in to grab my bag off the seat.

We walk up to his apartment holding hands, and there are nerves creeping in a little bit. They swirl around my gut, so I let out a slow, steady breath to calm myself. I have been with other men; I mean, of course I have, but this is different. I haven't ever been with someone I was in love with. I have never had such an emotional connection with someone before. Sam was my first kiss, and I know if things had worked out back then, he would have had all my firsts. But now, I know without a doubt, my first time with him will beat any other first.

He opens the door and I step in. I notice Donny's picture on his fridge right away, and it makes me smile. Sam sets my bag down by the couch and, without a word, leads me back to his room.

Even though it's the middle of the day, his room is dark. The curtains are drawn, and the covers on his bed are pulled back a little. That's about all I get to notice before he spins me toward him, his arms wrapping around me and pulling me in. I take a deep breath, inhaling his scent. I wish I could take this back with me, but he doesn't wear cologne. He just smells good all on his own. I tip my head and plant soft kisses to his neck as I am spun again and walked backwards until my legs hit the bed. Sam grabs me before I fall, and we both laugh a little.

"Let me see this tank top," he says in a gravelly voice.

I hold my arms out wide, then put my hands on my hips and lift a shoulder. My attempt at trying to strike a pose.

"Jesus, it looks better on you now and I'm trying to figure out how that's possible."

"I believe you said there were things you wanted to do to me the first time I wore this?"

"Oh, hell, yes." Sam steps closer and kisses me. Rougher this time, the tentative kiss we shared as teenagers has nothing on this. This is a man kissing me, owning me. His hands start to move, caressing every inch of my body but never landing on one place too long. It is overwhelming and not enough.

His head dips as he kisses down my neck and his hands move at the same time to cup each of my breasts. He squeezes them and I moan, tipping my head back. There is something so intoxicating about his mouth moving closer to my breasts as he kneads them gently. His kisses are a promise of things to come. He stops and pulls the scoop of my tank top lower, then stares at the rounded tops of my breasts. I may have made a quick trip to Chico's mall to get a few sexy new bras before coming out here. This one is white lace with a front clasp.

"You are so beautiful," he says, tracing his fingers over the swell of my breasts. "I think I would have had a heart attack if I had seen these in high school."

That makes me laugh. "I'm sure you would have handled it just fine."

He shakes his head. "That kiss we shared on your porch just about did me in. I left without trying anything else because I was so over my head. I didn't want to mess up." He admits, then lowers his forehead to mine, fingers still tracing, dancing along. "I love you,

Tammy. I thought I loved you then, but I didn't know what that really meant."

I pull back and look into his eyes before I tell him I love him too. I place my hand on his cheek. "I'm constantly torn between being sad about what we could have had, and being happy about what we have now, Sam. I know you in a way I could never have imagined as a teenager. The crush was there, the adoration, but now? I love you. I love who you are, what you stand for. I hate what you went through, but the man who stepped out the other side is—"

I don't get to finish that sentence because he is pushing me down on the bed and covering every inch of my body with his. His hands are tugging at my tank top and unbuttoning then pulling off my jean shorts. He does stop for a moment to appreciate my matching underwear, groaning as he lowers his mouth to my nipple. He sucks and bites through the bra, then with a quick flick of his fingers, he springs the clasp open.

"Tammy, I want to take my time with you and worship every inch of this gorgeous body, but if I don't get inside you soon, I'm going to embarrass myself." Sam tugs his T-shirt off and stands to remove his shorts.

I sit up, resting on my elbows, and admire the view. He's wearing a pair of black briefs and he strokes himself through the fabric. I know what he means. There is so much I want to do with him, but I can't think beyond wanting what he does.

He slides off his underwear and his hard cock springs free. I haven't seen a lot of guys naked, but I am still sure none of them are as perfect as Sam. His chest and shoulders are defined and strong, and his waist is trim. He doesn't have a six-pack, he's a little soft there with a dark trail of hair. I watch as he wraps his hand around his very hard cock. He gives it a few strokes and then grabs the sides of my white lace thong and pulls it over my hips and down my legs.

As he moves over me, hot and naked, there is nothing I want more than him. No previous experience has ever been this good. The want, the love, it's like my entire body is on fire and he is adding more fuel.

He rocks against me and I part my legs for him. He reaches between us and drags the head of his cock up and down my center. I arch into him and let my legs fall wider.

"God, Sam, you feel so good," I whisper into his ear, and that's all the encouragement he needs. He stalls and pushes in just a little bit, the head of his cock slipping in, before he pulls back and in one thrust seats himself fully inside me.

I gasp and cry out, the pleasure shooting through me.

"Fuck. I need a minute. You are so perfect. So perfect for me. It's like you were made for me, Tammy. Do you feel that? Do you feel how good this is?" He's kissing and mumbling against my neck, my ear, my cheek. He is everywhere all at once and my emotions get the best of me.

I nod, and a tear slides free. Sam catches it with his mouth, then moves along my cheek again with soft kisses. When his lips find mine, his hips start to move slowly. He's rocking and going deeper than I thought possible, hitting a spot I have only heard about. The intense feeling tumbles out as I chant, "Right there, oh God, right there."

THIRTY

TILL THE DAY I DIE

SHE'S MOVING beneath me like a woman chasing her pleasure and that is almost my undoing. When she chants, "Right there, and oh, God," I almost lose it. It takes all I have to hold it together as she completely unravels beneath me. Her soft moan starts soft and grows louder as I try like hell to maintain the same pace and rhythm, hitting that magical spot. When I feel her go, I am right there tumbling over the edge with her. My balls tighten and my hips stutter as I unload inside her. It goes on forever—the pleasure, the overwhelming love, the sensation of coming home.

I collapse on her, our hearts pounding the same erratic beats, dancing together as we come down from the high. I am slowly aware of her fingers moving up and down my back, gently tracing with no hesitation over my scars. My whole back is hers to explore, and I can honestly say that for the first time since my injury, I am enjoying someone touching me everywhere.

I lift and place a gentle kiss on her lips. "It's never been like that," I tell her, searching her eyes.

"No, Sam. It has never been that way for me either. Jesus, you are very talented."

That makes me laugh. "I was following your lead."

I slide out of her slowly and roll carefully to my side. I keep my left leg draped over her for support, and she rubs my thigh and hip.

"Are you okay? Did that hurt you?" she asks. I realize that there is no judgment in the question, only concern.

"No," I say, laughing a little at what I'm about to confess. "If I had lasted longer, it might have." I think about other positions that might be easier on me, and having her on top, taking charge. That makes my dick twitch with approval.

She smiles at me, then closes her eyes. I let mine fall too, enjoying the way my whole body melts into hers.

AFTER THE BEST nap of my life, Tammy and I eat a quick lunch at my apartment before we head out for our date. Not a traditional date by any means, I thought about re-creating what we had in high school, but that is impossible. We were different people back in '85, carefree and unburdened. Now? We are more than just us two. There is Donny and what today could mean for him.

We set off, driving north to Carson City. I told her there were a few houses I wanted to show her, but really there is only one that will work for us. Once she was able to forgive me for walking out, something I will be forever grateful for, things just started to fall into place. We have been planning our lives together, like us as a family is a forgone conclusion. That is stability I didn't know I was missing. Having her and Donny in my life has made me face my past, my failings and my wins. Fred really helped with that part. Therapy was so focused on the tragic events that shaped who I was, blotting out the good. Fred reminded me of the pride and sense of belonging I had in the military. It was an accomplishment that I alone achieved. Not my father, not my mother. It was for me and I grew up wearing fatigues.

When we planned for her to come here, she told me she hadn't been with anyone in over a year and is on birth control. I didn't elaborate to tell her it's been longer than that for me, but I did assure her I am clean. I've never had a relationship like this, tackling things before they become a problem. I give all the credit to Tammy on that front. I hope to be more like her one day, assured in my decisions, and calm in my confidence.

And God, is her confidence sexy. Seeing her take what she needed was my undoing. I loved feeling all of her, with no barriers between us.

Finally.

Not just a condom, I mean no walls, no misunderstandings, no confusion. It was just me showing her with all my heart, soul, and body that she is mine.

She reaches over and squeezes my hand, and I take a quick glance at her. "Peaceful Easy Feeling" by the Eagles is playing as the valley zips past us on Highway 395. Her long brown hair dances around her face as the wind from our open windows takes its liberties. Her lips are slightly parted, and I am mesmerized as they turn up into a smile.

"Eyes on the road, handsome," she teases.

I snap my gaze back to the highway and chuckle. The house I want to show her is on the south side of the city. It's close to the elementary school and would be an easy commute for me. If she likes the neighborhood, I'll consider that a win. The homes were all built in the eighties, so they are a little bit older, but have charm. She shared with me that the sprawling property her dad owned was overwhelming. When she lived in D.C. she had a small condo close to the archives. She took public transportation or walked most of the time. She wants small, simple, easy. Just like me.

"Oh, this is a cute little area," she says, letting her hand slip off my thigh. She is turning in her seat and looking around.

"Yeah, this is the first house. The elementary school isn't too far from here; we can drive by that next."

"Okay," I can hear the excitement in her voice.

I pull onto the street and see the Realtor's car waiting. He must see my Jeep because he's climbing out just as I pull up.

"Sam, good to see you again. This must be your wife, Tammy?" He sticks his hand out for me to shake.

"Someday soon, I hope, yes," I say. Tammy's hand tightens around mine but I don't dare look at her.

"Nice to meet you," she says, hand extended.

"Tammy, I'm Aaron. I've been working with Sam to find you both a great home. This one seems to be Sam's favorite. Are you ready for the tour?"

She nods, and we follow Aaron into the modest ranch-style home. Carson City is the capital of Nevada but still manages to have that small-town feel. There are cattle ranches and a ton of outdoor activities, museums, and history. It's close to South Lake Tahoe and Reno.

The house is a three-bedroom, two-bath. Decent-sized kitchen that is open to the living room thanks to the previous owner having done a little remodel. All of that is great, but it's the backyard that I know Tammy will like. I know when she sees it because she lets out a gasp.

"That tree is amazing." She walks to the sliding glass door that is at the far end of the living room. She can only see the trunk from where she is, and as she gets closer to the door, she turns to me.

"Sam, it's perfect."

I bask in the awe I hear in her voice. Aaron pulls the slider open and turns to smile and wink at me. I liked the house, but the backyard is what sold it for me.

There is a small patch of grass, drought-hardy plants and flowers that are in bloom lining the fence. The main attraction is, of course, the giant Jeffrey that sits just to the left. She walks straight to it and touches the trunk, looking up, just like I did for a sturdy branch.

"It will work for his swing, right?" she asks.

"Yeah, I think so. I thought we could put a barbecue over there and some chairs so we would be comfortable out here too. They get some snow, but I was thinking with these huge branches he could probably swing most of the year."

She runs to me and throws her arms around my waist, pulling me into a hug. "It's perfect," she says into my chest, then tips her head back and looks up at me. "What if it sells before we're ready? I have to list Dad's house still."

I shake my head and stroke my hand over her long hair, letting it spill between my fingers. "I can use my savings. We can put an offer on it today if you want."

"Really? Are you sure?"

"I'm sure," I tell her, because those are the only words I can manage without getting choked up. I pull her in tighter and look at Aaron, who is smiling like he just made a sale.

"Let's do it," I confirm.

"Fantastic. I'm going to go inside and call their agent and let them know to expect an offer today."

Tammy and I walk around the backyard talking about what we want to add. Then we head back into the house and I show her the bedrooms and bathrooms. The garage is adequate, but nothing like what she has in Bower. When we come back into the house, Aaron is smiling. The house has been on the market for a while, and he knows the owners are motivated to sell. They moved a few months ago to be closer to family and are ready to be done with this place.

"Their agent is confident that they will accept your offer. I should have an answer for you on Monday. He's calling them now, and I'm going to the office to get all the paperwork in order."

"Great. Thanks for your help with this, Aaron." I hold out my hand and he shakes it, happy with the straightforward process I imagine.

We drive around the town after that, looking at the school where Donny will attend and, of course, the library. She catches sight of the railroad museum and seems more excited about that than I thought she would.

"I love all the history here. I did a little bit of research once for a congressman who wanted to add the Northern Spotted Owl to the endangered species list. That made it so all the timber on federal land would be affected, so I spent hours upon hours going over the numbers and the effect it would have on communities close to here. There was a lumber mill just on the other side of the Sierra Nevada mountains that was hit hard because of the legislation."

"So maybe you could work at one of the museums, or even the capital?"

"There are a lot of options for sure. Of course, I need to get Donny settled first. Once we get him a routine, I'll feel more comfortable finding a job."

That brief glimpse of her selflessness is overwhelming. She has quickly morphed into a fierce, protective mother, one who will put her desires and interests on the back burner for her child. Donny and his comfort are her first priorities, and I find that incredibly sexy.

We spend the rest of the weekend in my apartment, more specifically my bed. Late on Sunday afternoon, as we lay tangled together talking, I know I need to ask her before she leaves. The ring I bought her sits in my nightstand, so I stretch my arm out and pull the drawer open. She moves a little with me, trying to help, even though she doesn't know what I'm doing.

Once I have it in my hand, I roll and get up on my knees. God, she is beautiful, hair spilling all over my pillow, lips swollen from my kisses. She's wearing that light blue Pink Floyd tank top and a white cotton thong, reminding me of all my teenage fantasies about her.

She cocks her head, questioning. "Did you want to go somewhere? I can get dressed."

I shake my head, trying to gather my nerves. "No, I wanted to ask you something." I slide my hand over the little wooden box, teasing the clasp open with my thumb.

"I don't know how I got so lucky running into you in Bower. I went there to reset myself. Give my brain a break from new things; get lost in the familiar. What I found was both. You are familiar and new. You hold my teenage heart that was so battered and broken, and you hold my heart now. The one that ran away, the one that almost died in a ditch." My voice cuts out, and I look up at the ceiling to regain some composure.

Tammy pulls herself up a little, resting on her elbows. "I love you, Sam."

"I know, and God, do I cherish that. I thought about you often over the years. In my mind, you had found love somewhere else, married, a few kids, me long forgotten."

She shakes her head and starts to say something, but I cut her off.

"I am so lucky that you were there in Bower. I am so grateful for Donny, who showed me how deeply and thoroughly one can love. I will stand in the rays of your love, a happy man till the day I die, even if it's on the edges."

"I don't want you on the edge, Sam. I want you right in the middle with me and Donny," she says softly.

I nod and swallow hard, willing myself to get through this without crying like a baby. I hold the ring box up and turn it towards her. It's simple, a single diamond set in a silver band. It's big enough to let the world know she is mine. "Tammy, will you marry me?"

Her eyes fly open wide, and she drops to her back, her hands covering her mouth. She sits all the way up then, wrapping her arms around me and pulling me down. She kisses me softly, then moves her lips slowly along my cheek and whispers in my ear, "Yes, God, yes. Always and forever, till the day I die, yes."

I break away from her and grab her hand, sliding the ring where it belongs. She takes a moment to examine it on her hand, then pulls me back to her. We kiss in slow, languid movements for only a minute. Our need for each other consumes us. I really didn't think I had another round in me, but with this beautiful woman who just agreed to spend her life with me, I am insatiable.

We make love, slow and sweet, connecting again in a way that I imagine heaven to be. There is a future here with her, with Donny. One I didn't picture, a life so far from what I imagined that it makes my heart soar.

I pump my hips slowly, deliberately, until the telltale signs that she is coming undone are pulsing around me and like every other time, I join her.

THIRTY-ONE

EPILOGUE

I TOLD Sam he didn't have to come back to Bower to help, but of course he did. C. J. and Paul offered to buy my dad's place as soon as I told them I was going to list it. It's perfect for them, and I know my dad would be happy that the farmhouse that raised me will continue to be filled with love.

We took the tire swing down so it could be at the new house, and the moving truck is packed and ready to go. I take one last walk around the property, flashes of my childhood at every turn. I say a silent thank you to my dad as I stare across the street at the rice field where I scattered his ashes, and then I head back to the truck.

Sam opens the door for me, helping me up into the cab. Donny sits between us, a clipboard full of paper, and his new favorite catalog to copy from. Paul brought it for him after a trip up north to see his brother. SkyMall is a mail-order store that has the most unusual things. Donny loves it. He has read each description over and over and seems to like the ad for some adjustable tint sunglasses. He has already started drawing it.

We plan to get married at the courthouse in Carson City, then have a small party at Poppy's Place. I don't want anything too crazy, because I want Donny there. Small and quiet suits us both. It seems like the adoption will be final before school starts in the fall, making everything a little easier on me. I've found a speech therapist who will work with him privately, and of course he will have one through the school. He doesn't qualify for occupational therapy anymore, since his motor skills have improved so much. His handwriting is better than most adults' and his drawing skills are quite impressive.

He seems to be excited about the move. Sam took a bunch of pictures of our new house, and C. J. helped me make a book for Donny explaining the entire process. I will miss her dearly when we are gone, but I know she is just a phone call away.

As the truck pulls out of Bower, I watch the rice fields fade into orchards. The perfect combination of both of us. I hope Sam can come to appreciate the place where he grew up, apart from the memories of his family and what they did. It's hard to hold all of that so close. He is working hard to come to terms with all of it. He and Fred talk a lot, and he has a counselor he sees every other week. I've noticed he isn't taking notes on things like he did the day I saw him again.

I glance down at Donny's drawing and see he's added the hot dog maker that is on the same page as the sunglasses. I'm grateful he's content just drawing these things and never asks for them. Especially in this catalog. There are some expensive gadgets in there.

We leave the valley and climb up and over the Sierra Nevada Mountains, and my heart lifts as we enter the tall redwoods. John Denver's song "The Eagle and the Hawk" plays in my mind. I want to dance with the west wind and touch all the mountaintops.

This isn't the life I pictured for myself. Sam appearing in Bower and all that happened to place Donny in my life and my heart—those aren't things I would have thought possible. I glance over at Sam. He has one arm resting on the open window and one on the steering wheel, confident and sexy as he drives his family home.

.   .   .

SECOND DATES, ten years apart, aren't for everyone. But they are perfect for us.

ABOUT THE AUTHOR

Born in 1970, Pamela Dean survived the '80s armed with Aqua Net, Wet n Wild makeup, and a loyal rotation of button-fly 501s pegged just right at the ankles. It was a time before cell phones, when love notes were folded into tiny footballs and passing one in class felt riskier than it should have.

She grew up staying out until the streetlights came on, where the soundtrack of her nights was crickets, frogs, and the occasional "get home!" echoing down the street. Raised in Redding and later escaping to Chico for college, she's a lifelong Northern California girl —and it shows up in every story she writes.

These days, she writes the kind of love stories she grew up on: a little messy, a little nostalgic, and a lot more fun without Wi-Fi.

If you enjoyed this book, you can find more of her work on Amazon and other online retailers. Follow along for new releases, behind-the-scenes moments, and the occasional trip back to a time when flirting required actual effort. And if you feel like spreading the love, leaving a review helps other readers find her too.

<u>Romantic Comedies</u>
And I Love Her Still
Box One of Two
From the PCT with Love
Free Bird